EARTH'S ANGELS

Book One of the Earth's Angels Trilogy

By Beth Worsdell

Cover designed by GermanCreative

Beth Worsdell
Visit my website at www.bethworsdellauthor.com

Printed in the United States of America

First Printing: October 2018
Beth Worsdell Publishing

Dedicated

To all the people who take the chance to follow their hearts and dreams. Thank you to all my supporters and test readers for your constant words of encouragement, feedback, reviews and sharing of my media pages & book posts. My favorite comment from a test reader on my first rough draft was, "Beth you vomited commas," which will always make me laugh!

"I never intended to write
a song, I never intended to write
a story. Sometimes these
things just write themselves."
Quote by Beth Worsdell

CHAPTER 1

We should have known someone or something would step in and save our planet. Who could blame anyone for trying to save the planet we'd been steadily destroying for centuries! Let's face it; we couldn't possibly be the only inhabitants of a planet in the whole universe. Especially when you consider how much evidence there was of ancient aliens and proof of UFO's being seen, not only recently, but in ancient historical records.

We had tried to change our ways; we really did. However, our farmers had already poisoned our soil with pesticides for decades; and purely for profit. Our oceans had been overfished by commercial fishing companies all over the world, and nearly all whales were already close to extinction.

Our oceans were being constantly diluted and

poisoned from oil and huge amounts of plastic, and it wasn't just all the oil rigs and tankers in our seas that were causing the pollution. It was also the amount of human waste that was being pumped into our waters.

Governments around the world tried to stop the ocean pollution from the big waste companies, but let's be honest, they couldn't be watched constantly. These companies would try and save or make their money any way they could. They didn't care what effect their actions had on our race or our planet; they only cared about their bottom-line profits and their shareholders.

Society was just as much to blame, with our overuse of plastics, and our throwaway culture. Plastic waste was constantly washing up onto shores all over the world, washing up on once beautiful beaches, as well as killing whales, turtles, and other marine life.

We had destroyed so much land to build new towns and cities; as well as extending the current ones. There were so few forests and jungles left compared to centuries ago.

We were constantly destroying natural habitats, forcing animals to scavenge for food any way they could. More and more wild animals were having to make their way into the cities to try and find whatever food they could. Then we had the audacity to complain about

We'd also become a throwaway race, and nothing was made to last anymore, unlike when my grandparents were young. Only some of us tried to use vintage things from a better time, buying household items from antique shops and thrift stores.

Then out of the blue; everything began to change. All governments around the world suddenly started taking everything seriously for a change. Finally, they were prosecuting companies for not following their new strict guidelines for emissions and waste. They started taxing them heavily if they didn't use green energy. Some companies were even shut down—when they didn't become environmentally friendly.

Soon, most companies and homes were powered by solar energy, wind turbines, hydropower, geothermal, and bioenergy. Massive changes were happening at last, all over the world.

Money was no longer important or an issue for our world governments. They were practically giving away solar panels, wind turbines, and hydropower units to anyone willing to use them.

Where once most people couldn't afford green energy, it was now easy and cheap to have a green energy-efficient home, thanks to government-sponsored commercials and programs. We were one of the first in our neighborhood to make the new changes, jumping at the chance to be green, and we were happy to do so.

The majority of us knew something big was going on. It was just so strange how governments and world leaders all started to take global warming so seriously. It was a total reversal of a global attitude.

Things began to change rapidly, with organic food being grown with natural peat moss and compost being sold in all food shops. Pesticides were being banned all over the world at long last.

Action groups were popping up everywhere; actually, supporting our governments, forcing companies to change to biodegradable everything. From all bottles being made from recycled glass to shopping bags and all paper being made of hemp.

Most people were actively trying to do their bit too such as making their own compost with kitchen waste, minimizing water usage, and trying to grow their own fruits and vegetables in their gardens or allotments. Fruit trees were being planted in public areas such as parks, library grounds, and schools.

We all felt that we were finally making all the changes to repair the damage we'd done; none of us realized at first, that it was too little too late.

Because we had abused our planet for so long

—our Earth was a disaster waiting to happen. Our planet was so over-populated; it was just too late to reverse the damage we'd already done. Even though we'd tried to change our ways, we didn't seem to be making any difference whatsoever.

Our ice caps were beginning to melt at an alarming rate, and temperatures were drastically rising all over the Earth. Hurricanes were hitting countries one after another; some of them were even classified as super hurricanes.

Places where storms were common, were now having to cope with horrendous lightning strikes causing horrific wildfires. It seemed as though all weather was becoming extreme across the world.

On top of all the extreme weather, permafrost was thawing, releasing long time buried infections such as Anthrax and unknown diseases never before encountered by mankind. These diseases were killing wildlife and people, spreading through our streams and rivers.

As far as I know, the end of our planet first started with the oceans. There was a supertanker that had sunk and had leaked oil, just in the perfect place to change our ocean currents. This was before we all knew that our Earth was already going through irreversible changes. We had no real idea of what was going on.

The tanker had an explosion on board, leaking its oil right where the warm water met the cold, and because the warm water and the cold couldn't mix anymore, it started a chain reaction, and so our oceans began to die.

The coral started to die first, leaving no living habitat for so many marine life, and then the seaweed and marine flora died off. The microscopic organisms that fed off the ocean flora and coral died. The shrimp, krill, and other mollusks died off too as their food sources vanished. Next were the fish, dolphins, whales, and then lastly the sharks.

After a while, marine life eventually stopped being eaten by other marine life and so the oceans were full of dead fish and mammals. Some were floating and rotting on top of the water, while larger sea life such as the blue whales rotted on the ocean floor. At first, the seabirds fed off the dead rotting fish floating in the seas, but all too soon, those carcasses were poisonous as well.

We began to see photographs and videos over the social media and the news stations, showing all the dead birds, fish and sea mammals, and hearing people's theories. So, we all realized that the situation was getting extremely critical.

Then all at once, our world leaders and governments leaped into action, using every possible resource and every scientist they could find from all over the world. Leaders from every country addressed their nations to tell us what was happening to our planet. They couldn't hide anything from us any longer.

Every day on the news, we learned of yet another animal extinction, and it was heartbreaking. Scientists around the globe were desperately collecting and freezing eggs, semen, and DNA samples from every species they could before it was too late. Other scientists were trying to figure out how to reverse the damage to our oceans while removing the dead sea life and the death sludge left behind.

So many people stepped up to help the scientists as much as they could. Fisherman and many people who just happened to own a boat helped to retrieve dead animals and capture whatever live sea life they could, collecting samples.

DNA collecting kits were sent to anyone who was willing to help; provided by all governments around the world. Huge storage facilities and laboratories were also created to cope with the growing need. For once, all our governments were working together for the common good.

We were, however, powerless to stop the chain reaction that had begun. When all our governments gave yet another public address, informing us that the rivers and streams were going the same way as our oceans, we knew it was the beginning of the end.

Our governments were beginning to prepare us for the mass extinction that was approaching. We were all finally having to come to terms with our dire fate.

We had taken our four kids out of school months ago. We didn't see the point in making them go anymore when it was no longer of benefit, especially as so many teachers were no longer turning up for work. Not that we could blame them.

We had both stopped going to work too, deciding to spend as much time with our kids as possible. Neither of us had jobs that affected anyone else, so what would have been the point in going?

We stocked up on as much food and water as we could get our hands on, even dehydrating food that we'd been growing in our garden. Anything that could give us a little longer with our kids.

Thousands of families in our state of California had already committed suicide, so they didn't have to watch each other suffer. Some did it to give the rest of us some more time. Especially the older generation, the grandmothers and grandfathers. They took their own lives, so there were more food and water supplies for their children and grandchildren.

It was truly heartbreaking, knowing that my husband's parents had done the same for our kids and us. James and I had already started rationing ourselves, so our kids had enough food. We understood why the older population and his parents were sacrificing themselves for the ones they loved.

All conflicts around the world had finally ceased, even the conflicts over religious reasons. Many believed that the end of the world was our punishment for all the wrongs we'd done.

Instead, everyone still surviving was helping each other. There was no point in fighting over a dead planet where money and power were now meaningless. It had taken our world to start dying for us to finally gain world peace. However, it didn't make us feel any better.

Everyone was doing the same thing as us; preparing to die. We just didn't know how we were going to die. Diseases were spreading like wildfire. The poorest countries were losing millions of people every day because their food and water supplies were running out so quickly.

Either way, my husband, James and I agreed that our deaths were likely to be slow and painful if we didn't take control. We'd already discussed ending it all as a family before that could happen. We had enough means in our house to enable all of us to fall asleep and never wake up. There was no way that we were going to let our kids suffer slow, painful deaths.

It was beginning to become very real for our kids too. Especially when they were outside finding dead birds and small animals in our garden, such as hummingbirds, mice, and many others.

At first, they were so upset finding the dead animals who were lying motionless on the ground. Tears streamed down their little faces, but after a while, the tears stopped, and they no longer showed us what they'd found. Instead, they either collected DNA samples to send off to the labs or buried what they discovered. We had many little graves dug in our backyard.

Once our rivers and streams began to be undrinkable, we all knew it was the end for all of us. We'd already used all our savings, at the beginning when things had started to get serious, to stock up on as much food and water as we could get our hands on when the shops were still open. Thank goodness, James, made us act quickly. It was as if he'd sensed that things were serious right away.

We stored all our supplies in the kids' bedrooms and our dining room, opting to all share the same bedroom. I suppose we were trying to make the most of being so close together and wanting to keep the kids safe.

When we saw the news updates about the insects dropping dead all over the planet, we knew that what little food was still growing would be the last. With no more insects, the plants wouldn't be able to reproduce, and our lead scientists around the world had all agreed that there was nothing more that could be done to stop it.

We no longer had any proper programs on our televisions or radios. Only news updates from our governments and world leaders. With the insects now dying, we had to explain to our kids that this was going to affect what little food supplies our countries had left.

Even our children seemed to grasp how horrific the situation was. My heart was breaking in my chest at their facial expressions. The looks of sheer fear and the color draining from their faces; their eyes wide with shock.

The last updates from our governments were letting us know that an ice age was coming. So, even if we didn't starve to death or die of diseases, we were all going to freeze to death. Nothing we could do could save us from the freezing temperatures or the amount of ice and snow that was going to hit the whole planet.

I didn't remember any of this, when I woke up, however ....

* * *

It was so bright when I tried to open my eyes. My eyes hurt from the light as they tried to focus. My vision was blurry, and my eyes stung and started to water. Both of my arms felt heavy and weak as if they hadn't been used in a while.

When I tried to lift them to rub my sensitive eyes, I felt a tug on my right arm as I raised it, making me stop. I laid my arms back down, deciding to give myself a moment to focus my thoughts and let my eyes adjust.

I didn't know where on Earth I was, and as I laid flat, I realized that I didn't know anything! Who I was, where I was, or why I was laying down. What was also very strange was that I felt no panic. In fact, I felt very relaxed, even woozy. I didn't like the woozy feeling at all, but I didn't feel in any danger.

Gradually, my eyes began to focus, and as I lifted my head to the side, I saw beds in a long row next to me; all occupied. The room was obviously massive because I couldn't see a wall at the end of the rows of beds. I assumed I was looking at people in the same situation that I was in, '*We must all be sick,*' I thought to myself.

The woman in the bed next to me looked so peaceful; she didn't look like she was suffering or was sick in any way. '*This place does feel like a hospital.*'

Everything looked so bright and clean, and I wasn't sure if I was seeing things, but the white ceiling and the floor both looked as if they were shimmering, '*Maybe it's my eyes still adjusting to the light?*'

The woman next to me was young, and she looked like she was in her early twenties, with a beautiful pale face and rich, dark chocolate brown hair. She was slender in her body shape, and she was obviously pregnant. I could see a definite small baby bump, covered by the white gown she was wearing, and a silvery, shiny sheet that covered her from just below her breasts to her feet.

The young woman was hooked up to what I assumed were monitoring machines, but they weren't like anything I'd seen before. It all looked a lot more advanced than what I thought they should look like. '*Have I been in a hospital before?*' I didn't know, but I could hear a repetitive small bleep sound, which I thought must be the woman's heartbeat or maybe the babies. The bleeping was soft and rhythmic.

As I took in all the visual information, my senses and body sensitivity seemed to be returning, and I realized that I didn't feel woozy anymore. When I looked down at myself, I saw that I was in the exact same situation as the woman next to me.

I was on a hospital bed with an IV-looking thing in my right arm, hooked up to my own machines. No wonder I'd felt the tug on my arm; I was lucky not to have pulled it out. I was wearing the same kind of white gown which felt like silk against my skin, and I was covered with a thin silvery sheet.

What shocked me the most was the fact that I seemed to have a baby bump as well, with no memory of ever getting pregnant or how I ended up there whatsoever. I was stunned when I looked down at my swollen abdomen. Lifting up my arm, I reached up and touched it, '*Yes it was real, and yes, it was a definite baby bump.*' By the size of the bump, I was around four months pregnant, but I wasn't sure how I'd even know that.

I laid my head back down on the bed feeling

totally stunned, trying to register this new development when abruptly a sharp stabbing pain racked through my stomach, taking my breath away. '*Is this why I woke up?*' The machines next to my bed started to make an alarming noise, making me jump.

I lifted my upper body and curling into a ball; my hands gripped my pregnant belly. I looked to the other side of me and saw rows and rows of more pregnant, sleeping women of all ages.

As my eyesight sharpened, I took in the images before me. I felt panic rising in my chest, making my heart race. It felt as if it was pounding in my throat.

The pain started to gradually subside, and I tried to breathe slowly in and out to subdue my panic. When my pulse slowed, and the pain started to ebb away, my ears picked up strange noises. The noises were coming from what I assumed was a corridor, or maybe another room at the opposite side of the long cavernous room I was in.

I could hear communication between whoever it was. However, it definitely wasn't human! I can't even describe to you how it sounded, other than it was like a watery whisper. Even though I could tell they were getting closer as their communication was getting louder, I couldn't hear any footsteps at all, which was really odd.

I maintained my slow breathing and laid back down on the hospital bed, pulling the thin, silvery sheet back up to the top of my abdomen, where it was positioned before.

I didn't understand what the hell was going on. So, I decided that pretending to be still asleep was probably the best option for now; until I knew more. I left my eyes open the tiniest bit, so they looked closed, but I could just about see who was entering the massive room.

CHAPTER 2

There were five of them, and they were beautiful. I couldn’t tell if they were male or female as they weren't wearing any clothing, and they didn't seem to have physical body differences like ours, such as breasts or visible genitalia. They were what I can only describe as angelic-looking aliens.

They glistened a mix of ice-white and the most beautiful shade of blue and silver. I could barely make out facial features from the distance as they glided across the room. Two of them made their way in my direction, and I assumed my bed, considering it was my machine that was making the loud noises.

As they approached, I noticed what appeared to be long, silvery-blue hair, running down their backs to their legs. They both had the most stunning blue eyes. They looked like the eyes on peacock feathers, and they sparkled like polished sapphires. I was in total awe of their beauty, and I literally felt as if I were in the presence of angels. '*Was I religious?*' I had no idea either way.

I didn't know where the other three went in the room, but the two who had reached my bedside were busy checking the futuristic-looking machines, pressing buttons, and discussing their findings, I think. Even up close, I couldn't understand what they were saying; their language was nothing that I recognized. I tried to keep my breathing slow and at the same pace as the other women, keeping up my sleeping pretense.

As I lay there, being as still as humanly possible and watching the angel aliens, I heard another machine beginning to make the same noises as mine had. I wondered if the woman was awake and confused like me, or still sleeping peacefully.

The two angels at my bedside started to move the machines, and I could hear them unclip things. Then I could feel their alien hands touching and examining me, but their touch didn't feel like it should. It was feather-light, and their gentle touch sent a feeling of calm throughout my body. Which was perfect timing, because I was beginning to feel another wave of sharp pain in my swollen stomach. However, the moment they touched me, it melted away, and I was so relieved. I don't think I would have been able to maintain my fake slumber if they hadn't.

I felt so confused, as I didn't know if I was in early labor and that's why I was getting pain, or if it was something else. My baby bump certainly didn't look big enough to be full term.

At the foot of my bed, they spoke to each other softly, and I was mesmerized by their sheer beauty and the graceful way they moved. They moved fluidly as if there was no gravity. Suddenly, my bed and the machines started to move on their own.

The alien angels were gliding in front of my bed with me gliding behind them, but there were no sounds of moving wheels, or metal scraping on the floor. '*Were they using their minds?*' I wasn't sure, but my bed and my body were now giving off the same shimmering glow of ice-white.

As we left the cavernous room and all the sleeping pregnant women, I picked up on some sounds behind me. '*Maybe more machinery*?' I wondered if another woman was following us with the other three alien angels. This would make sense after hearing another machine making the same noises as mine.

We entered a corridor, and I was really surprised just how pretty everything was. Not just the angels, but even the corridor. Its surface looked so smooth, and it had its own kind of pearlescent sheen of ice-white, but with a hint of silver and purple.

It looked like the inside of a shell, mother of pearl or maybe the inside of an ice cave, but the corridor didn't feel cold at all. In fact, the temperature was perfect for me, and I wondered what the walls would feel like to the touch. I felt so at ease too. Which I thought so odd, considering I still didn't seem to have any memories of who or where I was and why this was all happening.

While we traveled down the long corridor, I could feel waves of pain coming and going, and every time a wave of pain began, one of the alien angels would touch my hand, making it ebb away. Not only was I extremely grateful not to be suffering, I was also relieved that it gave me the chance to keep pretending I was asleep.

I couldn't see much as we traveled down the long corridor. I knew we were passing rooms, as I could just make out shadows through my eyelashes in my peripheral vision. A few minutes later, we approached a large decorative archway, and it was stunning. There were beautiful symbols at the top near the edge that I thought I recognized. The symbols were intricate and seemed to glow against the Darker background; they looked like Egyptian hieroglyphs.

We slowly entered the room beyond, and it was even larger than the one we'd just left. It was draped in sheer white shimmering veils, separating sections into cubicles on one side. The alien angels stopped, and my bed came to a gentle halt.

One of the aliens glided away while the other did something to the machines next to me. My bed was turned around and reversed gently into one of the white-veiled cubicles. Another bed glided past with another sleeping woman and the other three angels I'd seen earlier.

The alien angel next to me left, gracefully gliding away to the other woman's bed, clearing what little view I had, and then I saw the opposite wall. It was massive and was made of a glistening kind of glass. There, inside the wall, were hundreds of oval capsules, all containing baby animals.

I couldn't believe what I was seeing at first; my brain was trying to deny what my eyes were showing me. As I stared at the encapsulated animal fetuses, suddenly the machines next to me made a strange noise. I felt my whole lower body beginning to go numb from my breasts down. The machine was injecting me with something through the IV, and I felt something warm rush through my veins; the pain was disappearing, and it was such a relief.

Moments later, the five aliens all glided out of the room, giving me the chance to look around properly. I turned my head to the left and looked through the sheer veil.

There next to me was the other woman whose machine had also been making strange noises. She was still sleeping soundly and looked so utterly peaceful that I actually envied her. She had short black hair with oriental features and dark smooth skin. Her bump was slightly bigger than mine, although not by much from what I could see.

I looked back to the wall of oval capsules, and I was amazed at the selection of baby animals. There were lion cubs, dolphins, badgers, various fish and so many more. It then struck me that they were all animals; there was not one human fetus among them. They were all floating in the same sparkling fluid, just like the shimmering glow the angels had surrounding their bodies.

The baby animals were inside their amniotic sacs; their umbilical cords and placentas were attached to some sort of organic-looking device on the inside of every capsule wall. Each capsule pulsed its shimmer like a constant heartbeat rhythm.

While I laid on the soft bed processing what I'd seen so far, I tried to move my lower body, but nothing would happen. The only things I could move were my neck, head, and arms, and it made me feel so vulnerable. There was no way I could get up and run if I needed too.

The only thing that was stopping my panic was the logic that these alien angels hadn't hurt me so far, and they seemed to be making sure that I wasn't suffering. They didn't give off any negative or evil vibes either. In fact, they seemed to have a gentle and peaceful aura emanating from them whenever they were near.

While thinking about the whole situation and wondering why the animals were here, I heard them communicating as they were making their way back. I steadied my breathing and closed my eyes again, just enough so I could continue to watch them. This time, there were four of them. Each of the alien angels was covered in a sheer silvery-white veil and had gloves on their slender hands.

Each pair had a large glass capsule between them; just like the capsules in the big glass wall. Both capsules were glowing and were full of the glistening fluid, and inside were the organic devices attached to the sides.

Although they appeared to be carrying the capsules, they weren't actually touching them, and I assumed that they were using their minds somehow —it was like magic.

Two of the angels walked towards the sleeping woman in the next cubicle, and the other two came my way. As they approached, it occurred to me again just how much they looked like angels.

When the aliens stood and turned at the bottom of my bed, I realized it wasn't just their long shimmering hair, but also delicate silvery, feathered wings down their backs too. Somehow, that made me feel even calmer.

The capsule was left hovering in midair at the foot of the bed, glowing and sparkling gently. Then the two angels moved to either side of me, lifting the top of my bed up a few inches, and I wondered if the same thing was happening to the other woman.

I didn't like the feeling of going through this alone, even if she was still sleeping. I felt the angels pulling down the thin silvery sheet that was covering my lower body, and the gown I was wearing being rolled up to the bottom of my breasts.

The angel on my right hovered its hand over my pregnant stomach, and as soon as it started to move its hand, my skin started to glisten and glow a silvery-white. The angel was so close to me that I could see definite human-like facial features, which looked soft and female.

Her peacock eyes were such deep colors you could get lost in them. There was a marking on her chest that began at her neck, almost like a necklace. It ran down between where breasts would be and along the necklace line with what looked like tiny sparkling diamonds along her markings. She was beautiful.

The other angel ran its hands about an inch distance over the capsule, making it shimmer and pulse the same silvery-white as my stomach. When it finished, it glided to the left of me, and I noticed that it also had human-like features.

Its features were more masculine-looking, even with the silvery-blue shimmering hair. It was definitely a male with a face that had sharper angles, and he was slightly thicker set than the female.

There were no necklace-type marks on his chest area, but he did have beautiful markings around each wrist. There were two thin, dark silver bands on each of his wrists with symbols similar to those I'd already seen on the archway entrance, in between the bands.

When both angels were either side of me, they both hovered their hands over my pregnant stomach, making the silvery-white light grow brighter. At first, I wasn't sure what I was seeing; it still felt as if my eyes were trying to focus.

Moments later, the scene before me sharpened, and as they raised their hands, something slippery and shiny began to appear between them. It was slowly rising out of my stomach. At first, I could see some sort of membrane, then fluid, and as it carried on rising, I could see faint stripes and what looked like dark wet fur inside.

My mind was screaming, '*What the hell, I was pregnant with a bloody Tiger cub!*' I didn't know what to make of it, and my instincts were screaming at me to get up and run as fast and as far away as possible. My logic, however, was telling me, '*You can't run stupid, your body is numb!*' I continued to watch with a sick fascination, my eyes glued to the unbelievable scene before me.

The only thing that stopped me screaming aloud was the fact that my stomach wasn't being cut open like a caesarian section. There wasn't a drop of blood, plus I still didn't feel any pain.

The small tiger cub was passing through my skin as the light pulsed and flowed. It was contained inside the amniotic sack with the umbilical cord still attached to its small soft underbelly. It looked so peaceful, curled in a tight ball with its eyes closed, and its shiny, dark striped fur glistened in the amniotic fluid.

The alien angels raised the tiger cub between their hands with precision and ease and moved it to the hovering capsule at the bottom of my bed. Just as it had passed through my stomach into their hands, it now passed through the wall of the glass capsule until it was safely inside.

The organic device suddenly pulsed with the bright white light, and I watched in amazement as it seemed to draw the end of the umbilical cord and placenta to it.

When the placenta and device connected, there was one last pulse of bright light, and the capsule began to gently pulse rhythmically, just like the others across the room inside the wall.

I looked down at my now empty stomach and watched the silvery-white glow emanating from my stomach begin to gradually fade. There wasn't any scar on my stomach at all from what I could see, and I felt an immense relief. I did notice faint pale stretch marks, however, which confused me, as my pregnancy bump hadn't been that big. '*Had I been pregnant before? Had I carried other animals in my belly?*' I wondered.

I still wasn't feeling any pain, and I could sense the subtle feeling coming back to my body. My feet and legs were beginning to tingle; the feeling gradually moving upwards. The female alien angel lowered her hands and then she turned her head and looked right at me.

The kindness in her sparkling sapphire–blue

eyes went straight to my heart. I felt loved, and I couldn't explain the feeling, but I did indeed feel loved. Her eyes flowed with compassion, and as she looked at me, I wondered if she knew I wasn't asleep.

As she moved towards me, the male alien angel glided towards the exit with the encapsulated small tiger cub hovering between his hands. The female alien gently rolled down the white gown, covering my body with her power, and then she slid the thin silvery sheet back up to the top of my waist.

Moving her way to the end of my bed, I watched her as she raised a hand to her throat. When she touched her throat, the silvery-white glow appeared, and then she smiled at me again.

"My name is Zanika," she said slowly, her voice almost musical and very soft. "I know you are awake young one; you can open your eyes now."

As my eyes opened, they connected with hers, and again I felt love and peace coming from her straight to my heart. I weirdly felt no fear or anxiety, just totally calm.

"What is your name young one?" she asked.

"I don't know my name," I told her in a strained whisper.

"Do not worry young one; memory loss is common when you have been asleep for a long time."

'*A Long time?*' My mind screamed!

"How long have I been asleep for?" I asked.

She looked at me with kindness shining through her blue peacock eyes.

"I believe five of your earth years," she gently stated, "You have given your Earth six animals back; you should feel very proud."

My mind was reeling. Not only had I been asleep for five years, but I'd been pregnant with more than one animal. I was totally stunned, and stared at her in utter disbelief.

I began to take deep slow breaths, trying not to let the feeling of shock overwhelm me. Zanika must have sensed the feelings of anxiety flowing through my whole body as she suddenly spoke in her calm manner.

"I will get you something to drink and eat young one. We may talk some more when you have calmed your mind and body," she said.

With that, she glided towards the archway where we'd come in. As my emotions calmed with each deep breath I took, I began to try and sit up. There was no discomfort in my stomach at all, which surprised me considering I had basically given birth to a tiger cub.

The thought wasn't quite as disturbing to me as before, and I had to admit, my body felt great There were no physical signs that would indicate that

I'd been asleep for so many years either.

I used my arms and hands to lift my upper body until I was sitting on the bed, and once completely upright, I swung my legs to the side, so they dangled over the edge. It felt wonderful being upright, and I seemed to have all feeling back in my lower body which felt great. I looked at my bare arms and hands, amazed at how good my skin looked. I ran my hands up and down the upper part of my arms; my skin felt so smooth and soft.

The alien angels obviously took very good care of us, and I felt a great appreciation towards them. Next, I ran my hands down my hair; it was pale-blonde, long, thick and felt so soft as it slipped through between my fingers.

A movement to the side of me made me turn my gaze to the other woman in the next cubicle. She was just giving birth like I had done moments before. I couldn't look away as the other two alien angels, dressed in their sheer veils and gloves, did the same process to her, as Zanika and her counterpart had done to me.

They too were hovering their hands over the sleeping woman's pregnant stomach, and as the light glowed bright white, a creature was beginning to appear inside its amniotic sac. It was pure white in color, curled in a tight ball with soft, but thin-looking fur. It had small round ears that were flush against its head, and a tiny black nose. I realized it was a baby Polar bear.

They transferred the baby Polar bear to the glistening capsule at the end of her bed with precision. As I watched, I realized that with this second birth, I was starting to feel that it was a truly magical scene. The shock of it being animals instead of human babies was really starting to wear off.

One of the aliens began to exit with the newborn Polar bear in its capsule; the other one covered the sleeping woman's form with her white gown, and thin silvery sheet. I wondered how long she'd been asleep for and how many animals she'd birthed. I also wondered if we'd always birthed the same animals or if they were different each time, considering the number of different species that were inside the glass wall.

While my mind was going over these thoughts, Zanika entered the room again. Between her hands hovered a black stone tray laden with a drink, fruit and chopped vegetables. Some of which I didn't recognize, but as I ran my eyes over the selection, my stomach growled loudly which made Zanika smile. I couldn't stop myself from smiling back.

Her beautiful face oozed friendliness, and it felt good to smile.

"Thank you Zanika," I whispered as I took the tray from her.

I began to eat some of the large green grapes, and they were so delicious. I didn't think anything else could possibly taste that amazing.

"You have many questions I think," Zanika stated.

'*I believe that's the understatement of the year,*' I thought to myself.

"Where exactly am I?" I asked, between grapes.

"You are still on earth young one," she replied softly, "You are on one of our spacecrafts. This craft contains our medical units and our main control center. This is where all human females stay, while we heal your Earth and replenish your animal kingdom."

When she spoke, there wasn't any hint of judgement, only a soft kindness. Her sapphire blue eyes sparkled as she continued.

"We arrived just as your Earth's water turned to poison. Your people were starving and dying, your animals were dying out, and your Earth was failing," she said.

Still, there was no judgement, but as I listened to what she was telling me, I was judging us.

I couldn't believe my ears, '*How could this*

happen? Was it even possible?' Zanika seemed so sincere; she couldn't be lying. In my heart, I didn't really think she was capable of lying to me as she came across so pure.

"Is that why I just gave birth to a tiger cub?" I asked in a shocked whisper.

"Yes," she replied, in her musical voice. "There were no healthy animals left that we could breed to replenish your Earth. We have crafts like this one all over your planet. We had no choice but to return and save your Earth."

"Have you visited our planet before?" I questioned, my voice sounding a little stronger after sipping the freshwater.

"Yes, we have visited your Earth many times before. It is why your race calls us Angels or Gods and have created images and sculptures of us. We have been visiting your planet for as long as I can remember," she said.

'*No wonder I thought they looked like angels; they were angels!*'

CHAPTER 3

My mind was racing with so many questions and all the information it was trying to process. '*Angels, wow, Real Angels*!'

"I will take you to a room where you may feel more at ease," she said gently. "Please follow me."

Zanika moved away from my bed, allowing me the room to get up. Even though my body felt wonderful, my legs were still a little wobbly when I tried to stand. So, she patiently waited as my legs steadied.

I looked up into her beautiful face, and she reached out a hand to me. I lifted my own hand, and as I went to place my hand on hers, I felt her shimmering aura connect with my skin.

The most amazing feeling traveled up my hand to my arm. It coursed through my body, and it was a feeling of utter peace and calmness. Zanika led the way out of the massive birthing room, through another exit and into another corridor like the one we'd passed through earlier.

There were smaller archways along the corridor, which I assumed were smaller rooms. Every archway had different symbols glowing in the soft light at the top. Every so often, another angel would pass us by, and as they crossed our path, they would slightly nod their head at Zanika and smile at me.

They were just like her, the females and males alike. All of them were emanating peace and calmness. I didn't feel unsafe or unwelcome in any way, and it was very reassuring. The tension in my body had begun to gradually melt away. Within minutes, Zanika stopped at one of the smaller decorative archways.

"This will be your room for now, if you would like to enter and make yourself comfortable. I will come back later," Zanika said.

She swept her hand towards the entrance, inviting me to go inside. Nervously, I entered the room. The light inside was a warm, soft glow, and the room was stunning. Thin silvery veils hung from the ceiling to the tops of the smooth white walls.

The room was a circular shape, with a round bed underneath a large round window. There was a hint of purple in the silvery bed coverings and the seating area to the right of the room. On the left side of the room was a smaller archway that led to a bathroom with the funkiest toilet, shower and sink I'd ever seen.

I quickly realized how desperate I was for a hot shower, but first I needed to look outside. After what Zanika had told me, I needed to see the outside world for myself.

My nervousness grew as I walked over to the large round window. I placed my hands on either side of the window frame and peered out, and I was astonished at what I saw.

We appeared to be in seawater, and I couldn't tell whether we were in the middle of an ocean or on a coastline. As far as my eyes could see, there was choppy dark green and blue seawater.

The sky was cloudy with hues of pinks and reds, so it was either sunset or sunrise, but there was no way I could tell from the view I had.

In the far distance were what looked like futuristic-looking oil rigs, but if the angels were trying to save Earth, I couldn't imagine them mining for oil. As I strained my eyes to make out the white round rigs, I spotted something moving underneath the rigs and also on one side. It looked like flowing water, but how could water be flowing upwards?

I'd already seen enough to assume that the angels were using the same powers or magic that they'd used to move me in my bed without touching it. '*This must be what Zanika was talking about when she said they were saving our planet.*' I suddenly felt so tired which was ridiculous. I'd been sleeping for the last five years; so how on earth could I be tired?

Logic made me realize that it was probably the shock of everything that had happened so far. Waking up in confusion and panic, my discovery that angels are actually real and the shock of not only giving birth to a tiger cub but also learning that I'd given birth to other animals too. '*Yes, I seriously needed a shower and a good sleep!*'

It didn't take me too long to figure out how to work everything in the small bathroom. The toilet, sink, and shower all had the beautiful intricate symbols next to them, just like the ones on the archways but a smaller scale.

As I finished my business on the toilet, I started looking for something to wipe myself. I touched the wall next to me where the symbols were, and a small section opened in the wall. There on a small tray was what I assumed to be a cleaning cloth of some kind. It felt organic to the touch, which didn't surprise me considering what the angels were here to do. It felt almost like a thin ultra-soft leaf.

After finishing my toilet business, I approached the shower, removing the gown I was wearing, and I draped it over the sink. I lifted my hand to touch the symbols on the wall next to the shower area, and the ceiling sprang to life. Clear water began cascading from holes above in the ceiling.

The symbols had glowed a bright white at the contact of my skin when I touched them, and I wondered if they had somehow read my body temperature because the water flowing over my body was now perfect.

When I looked around for any kind of soap and shampoo, I realized that my skin was slightly glowing. I cupped my hands to catch the water and lifted my hands to my face to smell it. The scent of the water was fresh and sweet, not like I thought water should smell at all. I splashed the handful of water over my face, and as my hands smoothed over my features, I was truly amazed at how wonderful my skin felt. The shower water was better than a skin cleanser.

'*The angels really did take this planet-saving mission seriously,*' I thought. Respect was growing in me, and I truly admired the angels and what they were doing. I was desperate for more information about them and about myself. By the time I'd finished in the shower, I was more than ready for sleep.

Exiting the shower area, I started to scan the bathroom for some kind of towel, but my body appeared to be drying very quickly by itself. It felt so fresh, clean and alive.

When my feet touched the bathroom floor, another larger opening appeared next to the shower entrance. This time, there was a rolled-up garment on the tray, and as I lifted it up, it unrolled into a plain but stunning maxi style dress.

Long sleeves hung off thin silver shoulder straps, and I noticed that the dress was going to leave my shoulders bare. It was so soft to the touch that I couldn't help but run my hands down the material. It was beautiful and a very pale, silvery-blue color, like the sky on a summer's day.

I slipped it over my head, and the material was silky soft against my fresh shimmering skin. When I looked down in admiration, I noticed it had delicate symbols on it, just like the marks on Zanika's body, as if they were indicating that I was also female.

Walking back to the strangely shaped sink, I tried to figure out how I was going to clean my teeth and brush my hair. It was then that I spotted some smaller symbols just above the sink.

I touched one, and water sprinkled from small holes under the symbol. I touched another, and a small tray slid out of the wall above the symbols with a small dish inside. The dish had a pale green pressed powder inside, with a slight hint of mint and something else that I didn't recognize when I lifted it up to smell it.

Next to the dish was something that looked like the finger of a latex glove. When I looked closer, I saw that it had tiny bristles all around the end. I took the weird glove thing and slipped it over my finger. It didn't feel like latex at all, and I just did what my instinct was telling me.

I put my covered finger under the water for a second and then dipped it into the pressed powder. '*Here goes nothing,*' I thought to myself as I began to brush my teeth. The powder began to foam in my mouth instantly as I brushed, and it felt marvelous. The powder appeared to be toothpaste and mouth-wash all in one. I could feel the foam getting every-where inside my mouth, and when I'd finished, my teeth felt amazingly clean.

After I placed everything back on the tray, I looked around for a hairbrush or comb, subconsci-ously running a hand down my long hair. I instantly realized that I didn't actually need one. My hair was so soft and tangle-free already, '*Damn, that water is amazing,*' I thought, smiling to myself.

I made my way to the circular bed and laid

down on top of the sheets, my mind actively going over everything I'd seen and done so far. My eyes felt so heavy, and it wasn't long before sleep took me.

My dreams were like memory flashbacks—with images of floating, rotten whale carcasses in the sea, and a grass lawn scattered with dead birds and butterflies as if they'd dropped from the sky.

Then faces started appearing of a man and some children. The man was handsome and rugged; the young children were angelic with pale blue and green eyes.

As their faces appeared, my heart ached; it throbbed so hard in my chest that I awoke with a start. Sitting up on the bed, my mind reeled from the vivid dreams. '*Were my memories trying to reach the surface? Who were the man and children to me?*' My heart ached again in my chest, and I felt like I should know them.

I felt instinctively protective towards them as if they were family like they were mine. While I attempted to collect myself—get control of my emotions and thoughts, Zanika appeared at the entrance to my room.

Seeing her standing under the archway, I was again reminded of how beautiful she was. However, she wasn't alone this time. The male angel who'd helped her deliver my tiger cub was standing next to her, with the same expression of love and compassion. He really was just as stunning as Zanika.

They began to approach me, and as they glided in my direction, the male angel touched his hand to his throat. The white glow shone at his throat just like it did for Zanika, and I understood immediately that he wanted to talk with me too.

Sliding myself to the edge of the bed, I stood to greet them. Zanika was starting to feel like a friend already, and I wanted to show them my respect and admiration.

The male angel was the first to speak, and although his voice was soft and musical like Zanika's, it had a definite muscular tone to it.

"Welcome young one. I am Harrik; you look well-rested; may we talk a while with you?" he asked.

"Sure," I replied.

I was desperate for more information, and it looked like it was my chance.

Zanika raised her arm and pointed to the seating area. There were four soft-looking chairs arranged in a semicircle around a small low table.

"Let us sit and talk while we await our meal," she said.

Harrik led the way to the chairs, gliding

gently in front of Zanika and myself. He really was very masculine once my eyes and brain accepted what I was seeing. We all sat down in the soft chairs Zanika and Harrik looked very relaxed and composed as they looked and smiled at me. I felt like I should say something before it began to feel awkward.

"Thank you for taking care of me and making sure I wasn't in any pain," I told them both, with total sincerity and gratitude.

Harrik smiled kindly at me while Zanika reached out to touch my hand.

"You are welcome young one; we do not want to hurt anyone," she said softly.

"Do you have many questions to ask us?" Harrik inquired.

"Yes, I do," I replied.

My voice sounded stronger now, no longer the strained whisper it was before.

"Firstly, where did you get me from?" I asked them both.

I had so many questions, but I knew I'd have to be patient.

"Our searchers found you, but I do not know the exact location. We were trying to find as many survivors as possible, and you were the first human we found," she said. "If there were any other humans with you, then the women would have been taken to a structure like this one," she explained, raising her arms for emphasis. "If there were any children or male survivors, they would have been taken to one of our healing crafts," she added.

Harrik seemed to sense the despair emanating from my whole body. He gently touched my arm, and calmness flowed through me from my head to my toes.

"I am sorry we cannot give you more information young one," he said with so much feeling that I actually felt bad for him.

"There were so many human's dead already. We had to act fast, to save as many of you as we could. We also had to try and save as many of your Earth's animals as possible too. So, we could not take time to record every detail as it would have slowed us down greatly," Harrik explained.

What they were both telling me made perfect sense. I thought to myself that if I'd been in their shoes so to speak, I would have acted the same way.

"Why do you call me young one?" I asked.

They both smiled at me with affection– Harrik's hand was still touching mine, and I think he left it there as a comforting gesture. He squeezed it gently as he explained.

"We are what you humans call ancient," he

told me. "We have lived as a race for more of your Earth years than we can remember. To us, anyone who is not of our race is young," he added.

I must have had a funny look of amazement on my face because as they continued—they both had what looked like humor dancing in their blue-sapphire eyes.

"We also cannot die," Zanika said, "our bodies start to heal instantly if we are injured. We are healers of worlds, young one. We have saved many planets since we came to be," she explained.

I was in awe of them, these angels who spent their lives saving planets, races, and their wildlife! It suddenly dawned on me why they were loved, adored, and worshiped by so many of us humans.

"Why have you visited our planet so many times and spoken to people here?" I asked, while images of angel pictures suddenly popped into my head.

I began mentally ticking off the questions they were answering. Zanika and Harrik then explained to me that Earth had had a number of mass extinction events. The Cretaceous era was the most recent event before now, and there had been four mass extinctions before that.

They hadn't been able to save the dinosaurs because the event had happened so fast. They were, however, able to save some sea creatures, insects, and other creatures, enabling Earth to heal and recover.

They'd kept returning to monitor our planet, and once humans evolved, they knew that they would have to be vigilant because of our natural desire to learn, develop, and spread ourselves across the land. Which they understood could impact our Earth and everything on it.

They had appeared to some of us by accident, but when that happened, they'd spoken with the humans, so they weren't scared. However, most of their encounters were intentional.

They explained that they had built relationships with many of our ancient ancestors, such as the Mayans and Egyptians. Civilizations who were willing to live in harmony with each other and, more importantly, nature. The angels had shared their knowledge of natural healing, farming, and showed them how to read the stars.

I totally understood why they were worshiped by so many—as they were pure souls only wanting to do good.

"Would you like a name young one?" Harrik asked.

I was very pleased he'd asked, as I wasn't too keen on being called "young one" all the time.

"Yes please, I would like that," I replied.

Zanika and Harrik looked into each other's eyes as if they were communicating with each other with their minds. There were no head or body movements at all, but as I watched them stare at each other, the blue in their eyes started to sparkle with silver. Then the silver sparkle began to spiral, making their eyes look like sapphire blue whirlpools. After a few moments—they broke their eye contact, and both turned to face me again.

"We think, Elita, would be a good name for you until your memories return. It means chosen one, in one of your Earth's languages," Zanika stated.

"Thank you," I said.

I meant it; it seemed like a beautiful name, and as I said it in my head, it sounded perfect to me.

Just then another angel entered the room with a large, black stone tray, hovering between her hands. She was just as beautiful as Zanika and Harrik with the same silvery-blue shimmer to her hair and wings.

"This is Hulaz," Harrik stated.

He looked up at Hulaz with such adoration that I wondered if they were together. Hulaz smiled lovingly at Harrik too and placed the tray on the small table in front of us. She turned her gaze to me and touched her throat, making it glow.

"It is a pleasure to meet you, young one," she said kindly.

"The young one's new name is, Elita," Harrik told her.

Hulaz turned to look at me.

"It is a good name for you," she said.

Her eyes sparkled as she smiled warmly.

We all thanked Hulaz for the tray of food and she bid us farewell, and dipping her head in respect, she gracefully left the room.

The stone tray was laden with exotic fruits, vegetables, and white cups which looked as if they were made of shell. Inside was a delicious smelling fruit juice; my mouth watered just at the sight. I wondered if the angels were vegetarians or whether they weren't eating meat due to our animals dying. '*Maybe I would find out later.*'

We ate our meal which included carrots, mango, various salad leaves, and many other foods I didn't recognize, but still tried. I asked lots of questions, and just as I was asking one question, another would pop into my head. Zanika and Harrik were so patient with me, and they answered every single one.

They explained that they'd never been told to save planets, but they all knew it was their purpose in the universe. They had many gifts emanating from an inner power within their bodies. It was how they were able to move things with their minds and how they could understand and speak any language at will. They could also use that power to calm someone or remove their pain.

I was fascinated by these amazing angels. I could feel my admiration and respect growing with every word they said. As we finished our drinks, I couldn't help asking them some more questions.

"What's your plan, and what are those rig-looking structures that I saw out of the window?" I asked.

"Come," they said together as they stood from their chairs.

"We will show you what we are doing right now and what our plan is for your Earth," Zanika said excitedly.

She was obviously pleased to be able to show me.

They began to move towards the archway entrance, so I got up to follow them. The floor felt warm on the bottom of my feet as I walked after them. The thought of them not giving me shoes tickled me, '*Why would they think of shoes; they don't even wear clothes!*'

We entered the corridor, turned right and walked for about five minutes. Well—I walked; Zanika and Harrik glided gracefully. We passed numerous decorative archways which I assumed were other rooms, maybe like mine.

Each archway had different symbols on them, all were beautifully ornate and glowing against the frames of the arches. I wished I could read what the symbols said.

Two other angels passed us as we traveled to wherever we were going; they were just like my two chaperones apart from their hair. Their hair was just as long as Harrik's, Zanika's and Hulaz', but these angels had a green shimmer to their long hair.

They were both males I guessed as their forms were thicker set like Harrik's. As they passed us, they dipped their heads slightly at the three of us. I wondered what their jobs were. '*Were they medical like Zanika and Harrik or did they work on the rig structures?*' I guessed I would eventually find out.

CHAPTER 4

Before long, we arrived at another massive archway, which was much bigger and grander than the entrance to my room and the other archways we'd passed. There seemed to be more symbols on this one too than the archways I'd seen so far. The extra symbols made the archway look a lot more important and impressive.

Harrik led the way in, and I followed with Zanika taking the rear. As we entered, there was a humming sound; not loud, just a soft collection of sounds blended together.

The room was a large half-circle shape, and it was also very wide and full of angels. The front wall ahead of us was made completely of glass, glistening exactly like the wall of encapsulated animals in the birthing room. Through the glass, I could see the ocean waves, crashing against waves and flashes of white tips. There among the turbulent waves were more of the white rig type structures.

I couldn't count how many there were. There were rig structures miles away in the distance, but some were closer, and I could see the seawater flowing in and out of them. It was an amazing sight.

"Please follow us," Zanika said as we began to move through the bustling room.

There were curved shaped consoles everywhere; so many buttons and dials flashing in all directions. All the consoles were facing the huge glass window.

The consoles were all occupied by male and female angels, all with the beautiful green shimmer to their hair and wings down their backs. They were all very busy, but everyone that I looked at had the same look of peaceful contentment on their faces. They obviously loved what they did. None of them seemed to notice us as we went by; all were clearly focused on their jobs.

Zanika and Harrik led me through large glass doors to a side room. It was spacious and bright inside with a small table in the middle, and the same style comfy chairs as in my room, three of which were occupied by more angels. They were all female with silvery-red hair and wings, and all had kind calm faces.

As we entered the room, all three smiled at me and dipped their heads, and then they raised their hands to their throats making them glow white. Lowering their hands back down, the angel in the center spoke.

"Welcome, Elita, please join us and sit, we would like to talk with you," she said kindly.

She had the same soft musical voice as Zanika and Hulaz.

"My name is Christik, this is Livik and Jakiz," she stated.

She raised her arm to indicate who was who, and all three had the same kind of aura as those I'd already met, which was peaceful and kind. The three of us took seats in the other chairs, and I looked into the sparkling blue peacock eyes of Christik.

"Thank you for taking such good care of me," I told her, hoping she could hear my gratitude.

She gave me such a look of warm affection as she smiled at me that I felt an instant connection with her, and it warmed my heart.

"I asked Harrik and Zanika to introduce me to you, Elita, as you are the only human woman to wake in all the years we have been here," Christik said softly. "The human men and children in our holding structures only socialize with each other. We do not have any contact with them—other than delivering supplies every day and seeing to their medical needs," she explained.

The look on my face must have reflected my utter disappointment, because Christik suddenly looked concerned for me.

"Do not worry, Elita," she said, "we do that, so they may bond as a community, without any interference. We do explain to them, that we are here only to help when they arrive at our holding structures."

I felt a little relief flow through me at her statement, but in my heart, I just felt a great sense of loss with no understanding why. It was so confusing. I needed to remember who I was, and I couldn't imagine myself being alone with no loved ones. I must have at least a mother and father or some other relatives wondering where I was.

"Let us show you something, Elita," Livik said.

With that, she lifted her arm with her palm facing outwards towards the middle of the table.

Instantly in front of us was an image of Earth turning slowly. It was a sharp image like a TV screen but more like a hologram hovering above the table, and I was mesmerized by the sight.

"Your Earth was dying when we arrived," Christik stated. "We arrived just in time; I think.

Your oceans were dead; your fresh water was no longer pure and drinkable, and your animal kingdom was virtually extinct."

She had such a sad look on her face as she spoke which didn't brighten as she continued.

"Your fellow humans were also dying from disease, starvation, thirst, and from killing each other over what few resources were left. Elita, your race was on the edge of extinction."

I was stunned at the severity of what she was telling me but also the heartbreaking sadness in her tone and body language. As she was describing the scene they had encountered, the images changed before us, showing me just how horrific the status of our planet had been.

First, the image was of the sea. It was a dirty-brown color and was thick with lifeless rotting fish, with whale carcasses and birds floating on the top. The water was slick with slime which turned my stomach. Next were images of rivers and streams; the water was a darker brown which didn't flow properly. It looked thick and slimy with an occasional dead, rotting fish moving in the slow flow of sludge.

The vegetation on either side of the rivers and streams was brown and dead, limp in the hard, dry soil. I could feel tears welling up in my eyes and a lump forming in my throat as I witnessed the reality of their words.

Then the images changed again, showing cities and towns; none of which I recognized. The picture zoomed in displaying people of all races and colors dying in their homes and many in the streets. '*Were they trying to escape or were their instincts telling them to run for help?*' I thought.

Women, children, and men were lying helpless on the ground, racked with terrible diseases. Their bodies were showing their illness and starvation. Others were dying from injuries due to fighting; they had horrendous, open gunshot wounds and massive gashes due to knives or god knows what.

By this time, tears were streaming down my face. I couldn't stop myself from sobbing at the sights I was witnessing. '*No wonder they came to help us!*'

I looked into my hosts' eyes, and they all looked back at me with such great sadness. There was no anger, frustration, or judgement in their sparkling blue eyes about what we had done to our planet, our Earth. Just an utter sadness. Jakiz continued the explanation.

"Because humans were fighting over the last of your resources, we had to act fast to try and save as many of you as possible," she said. "We decided that the safest and quickest way for you all was to make you all sleep," she explained.

Again, the image changed to show what must have been their spacecraft, flying from space and through our atmosphere. All were going in different directions, and then some stopped over major cities. I assumed their crafts were all over the world, as the images were changing from one landscape to another.

Some places looked dry and hot with the population spread out in hut-like houses. Others were built-up cities with large older townhouses where there was lots of snow and ice. Some places looked a little familiar to me, but I couldn't tell you where they were.

There seemed to be different types of spacecraft of various shapes, colors, and sizes which I thought was very strange. However, my logical mind thought that maybe it's like us humans and our cars. We have different types such as cars, trucks, and tanks for different functions.

Livik closed her hand and opened it again, making the image instantly dissolve and then reappear. This time, I was watching other spacecraft moving to different locations. They landed next to massive rivers and in mountain areas next to lakes.

Some were landing in the oceans while others

landed in dry, dead fields and prairies. I noticed that the crafts landing in the oceans or next to the rivers were the white rig shaped spacecraft that I'd seen out of the windows.

The next images were of a large town with old-fashioned cobblestone roads. It was lined with black and white old-style houses, and the people were falling to the ground.

It looked like a pulse—some kind of light—was emanating from the spacecraft, which was hovering above the town. As the light hit the earth, the people fell to the ground. It wasn't like a fast faint but more of a slow-motion fall to the floor. There was no violence in the action; it was just the same as feathers falling to the floor.

"As you can see, Elita, we do not mean any harm to your race," Christik said with her lovely, soft smile.

Zanika placed her hand on mine, and I felt calmness spread throughout my body. I was grateful to her for helping calm my emotions. I could see from what they were showing me that they weren't a threat to us.

Next were images of the angels appearing on the ground in the city. There were more angels than I could count. They were finding a human and then using their power to elevate them off the floor, then they'd abruptly disappear in a white flash of light.

The image changed yet again as I watched the angels reappear inside one of their ships. The angels moved the elevated and sleeping humans into large hospital-looking rooms.

The rooms were draped with the same sheer veils, like the veils in the birthing room, and they laid the people gently on the beds. There were rows and rows of adults and children.

Fascinated, I watched as angels with the same blue hair color as Harrik and Zanika clean one of the children, who looked about 10 years old. They were seeing to the female child's wounds, using their power to heal her and then putting an IV-looking device into her arm.

My heart ached in my chest as I took in the horrific state of the child. She was skin and bone with her eyes sunk into her once beautiful little face. Her curly black hair was matted with dirt, and her little cheekbones were far too pronounced in her small face.

I bet I could have counted every little rib in her tiny thin frame. I could see that she had been starving and was severely dehydrated. I thought I could see sores around her mouth—on her small hands, and down her shins, just below the hem of her filthy blue shorts.

The image changed again, showing the same little girl, only this time she looked perfect. She was lying on a hospital bed, dressed in a white gown and covered with a thin silvery sheet. Her long, black, curly hair was shiny and clean, splaying out in a halo.

Her soft skin was now glowing a rich, deep brown. There were no sores anywhere that I could see, and her beautiful little face looked so peaceful. She looked so healthy now she had put on weight.

"Wow," I said aloud.

All the angels smiled at me. They all looked so utterly pleased with themselves, and I wondered if it was because of what they had done, or my response to it. Either way, they obviously really cared about us and our planet. I quickly felt humbled to be in their presence.

"As you can see, Elita, we have healed all your people," Jakiz said warmly.

The image changed to the little girl again, who was now in a large room with many other children and adults. All were dressed in white smocks and trousers or white dresses. They were sitting in a huge semi-circle, surrounding two angels who were obviously talking to them. Neither the children nor the adults seemed afraid, and they all looked the picture of health.

"Once they were healed, and we introduced

ourselves, we explained to your people why we were here, Elita." Christik stated. "We then transported them to our holding structures, where your people could develop and build new communities. They help each other heal from all the trauma and loss that they have been through."

Again, the image before us changed, showing the inside of a holding structure with happy, healthy people. They were talking, laughing and were so relaxed it made my heart happy to see them.

"If I've been asleep for five years....."

I started to say, but suddenly there was the sound of a huge explosion some distance away. The whole room shook from the force of it. It was so loud that I thought the glass doors to the meeting room were going to shatter to pieces.

It was truly terrifying, and all five of my hosts jumped up from their seats. The image before us instantly disappeared. I followed quickly as the angels moved hurriedly to the massive control room that I'd seen when we'd entered.

There were alarming noises and flashing lights in all directions. I could feel the panic in the room and the fear the angels were feeling. As I looked out of the massive, glistening window and into the distance, I watched in horror as another explosion erupted from one of the rig-shaped crafts out to sea. It was already an inferno. Flames were engulfing the craft in a blaze of red, orange, and green smoke that billowed into the clear blue sky.

The look of horror and sadness on the angels' faces that surrounded me told me that there were angels on the rig craft. I could feel the despair in the air, it was so strong.

I stood frozen to the spot, wanting to help in some way but knowing there was nothing that I could do. It felt like slow motion as the angels moved around me, giving urgent commands in their own language.

Then swiftly, every one of the angels moved in front of the massive, shimmering window. Rows and rows of them, all facing outwards towards the fiery scene. One by one, they raised their arms with their palms facing in the direction of the ocean and the burning rig craft. Their palms began to glow a bright white, and as my eyes diverted to the burning inferno, I wasn't quite sure I believed what I was seeing.

Flashes of bright, white light shot out of the tall flames almost like fireworks. They traveled up into the air and then arced. Their speed slowed rapidly as they began to fall to the sea about a mile from the rig craft. As they made contact with the water, the bright white light instantly changed into a solid form, '*Angels. They were the angels from the rig craft.*'

The water around the rig was starting to move in a circular motion, slowly at first but getting faster with each second, forming a whirlpool. Faster and faster the seawater moved and then it began to move upwards. Gradually, it started swallowing the rig, encasing it until all I could see was a dome of moving seawater. Steam rose up from the water dome in huge tendrils, rising high into the air.

In the distance, something else was happening in the sky above. I could see small spacecraft quickly flying to the scene. Beams of light pulsed down from the crafts to each of the angels who were floating motionless on the water's surface. My mind was taking in the sight as the bodies of the angels were pulled by the light beams and into the crafts.

The dome of water surrounding the destroyed rig started to gradually lower, and the amount of steam rising from it was becoming less and less. The rig craft was black as it began to appear. Once the water slowed and receded into the ocean, all the angels in the control room lowered their arms.

As they began to turn in my direction, I saw many angels with glistening, silvery tears streaming down their faces. The sheer sadness I felt in the room was echoed in those beautiful faces. Wiping away the tears from their cheeks, all the angels started to make their way back to their control areas.

I looked around for my hosts, and I saw Christik talking with her colleagues, all looking very somber. I didn't quite know what to do with myself, so I just waited patiently for them.

After a few moments, all five of them app-roached me. I could tell they were trying to handle their emotions, just like I was trying to get a grip of my own.

"Will your angels be okay?" I asked Harrik. I was choking back the tears that threatened to over-whelm me.

I felt such a strong bond with the angels already, and their pain felt like it was my own.

"Do not worry, Elita. As we told you, we cannot die. We are hurting because we feel their pain and their suffering," he said.

I couldn't imagine feeling all the pain of the angels that were burned in the explosions. It hurt my heart just thinking about how much agony they must be enduring.

Christik turned to me and smiled warmly,

"Come," she said, "we will finish our talk with you."

And with that, they all began to glide back

towards the room we'd left moments before.

We entered the meeting room again and sat in the comfortable chairs. Just as my backside touched the seat, another angel entered with drinks on a stone tray hovering between his hands. As he placed it on the table between us, I was suddenly aware of how dry my mouth was.

I wondered if it was shock setting in from all the extreme emotions we'd just been through. I gratefully took one of the drinks, and as my hand cupped the container, the male angel placed his hand on mine. I felt the stress and negative emotions instantly ebb away.

"Thank you," I told him with all my heart.

I think he must have felt my utter gratitude flow from our touch because when our eyes met, I could tell how much my gratitude meant to him. When he left the room, I took stock of my emotions and realized how much better I felt, back in control of my emotions and not feeling so shaken. Not only because of what the angel had just done but also because of Christik's reminder that the angels on the rig craft couldn't die.

After finishing my drink, I placed my cup back on the table in front of us like everyone else. Looking up at my hosts, it was as if they were aware of the emotional roller coaster I'd been on. I could feel their love and compassion for me, and I could see it in their sapphire blue eyes as they looked at me.

"Are you ready to begin again?" Livik asked.

"Yes, I am," I replied, trying to sound as calm as they were.

She raised her palm again, and the image re-appeared in the center of the table. The image was the same as before. It showed the many different spacecraft, but this time when they all started to move to their different locations, the image stayed with one of the rig structures and Christik began to explain.

"While some of our angels were saving your people, other angels were trying to save your Earth," she stated.

I watched the image change before me. It showed a rig craft structure landing softly in an ocean, the water thick-brown and covered in oil slicks. As the bottom of the craft touched the water, there was a glimmer of ice-white and silver.

The craft began to steadily rise, and as it rose from the water, mechanical-looking legs started to appear from underneath it, and they lowered into the water. Within minutes, the spacecraft looked exactly the same, as the futuristic rigs that I'd seen out of the window in my room and the control room.

The image changed again, and I assumed that this time I was seeing the inside of the rig craft. When the images changed, Jakiz began to explain what I was being shown.

"With the craft that you see here and the others like it," she said, "We clean your oceans, trivets, and your underground aquifers. By the time we arrived, all your water was poisonous to humans and animals. The most desperate animals and humans, who had run out of clean water supplies, were trying to drink from the rivers and streams. So, we had to act quickly," Jakiz added.

I watched the image, totally amazed at what I was seeing. There were angels monitoring futuristic machinery, busy moving dials, and activating various buttons with their power. The machines were sucking up the bad water through one side of the rig craft, and clean, pure water was flowing out of the other side. What truly amazed me was that the fresh, clean water wasn't mixing back with the bad. It looked like the same chemical reaction as oil and water.

There was a white glow around the massive inlet pipe and around the outlet pipe of the rig craft, which was just as large. So, I knew that they were using their power to suck the water up and pump it back out.

"Not only are we cleaning your water, but we are also healing your Earth," Harrik said, his voice full of pride.

Then the image changed to show many half-circle spacecrafts. They were landing in various wild areas such as jungles and great forests, prairie lands, and fields. My eyes were glued to the images before me—it was fascinating. As one landed in a wild prairie, the bottom of the craft started to glow just like the rig craft had.

I was in awe as silver vine-looking veins started to appear at the base of the craft. One singular vine became two; then two became four. The further out the vines spread, the more they split. It was amazing to watch, as not only did they spread outwards but smaller vines were appearing and entering the ground all around the craft.

The earth closest to the spacecraft began to change color before my eyes. Instead of tinder-dry brush and pale-dry dirt, it was changing slowly to moist earth and lush vegetation. Relief flowed through me as I witnessed the amazing work the angels were accomplishing with their knowledge and power. I was humbled by their unselfish compassion for us humans and our planet.

"There is more to show you, Elita; however, I am needed elsewhere," Christik said. "Zanika will take you to your room to rest and eat for now."

Christik rose out of the chair, and we all followed suit.

"We will talk more soon," she said.

She smiled as she and the other angels glided out of the room, leaving just the two of us. I was speechless. My mind was so full of all that I'd been shown.

"Come, Elita, I think you are weary. I will take you to your room now," Zanika said, smiling her beautiful smile.

CHAPTER 5

Zanika and I walked out of the room and back through the main control room. Everything seemed back to normal. The angels were busy working at their consoles, their demeanor now calm. I looked out of the window as I passed through, and I could see the decimated rig structure charred black in the water. Smaller craft were hovering over it, sending beams of white light down, flashing all over its surface. I couldn't see much detail from that distance, but I was pretty sure they were repairing all the damage.

We carried on walking through to the main corridor, and Zanika asked me what I thought about everything I had learned so far and about what they were doing.

She seemed genuinely interested in how I felt about their work, and as we talked, many angels seemed to be hurriedly gliding in different directions. I could see the urgency in their movements and felt a sense of worry.

"Do you know what's happening Zanika?" I asked. "I feel as if there's something wrong."

Zanika looked just as concerned and confused as I was. I could see the confusion in her lovely face.

"I will try to find out what is happening while you eat and rest, Elita." she stated. "I will come back for you when I know more."

We arrived at my room, and once we were inside, Zanika dipped her head in respect. I reciprocated, and she politely left my room. She was obviously keen to go and find out what was happening to make the other angels act so frantically.

Standing just inside the entrance to my room, I surveyed the scene before me but unlike before when I was still in shock, this time I took in more details.

The shape of the room itself was a perfect curve, and everything looked and felt so natural. The precision that went into everything they did or made was quite extraordinary, and I guessed that everything was made from natural materials.

There were no synthetic materials that I could see, and I couldn't imagine that a race who wanted to save planets would ever use or make something that wasn't a hundred percent natural and biodegradable. I could feel my admiration for them reach an all-time high.

Glancing at the table, I saw a fresh stone tray of food with fruit juice and water. It was no wonder my body felt so good; they really did eat and drink well. I wondered what they ate and drank on other planets. '*Did they eat whatever they found on the planet they were on; or did they travel with their own food supply?*' I thought. I was sure I'd find out at some point.

Enjoying my own company, I leisurely ate the food and drank the fruit juice while going over in my mind everything that had happened so far and everything I'd learned.

It wasn't until I'd finished my meal that I admitted to myself how utterly tired I was. It wasn't surprising, considering how much had happened with the rig craft explosions and how much information I'd absorbed since waking from my very long slumber.

I decided to have a relaxing shower to wash away all the negative emotions I'd felt during the long day. By the time I'd finished freshening up and changed into the fresh gown that had appeared in the bathroom wall opening, I was more than ready to sleep. As I made my way to the circular bed, I could feel my eyes getting heavier, and by the time my body began to relax as my head hit the bed pillow, I was gone.

I slept deeply, but dreams or memories kept appearing and it was the same faces as before. This time they were clearer, and I was calling out their names. I watched them in a garden. The boys were playing with a football, and the girls were sitting on the lush green grass picking daisies and making daisy chains.

"Abigail, Holly are you making me another beautiful daisy chain necklace?" I asked.

Then my dream changed to us being in a park. I was pushing the girls on a set of swings and a short distance away; I could see the two boys and the man unpacking a picnic.

"Right my fair ladies. Harrison and Anthony have helped me with the food, so let's tuck into this sumptuous feast," he said, in the worst old English accent ever, making me giggle.

"We can't wait to devour your sumptuous feast, Sir James," I replied, in an even worse attempt at the old English accent.

The girls stopped themselves on the swings using their feet to slow them to a halt. Scrambling to get to the food, they raced each other and giggled.

Next, we were all sat around a dining table, eating a meal together, and discussing their day at school. Flashes and flashes of dreams appeared and then vanished. I don't know how long I'd slept for, but when I woke, the faces of the man, James and the children, Anthony, Harrison, Abigail, and Holly were still fresh in my mind.

My heart ached in my chest so much it felt painful. I put my hand over my heart and had to take deep breaths to steady my pulse. After a few minutes, I made my way to the bathroom area to freshen up. It felt good waking myself up properly, but I still felt shaken by the dreams. I had a longing in my heart that just wouldn't leave.

When I walked back into the main part of my room, I was clean, dressed, and ready for the new day. Zanika was there waiting for me in one of the chairs next to the small table.

There were fresh drinks in front of her including fruit juice, and if my sense of smell didn't deceive me, coffee. I could actually smell hot, delicious coffee. My smile must have been huge because Zanika broke into a big smile too. '*How on Earth did she know that I was craving coffee?*' I didn't get a chance to ask her.

"Sit with me, Elita. I have news for you," she said.

I sat beside her, and she handed me the steaming, hot coffee. I couldn't believe it and couldn't stop myself from bringing the stone cup up to my nose to breathe in the delicious aroma. It was to die for! I sipped the coffee and looked up to Zanika, so she knew I was ready to hear her news.

Zanika suddenly came across nervous.

"I found out from Harrik that something has indeed happened," she said.

I stopped sipping my coffee immediately and gave her my full attention.

"What, what's happened?" I asked.

"Do not worry, Elita; it is nothing as bad as the explosion on the water cleaning craft. Harrik has informed me that a group of men had left one of our holding structures. They have made their way here to this craft and are trying to find their females," she explained.

Flashes of faces appeared in my mind from the dreams or memories I'd had in the night.

"Where are the men now? Can I see these men?" I asked her.

I needed to see if any of these men included the man I saw in my dreams or memories. I was hoping for the latter, and again my heart ached painfully in my chest.

"Zanika, I think I may have a husband and

children," I told her, "Please let me see if any of these men are my family," I begged.

Zanika seemed genuinely concerned and then she smiled warmly.

"We will go to find Christik together and ask her if it is safe," she said.

"Why would it not be safe?" I asked her, feeling very confused.

She smiled reassuringly.

"It is not the men I worry about," she said. "It is the explosions on the watercraft that concerns me, Elita. Our crafts do not usually explode."

I totally understood where she was coming from, and I couldn't blame her caution.

"Come, we will go to Christik now," she stated as she rose from the chair. I decided to take my coffee with us, not wanting to leave it behind as I was enjoying it so much.

We found Christik with Harrik and their colleagues in the control room. It seemed like business as usual apart from a slight buzz in the air. As we approached them, they all dipped their heads in welcome. Zanika and I responded in the same way.

"Elita believes she has family and would like to see if any of the men belong to her," Zanika stated, getting straight to the point.

Christik looked at me kindly.

"Of course, Elita. However, these men showed much aggression when they arrived at our ship. I worry that they may be aggressive towards you," she said.

I was confused as to why they'd be so threatening. I couldn't comprehend why the men would be aggressive when the angels were only here to help and had already done so much for us.

Then it suddenly occurred to me. Of course, they're being aggressive. These men were probably grandfathers, fathers, husbands or brothers, of women who had been taken from them. They were probably desperate to find the women in their lives who they love.

"I don't think I'm in any danger from these men," I told Christik and the other angels.

"You have to see things from their point of view," I said calmly.

I could see the confusion in their faces.

"They know you are saving us all and our planet, but they also know that their women are missing," I explained, "They are missing their wives, sisters or daughters, and are probably feeling frantic with worry."

The angels' faces showed their realization of the situation.

"Please let me talk with them and explain to them what's happening," I asked.

They all looked at each other as if they were in silent discussion. Their sapphire blue eyes swirled with silver, and then Christik turned to me.

"Yes, you can talk with the men. Zanika and Harrik will accompany you for your own safety, Elita," she said.

"Ok, thank you," I replied.

I was so grateful my heart began to race with anticipation. '*Could one of them be, James?*' I really hoped so.

"Are you ready, Elita." Harrik asked.

"Yes, I am," I replied.

With that, we all dipped our heads in respect to each other. Harrik turned and began to leave the control room with Zanika, and I followed after them.

We seemed to walk for about ten minutes down the main corridor, passing all the other rooms that were like mine. We even passed the massive room where I had woken up. Seeing the room again stirred my thirst for knowledge, and I was desperate to know more.

"How many species of animals have you managed to save?" I asked as we walked on past the cavernous room.

"We have managed to save all the creatures that your scientists were able to get samples of," Zanika stated. "We also were able to save the creatures that had died out before our arrival by finding their DNA. Your people did well to prepare as well as they did, collecting samples. It has made it easier and quicker for us. We will release the insects first, to help your plants and trees thrive. Then the other animals will be released in stages, once your Earth has healed enough," Zanika said with a total sense of pride.

The angels took their vocation very seriously, and again, I was in awe of them.

"Are they all still babies like the ones I saw inside the glass wall? I asked.

"Yes," replied Harrik, "they are all still babies. We are still replenishing your animal numbers right now. We will reintroduce the creatures slowly to establish new colonies and packs," he stated.

"Are all the human women birthing the baby animals," I asked, extremely curious.

It was Zanika who answered my question this time.

"Only your human females who are over twenty of your earth years, and no females who are over sixty earth years. We do not want to harm your females," she added as we carried on.

"And do the people in the holding structures know where their women are and what they are doing here to help you?" I questioned.

"Yes, Elita, we explained to your people when they arrived at the holding structure that their females are helping us to repopulate your animal kingdom," Zanika answered.

I stopped in mid-stride and looked thoughtfully at them both.

"When I was in the birthing room and found out that I was pregnant with an animal, I was totally shocked and horrified at first," I told them. "Can you imagine the fear and confusion of these men when they think about their women giving birth to animals?" I asked.

Zanika and Harrik looked at each other in total confusion, so I began to elaborate.

"Human females are only supposed to birth human babies for forty weeks. Their families are probably horrified at the thought, the same as I was. They're probably thinking that their females are having to go full-term with the animals and are suffering," I explained. "Some of our animals are massive!"

Both of their faces showed the realization of my words.

Zanika took my hand in hers.

"We will help you to explain everything to the men, Elita. We do not want your people to be afraid or to think we are capable of such things," she said kindly.

I think they were beginning to really understand why this situation may have arisen. We carried on down the long corridor. I'd never been that far in that direction, so I was fascinated by what I was seeing. Zanika and Harrik could tell I was obviously interested and were kind enough to explain everything new I saw.

We passed large storage rooms, some of which were temperature controlled for the fresh fruit and vegetables, and I could see the condensation on the glass doors. They explained to me that our human scientists had managed to save most of the seeds from all over the world.

So, while some angels were cleaning the earth and water, the other ships and angels were growing new healthy plants and trees ready to replant. They were even growing ocean vegetation such as seaweed and coral in massive tanks full of seawater that they'd already cleaned. They'd even managed to replace the microscopic organisms in the seawater.

They explained to me that underwater plants were just as important to our planet as the plants on land. Apparently, it was the coral and marine flora dying that began the process of our ocean's demise and that an ocean oil spill had sped up the beginning of the end. I had no idea just how important our oceans were to our planet, and they told me that our oceans not only produced oxygen, but they controlled our climate too.

What also blew my mind was that apparently, they were using agricultural techniques that they had taught our ancient civilizations. They had massive tanks full of water with fish inside. Then on top were the plants; their roots were growing into the water, and the fish were feeding off the algae.

Zanika explained that this process was the most effective way of producing plants and healthy fish as well as saving water too. We passed so many more rooms on our way, and I was beginning to realize just how vast the main spacecraft was.

Finally, we came to the room where the men were. I could tell it was the right room because there were four purple-headed angels outside the archway entrance. They didn't look like guards or soldiers. There were no weapons on them that I could see. They seemed no more threatening than Zanika or Harrik, but then why would they need weapons with all the power they held inside?

The four angels greeted us politely, and when

they saw me, they all touched their throats making them glow white. I appreciated them wanting to speak my language, so I could understand what they were saying.

"The men are still agitated and angry. We have offered them food and water, but they refused," one of the angels stated.

Zanika smiled at them warmly.

"Elita will talk to the men; please wait here," she said politely.

Zanika led the way into the room with her usual graceful glide. There was no glass door like some of the rooms we'd passed; instead, the entrance seemed to have a silvery, shimmering barrier. Zanika raised her palm just before she was about to come into contact with it, then passed through as if it wasn't there. Harrik and I followed behind her. I turned around, and the barrier was whole again behind us where the other angels were waiting outside.

There were seven men of various ages, and they were all sat around a long table, similar to the one in my room, only taller like a dining table. There was fresh food and drinks left untouched in the middle, and even though the men were sat in comfortable chairs, they certainly didn't look comfortable or relaxed at all.

As we walked towards them, they all looked

up and when they saw me with my companions, their surprise showed on each of their faces. I smiled warmly at them and hoped it was a reassuring smile, but they just seemed stunned.

"Hello, my name is, Elita." I said kindly, trying to sound a lot calmer than I felt inside.

"I'd like you to meet my friends. This is Zanika, and this is Harrik," I told them.

As I gestured towards my companions, they both dipped their heads in respect to the anxious men. Quickly, I scanned the faces of the men and there, at the far end of the table, was the man of my dreams, literally.

"James," I said under my breath in a whisper.

My eyes connected with his, and my heart started to pound quickly in my chest. My pulse was instantly racing so fast I thought that I might pass out. Zanika as always was attuned to my emotional state, and she reached out and placed her hand on mine.

I broke my eye contact with James, and when I looked at Zanika, she smiled kindly at me. I hoped that my returned smile said thank you. As my heart and pulse rate slowed, I looked back to the anxious men in front of me.

"I know you have many questions like I did, and I'm happy to answer as many as I can. May we sit down?" I asked.

A couple of the men nodded, so the three of us sat in the spare chairs nearest the entrance.

"Please help yourself to the food and water," I told them indicating the food.

While taking some of the strawberries off the tray myself, I hoped to remove some of the tension in the room. My small gesture seemed to do the trick. One of the older men who had a kind face spoke first, and he got straight to the point.

"Are our women alive?" he asked, politely but bluntly.

I appreciated his directness and I smiled at him, trying to show him we were no threat.

"The women who were still alive when the angels arrived are safe and well," I told them all.

"They were all healed just like you all were," I explained.

"Where are they now?" Another of the men asked.

"They are sleeping in one of the rooms here," I answered.

Again, I looked into James' eyes feeling dra-wn to him.

"Have you been told about the role we women have right now?" I asked him.

"Yes," he said, in a deep, husky voice that spoke directly to my heart and made my skin tingle.

"We were told that our women are helping to repopulate the animal kingdom," he stated.

The older man spoke again, his emotions spilling over into his words.

"The angels told us what our women were doing here. However, a few of the angels at the holding craft told us a different story. They told us that our women are being tortured. Made to give birth to animals and that they were here screaming in pain," he said, his voice getting louder and more desperate.

He stood from his seat, his body full of tension and his voice shouting by the end of his sentence. His desperation and horror were flowing off him in waves. All of a sudden, the tension in the room was escalating dramatically.

The anger and frustration from all of the men was flowing over me. I looked to Zanika; and Harrik and with that, Zanika slowly stood, raising her arms. As she rose her arms out from the sides of her body, she began to glow brighter.

The bright, white light emanated from all over her body. I could feel her calming power flow over me, and when I looked over to the men around the table, I could see them visibly relax and calm in their seats.

My mind was rapidly going over what the

older man had said. He'd been lied to; they'd all been lied to. When I glanced back over to Zanika and Harrik, she was lowering her arms, and her shimmer was beginning to dim back to normal. Harrik looked just as confused as I was with this new information.

"You have been lied to," I told them with as much conviction as I could muster.

I stood from my chair, leaned forward with my hands on the table, and made eye contact with each of them.

"I assure you we have not been tortured or harmed in any way, and I'm confused as to why some of the angels at the holding structure have told you differently," I stated, feeling angry that they'd been deceived.

I looked again to Zanika and Harrik.

"I do not understand either, Elita." Harrik said, "We need to inform Christik of this new development."

"You go and tell her Harrik. I will stay with, Elita and the men." Zanika told him.

Harrik rose and dipped his head to the men and us and then left the room hurriedly.

"I will tell you everything I know so far," I said to the worried men.

"But first please eat and drink something as it will make me feel better," I told them warmly.

The men were kind enough to start helping themselves to the spread of food before us, and I wasn't lying, it did make me feel better seeing them eat, drink, and relax. James' eyes never left me, and I could feel him studying me. As I looked up at his handsome face, my heart began to pound again in my chest. I looked down at his hands that were resting on the table, and I saw a wedding band on his left hand.

"Are you my husband?" I asked.

Our eyes connected again, and he smiled the most amazing smile.

"Yes, I am fair lady," he replied with a sexy smirk.

I couldn't help the smile that spread on my face; I was thrilled that my dream was true. Knowing he was mine meant the kids in my dream were mine also.

"I think you and I need to talk later," I said to him, still smiling like an idiot!

I tried to steady my heart by taking a deep breath. I cleared my throat and looked around the table. When I spoke to the men, I tried to be as clear as possible. Starting from the beginning, I told them pretty much everything, from the moment I woke in the cavernous room where their women were sleeping.

I explained about the whole birthing process I'd experienced, and I could see them visibly cringing, especially James. He looked the most shocked and horrified!

"We're saving the planet by birthing the animals," I explained to them, "We don't go through a full-term pregnancy, and we don't get cut or anything like that during the birth," I stressed. "It's like having a C section, but the baby animal magically passes through our stomach as if our skin is a force field."

I wasn't sure if I was relieving their stress and tension or adding to it. At that point, I just couldn't tell. James' eyes were still not leaving me in the slightest. A blonde-haired man with a young face and freckles across his nose spoke next.

"Why are our women being kept asleep the whole time?" he asked angrily. "It's like keeping them in a sleeping prison," he added, getting more irate by the second.

I looked at Zanika, and I think it dawned on us both how the situation must look. I could totally understand what they meant when I looked at the situation from their point of view. I'd been so relieved that the angels were here saving our planet that I didn't focus on the fact that I'd been sleeping for five years, and the other women were still sleeping.

"Don't get us wrong here lass, we appreciate what you're all doing," the older man said to Zanika, interrupting my thoughts.

"You're saving our planet and healing us and all, but our women should have the choice if they want to have animals inside them surely?" he added, slightly less agitated but obviously trying to calm himself down.

Zanika looked unsure of what to say, and that made two of us.

CHAPTER 6

There was an awkward silence that seemed to fill the meeting room we were in. Zanika spoke to the men, and her voice was soft and so full of remorse that my heart broke for her. This time, it was my hand reaching for hers trying to reassure her.

"We are very sorry," she told them.

We could all hear the total sincerity in her voice.

"We have only wanted to save you all and your planet. We thought we were doing the right thing by letting your women sleep while helping us," she added.

"Our women should not only be able to choose to help to save our planet, but they also need to be with their families while they do it Zanika," James told her kindly.

He locked eyes with me again, taking my breath away.

"Their men and their children need them," he added.

It was as if he was talking directly to my aching heart.

"Do I have children?" I asked him, quietly from across the table, as tears started running down my cheeks.

James nodded his head with his eyes never leaving mine. He held up his hand indicating four.

"I dreamt of you all," I told him softly.

Zanika rose gracefully from her seat.

"I will go and speak with Christik also. We will all talk again very soon; please relax here. You will be taken to your rooms very soon," she told them.

She then turned to me.

"Elita, I will take you and your husband back to your room while I talk with Christik and Harrik," she said, as she moved away from the table.

James and I rose from our seats too, both of us eager to be alone. Zanika and I dipped our heads to the men and began to leave with James. I seemed to be picking up the angels' ways already, and it made me smile to myself.

As we left the room, James slipped his hand in mine, and it felt so familiar and good. It made my heart race, and I was sure he felt it too.

"Your name is Melanie by the way, not, Elita," he said quietly, "My, Mel!" he added, and he gave my hand a gentle squeeze.

Zanika was kind enough to point out the various rooms to James as we traveled back down the corridor to my room. He seemed genuinely impressed with what the angels were doing.

"They take this all very seriously don't they," he said with a smile.

"They sure do," I replied, returning his beautiful sexy smile.

We soon arrived at my room, and Zanika said farewell to us, telling us she would return for us shortly after talking with Christik and the others.

Still holding hands, I led James into my room. As we entered, I noticed fresh food and drinks on the small table. Also, on the bed was a fresh tunic and trousers for James. '*The angels really didn't miss a beat when it came to details,*' I thought to myself.

"Would you like to eat before you freshen up?" I asked.

"That would be awesome; it's been quite a day and a long trek to get here, and I'm starving," He replied with a grin.

He hadn't let go of my hand, so I led him to the small table and chairs. As we sat down, I could feel my body starting to relax.

"Is this craft the same as the holding structure you were in?" I asked.

"No, it's very different," he answered.

Then he explained that everything was different apart from a few things. Apparently, at the holding structure, they had a beautiful circular courtyard in the center of the structure with tables and seating. It was filled with colorful plants and flowers, and it was all open, so everyone could socialize together. They felt that the angels wanted to encourage the feeling of community between them all, and it seemed to be working from what James said.

"I'll go and get freshened up," he said as we finished our food.

He stood up and walked towards the bathroom. Picking up the fruit juice from the table, I took a sip, and my eyes roamed the room. His fresh clothes were still on the bed; he'd forgotten to grab them before he went into the bathroom. So, I picked them up and made my way to the bathroom, and when I got there, James was already showering. I stopped dead in my tracks. My breath hitched in my chest, and my pulse began to race.

My husband was magnificent! I couldn't help but take in the sight of the water running down his handsome, rugged face and muscular body. Before I knew what, I was doing, I dropped his clothes on the floor. As he turned and faced me, I slipped my gown off my shoulders, letting it slide down my body to the bathroom floor.

He gave me the sexiest smile I'd ever seen and reached out his hand to me. I walked towards him feeling suddenly nervous but excited, and I took his hand in mine.

By my next breath, I was already in his arms with the warm water cascading over us.

Our bodies melted together like they belonged; the heat from his skin warmed me through to my soul. He felt so perfect. He felt like he was mine. His hands cupped my face drawing my hungry lips to his, and he tasted like he was mine too.

As we deepened the kiss, his tongue teasing mine, his hands caressed down my back sending a shiver down my spine. Moving further down, James's hands smoothed over my backside, and then cupping it, he lifted me up. I curled my legs around his body melting into him.

His hard arousal entered me slowly, and he gasped at my tightness. My hard nipples brushed against his muscular hairy chest, his hairs adding to my sensitivity. Slowly, he raised and lowered me with his hardness gliding in and out with ease.

With each entry—my climax built—James's

hands were gripping my buttocks harder as he got closer too. Before long, my orgasm exploded inside me, and as my body tightened around his hard-throbbing arousal, his orgasm peaked.

He groaned loudly at his release, his hands drawing me closer against his body. He held me as I kissed his neck softly, running my fingers through the wet hair at the nape of his neck.

We made love again there in the shower reminding each other of our love. It was perfect, and because I still had no proper memories of our life together, it was like the first time for me.

About an hour later, we were clean, dressed, and lying on the bed facing each other and talking quietly.

"I don't have any memories of our life together or our children, James," I said.

Tears sprung to my eyes as I said the words and felt the loss.

"Please tell me about our children. I don't want to feel like a stranger when I meet them," I told him.

"They are just like you," he said, smiling at me with love.

"They have your thick hair and your beautiful eyes, your strength, and your compassion. Plus, their dad's awesome sense of humor," he continued.

I couldn't help but giggle at the cheeky face he made.

"Our twins Harrison and Abigail are fourteen years old now," he said, "Holly is nineteen, and Anthony is twenty years old now."

"I've missed so much of them growing up; years and moments I'm never going to get back," I told him, again feeling a huge loss.

James began to softly and reassuringly run his hand down the side of my body.

"Are they all okay?" I asked, "I don't remember anything about what happened before the angels got here. Although the angels did show me how Earth was dying."

James looked deeply into my eyes and took a deep slow breath to calm his emotions. I'd asked him, but suddenly I wasn't sure if I wanted to know or remember. What the angels had shown me had been bad enough.

"The kids are great, but things were extremely bad, baby. Just before the angels arrived, about eighty percent of the human population had died already," he said. "Some through starvation, others through dehydration or worse. People were trying to drink whatever water they could find, and others died through some really nasty diseases. I'd never seen anything like it. Towards the end, many died from fighting over what little was left. There were so many committing suicide, because they didn't want to suffer anymore, or because they'd already lost their loved ones," he explained.

He stopped, and tears started to slowly run down his face. The pain and emotion were written all over his expression.

"I think all our family is dead, Mel, and our planet was all but dead with barely any animals left. There was no drinkable water and no food supplies left," he said. "We were on the verge of ending things as a family ourselves. We didn't want the kids suffering, but it had already gone too far.

I think we'd all just fallen into an exhausted sleep. When the kids and I woke up, you were gone. We found ourselves in a hospital room being looked after by the angels," he added, with sadness in his voice.

James had obviously nothing but gratitude towards the angels for saving our children and us.

"When I asked where you were, they told me you were alive and healed," he explained. "They did explain that you and the other women were helping them with the animals. I understood how important that was, but it didn't make it easier being without you."

The angels had obviously kept the details to

a minimum, not really understanding that humans needed as much information as possible. James and the kids had clearly understood just how important it was for the angels to replenish the animal kingdom. I listened patiently as James continued.

He explained that they and the other children and men had come to terms with their women not being there. They knew it was for the greater good and knew it wouldn't be forever.

However, after years of trying to be patient, their patience had begun to run thin. Especially with so little information and no proof of the explanation they'd been given. They'd been repeatedly asking for their women and had been told repeatedly the same thing.

Until one day, when the angels changed over again, and a few new ones appeared at the holding structure with the replacement shift. Just as James was about to tell me more, I heard Zanika's voice from the archway entrance to my room.

"Can I enter, Elita," she asked.

James and I quickly rose from the bed, "Of course," I replied, smoothing down my dress.

We walked towards the entryway, and Zanika entered my room. She dipped her head at us both and took my hand in hers.

"We are going to need your help, Elita," she

stated softly. "We want you all to be happy, with what we are doing," she added "However, we do not have your human social skills. Will you help us to resolve the issues that have arisen, so that we may move forward in our goals?" Zanika asked.

"Yes, of course, I will," I replied, "And by the way, apparently my true name is, Mel," I added with a huge smile.

"That is a beautiful name," she said "We can tell the others now. We are to meet them, with the other men in the larger meeting room," she added.

We left my room and made our way down the pearlescent corridor towards the control room. James was holding my hand once more. It was as if he was afraid to lose me again. I gave his hand a gentle squeeze,

"You're not going to lose me again you know," I said softly.

"I'm not taking any chances," he replied in a hushed voice full of emotion.

Zanika broke the emotional tension between us.

"Everyone is looking forward to hearing more, James," she said, "We very much want to hear why you were told we were torturing your females. We are very distressed by this new information. We would like to find the angels who told you these untruths," she added.

"Yes, I'd like to know why they lied to us too. We've all been through hell and back, all believing the worst, imagining our women were screaming for us in pain," he told her.

James was subconsciously tightening his grip on my hand as his emotions became stronger. I stroked his arm reassuringly, reminding him that I was there with him. I knew it worked. I could tell by the shy smile he gave me that he was getting his emotions in check.

In next to no time, we arrived at the control room. It was interesting to watch James's expression when he looked around the massive room, with all the angels busy working at their consoles. Like me, he seemed in awe of his surroundings. Especially when he looked out of the huge glass window and saw the ocean outside, with the big rig structures in the distance.

When I followed his gaze, I noticed that the once destroyed rig craft was now as good as new and working again. It was amazing how quickly the angels worked their special kind of magic.

Zanika led us through the control room to the meeting room beyond. Harrik, Christik and their colleagues were already waiting for us inside, and so were all the other men who'd come with James from the holding craft.

The tension that I'd felt coming from the men before at our first meeting was now minimal, thank goodness. I was so relieved that I hadn't realized how nervous I'd grown on our way to meet them. The room had been prepared for us with the smaller table now replaced with a larger and longer one with enough chairs for everyone.

On the table was an impressive assortment of foods; some were familiar, and others weren't. There was quite a feast with an assortment of fresh vegetables and fruits. Plus, there were plenty of fruit juices and fresh coffee for all.

The men still seemed to feel out of place; all stood in their own little group talking quietly while the angels, relaxed and intrigued, watched them from a short distance away.

We dipped our heads in welcome to the angels and men, then took seats together around the long table. James didn't leave my side and appeared very at ease with Harrik sitting next to him. The men, on the other hand, all sat together, forcing the angels to do the same.

There was a definite, them and us, situation going on. I hoped that the situation would remedy itself with time and that the men would eventually have the sort of relationship that I had with the angels.

“Welcome humans of Earth; my name is Christik,” Christik greeted warmly, “We are pleased with your visit, even though it was initially for negative reasons,” she said, not unkindly. “We hope we can turn that negative into something positive together as we still have much work to do here to save your planet.”

The men nodded at her greeting but didn’t say anything, so she continued.

“Zanika and Harrik have told us all about your initial meeting. It is worrying for us that our own kind would lie to you about your women. Our race never lies; it is not in our nature,” she told them.

“I would like you to meet Livik, Jakiz, and Hulaz,” she said, gesturing to the other angels who were sitting at the table.

The angels all dipped their heads in respect to the anxious-looking men.

“You have already met Zanika and Harrik, and of course, Elita, known also as, Mel,” she said, smiling at me warmly.

I really liked Christik as she was so honest and direct. Christik continued as the nervous men looked on.

"We are going to make some positive changes today. We want you to see how much we are dedicated to saving your race and your planet," Christik told them as she looked into all of their faces.

"Before we do, however, we need to find the angels who lied to you," she stated. "We believe they may be responsible for the explosions on our ocean cleaning craft, and the great suffering of our race, who were on it at the time," she said sadly.

Harrik sat forward and spoke to the men.

"Would you be willing to help us find the Fallen ones? They pose a real threat to our work together and the survival of you all," he stated.

The men glanced at each other as though communicating with thought, which, of course, they couldn't. So, I assumed it must have been an acknowledgement of something they'd agreed between themselves earlier. It was the oldest man who spoke for the group.

"Yes, we will help you find them," he said with conviction. "We want to help save our planet too, and now we have the chance to do it," he added.

The angels dipped their heads in agreement, and Hulaz stood up from her seat. When she raised her palm towards the middle of the table, I knew we were going to see something. Her hand glowed with the bright, white light, and an image began to appear in front of us all. It was the holding structure where the men had come from.

I could see angels working outside of it, unloading supplies of food and other essentials, such as clothes and bathroom items. They were using their power to elevate and move the items from a small land craft and into the building. The image zoomed in on one of the angel's faces.

"We will show you all the angels who have helped you and your new community. Please tell us which of them lied to you," Christik asked.

"We will," James told her.

He gently squeezed my hand and gave a nod to the other men around the table.

"No, he's not one of them," he told her, as the image zoomed in on the angel's face.

The image moved to another angel and another.

"No, No," The men stated as the images changed.

It was just like a space-age mugshot display or line up, and after about ten minutes, James suddenly stood from his chair.

"Yes, she is one of them," he almost shouted.

The image showed a female angel. She had the same markings as Zanika, but as we all looked on, the image glowed brightly. Abruptly, the diamonds on her markings turned a dark grey almost black, and her long red hair turned to a dark silvery-grey, as did the shimmer of her skin.

"She has been marked for removal; only we can see the changes for now," Harrik told us. "We still need to find the others."

James sat back down, and the images continued. Every time one of the men recognized one of the liars, Christik would mark them in the same way, turning their colors into dark grey.

There were six of them in total, and I could sense the anxiety emanating from the angels in the room. James started to gently stroke his thumb over my hand. I think he felt it too.

"Why would they lie to my people," I asked the angels. "I just don't understand what reason could be behind this," I added.

Christik looked at me with worry all over her beautiful face.

"We do not understand it either, Elita, sorry, Mel," she said. "We are a peaceful healing race; it is what we do. It is what we have always done," she continued. "It is not in our nature to deceive or have ill intentions towards another race or each other."

"We are very confused," Hulaz added.

"We will find out, Elita, do not worry. Now we know who they are, let us eat, and then we all have work to do together," Christik said to everyone in the room.

The atmosphere in the room had changed dramatically while we all ate and drank together. The angels asked the men questions such as "How do you like the holding structure? "How did you survive so long before we arrived?" and so on.

The men answered warmly, and I think the conversations were breaking the ice and the barriers between them. James and the men asked the angels questions too. They were genuinely interested in what the angels were doing and what they'd accomplished so far. They couldn't help but be impressed like I was. I also noticed a sense of determination coming from the men, including James.

As I watched them all, I thought to myself that I shouldn't really be surprised. These men, these survivors had witnessed famine, drought, and disease as well as fighting and the deaths of humans, animals, and vegetation.

It just showed how resilient we were as a race. I felt so much pride forming in my chest, I thought I might burst as I sat there at the table with my fellow humans and the angels.

After we'd all finished our meal and the last piece was eaten, Christik took that as her cue. Rising from her seat, she addressed us all.

"I believe we are forming a wonderful friendship with you all. We would like you to feel welcomed by all, and we want you to trust us," Christik said. "So, moving forward, we would like you all to work alongside us to help us achieve our goals, and we will start right now," she added with a lovely smile.

The angels rose from their seats and began to glide towards the exit, the men smiling at each other with, I think, excitement followed suit.

We walked back through the control room, and as we passed the angels working, the angels greeted the men with smiles and dipped heads of respect. It was as if they all knew what had been said and were happy to be all working together. I wondered if the angels were just as curious about us as we were about them.

As we walked into the corridor, the oldest man came alongside James and me and introduced himself.

"I'm Derek, ma'am," he said, with a very thick Scottish accent.

He had greying hair and a kind, slightly lined face with lots of character. That gave me the impression he'd seen and experienced a lot, even before the end of our world started to happen.

"I wanted to say how much me, and the lads appreciate what you're doing lass," he said.

"You're very welcome," I replied, giving him my best smile. "I'm starting to think that my waking up was fate," I told him.

"Aye lass, you could be on to something there," he responded with a chuckle.

I liked him instantly! As we walked down the long corridor, I soon realized that the men had already been told what the rooms were and for what. I could hear them asking the angels questions such as, "So what temperature do you keep the new plants at?" and "Do you have seeds and stuff just from our country or from other countries too?"

They'd obviously had time to process the information they'd already received and wanted to know more. I was starting to think it was the beginning of a beautiful friendship—between the angels and us.

When we finally stopped, we were outside the cavernous room where I'd woken from my long sleep.

CHAPTER 7

At the archway entrance to the sleeping room, Christik moved to the front of everyone in our group and she spoke in her calm demeanor.

"This is the room where all your women are. Please do not be alarmed by the machines; they are feeding your women, keeping them healthy and in a peaceful sleep," she explained kindly.

As soon as she said the words, I could almost hear the men's pounding hearts around me, beating and thumping in their chests as their excitement and trepidation grew.

"We will find your women one by one, and we will wake them for you," she told them. "I must warn you that many of your women may not have their memories for a time, unfortunately, like, Elita."

I think we all felt their disappointment at that point.

"Please don't be upset everyone. I started to

dream about, James, and our children straight away," I said reassuringly.

I looked at my husband and smiled at him, our connection feeling stronger with every hour we spent together.

Christik continued addressing the anxious group.

"We will walk through the room together. When you recognize your female, please tell us," she told them.

It was probably only natural that I was just as nervous as the men. I was nervous for them and excited for them too.

We walked into the massive white room, and the men took in the sight of the rows and rows of sleeping women. The highly intelligent machines were all humming in unison, and the soft beeping of the women's heartbeats were actually quite soothing.

The men excitedly led the way down the first row of women, looking at their sleeping faces. They all looked like sleeping beauties, and all of them had a healthy glow emanating from them. The women were all different shapes, sizes, and colors. They all had growing pregnancy bumps at different stages, hiding beneath the thin, silvery sheets and white gowns.

Derek probably said what all the others were probably thinking.

"Are all these lasses pregnant with the same kind of animal?" he asked no one in particular, not taking his eyes away from the sleeping women.

"They are all carrying different animals," Zanika replied. "If you look at their left hands, it will show you what creature they are pregnant with," she stated. "The silver mark disappears once the baby animal is removed."

I hadn't noticed any mark on my left hand when I'd woken up, but I suppose I was too stunned to notice. This was understandable after waking up in a strange room with the other women and not knowing what was going on.

Sure enough, when I looked at the left hand of the nearest woman, there was a silvery-white mark on her hand, and it was a deer. I could only just see the antlers on its head. '*Thank goodness the women only carry for a short time,*' I thought to myself.

It was as if Harrik read my mind. It was quite spooky how these angels sensed what you were thinking and feeling.

"Your women are only pregnant for a matter of weeks, depending on what animal they are pregnant with," he explained. "We did try to simulate the whole animal pregnancy process. Unfortunately, we cannot simulate the amniotic sac or the placenta. Your Mother Nature is very complicated and not easily copied," he added.

"That is why we had to do this," Zanika said, as she pointed to the nearest sleeping women.

"We felt we had no choice or other options open to us," she explained.

Abruptly, one of the men came to a halt at one of the beds. We all stopped and watched him as he stared at the sleeping woman.

"Julia," he whispered so softly I barely heard him.

He seemed to be taking in the whole scene before him, his eyes looking over her lovely face, her body, and the machines next to her bed. Julia was sleeping peacefully with her soft, light blonde hair framing her pale skin.

She was a beautiful curvy woman who was around 5'5 tall I guessed. There, on her left hand, was the silvery-white marking of a gorilla. I could just about make out the muscular shape of its body on her pale hand.

Her breathing was soft and regular, as her full-breasted chest rose and fell. Her pregnant belly was roughly the size of a small soccer ball. He turned to face Christik who was next to him,

"Can you wake her please?" he asked quietly.

She smiled at him warmly.

"Yes, we can, but remember, she may not remember you or what has happened to your planet. She has been sleeping for a long time, Barrie."

I assumed the men and the angels had introduced themselves while they had waited for James, Zanika, and I to arrive at the meeting room. Which I took as a good sign. At least they were trying to get to know each other; it was a step in the right direction.

I made a mental note of his name. I assumed that from now on we would all be working closely together. Well, I hoped we would be. The men gave me the impression that they wanted to be involved in saving our planet, which pleased me greatly. I was sure they didn't want to be stuck back in the holding structure anymore, and I couldn't blame them.

Zanika and Harrik moved to the side of Julia's bed where the machines were.

They didn't turn the machines off, but they did adjust some lit buttons which changed color from white to silver. Then both angels hovered their hands over the top of her still body. Their glowing hands were scanning her from the top of her head right down to her toes.

When they'd finished, they moved away from Julia, and Barrie slid past them and slipped her hand in his. We all stood there avidly, watching for any sign of her waking up. Even the angels were studying her lovely face for signs of her stirring.

James, who was still stood right next to me holding my hand, let go and wrapped his arm around my waist, pulling me closer. I looked into his eyes and kissed him gently on his soft, full lips. He smiled his sexy smile and lowered his head, so his lips were brushing against my ear.

"I really wish I'd been here for you when you woke up baby," he whispered.

He raised his head and looked deeply into my eyes; they were so full of emotion.

"Me too!" I whispered back, and I really mea-nt it.

We both turned back to Julia's still form on the bed. I wasn't sure if I was seeing things, but I thought I saw her eyes move. As if confirming what I thought I'd seen, Barrie gasped as Julia's eyes started to flutter open.

No one breathed a word as she tried to focus her eyes. I guessed she was trying to not only focus her eyes but also focus her thoughts, as her brain took in the surrounding noises of the machines. Just like I did when I woke up.

"Julia," Barrie said again, in a soft loving voice.

She turned her face towards him, "I know you, don't I?" she whispered gruffly.

"Yes Darlin, I'm your husband Barrie," he told her, worry written all over his face.

She smiled at him so sweetly it was heart-warming. I think we all felt the love that was flowing between them.

"Yes, my husband," she whispered to him.

Barrie's resounding smile was glorious to see. He was obviously thrilled that she appeared to be gradually recognizing him. She slowly lifted her head to look around, and that's when she saw the rest of the men, myself, and the angels. Her eyes grew wide as she took in the sight at the end of her bed.

Zanika approached the bed, smiling warmly at Julia and showing her palms emphasizing that she wasn't a threat.

"Welcome Julia, please do not be afraid. We are angels, here to save your race and your planet," she told her.

As Julia registered Zanika's words, she started trying to sit herself up, and Barrie moved forward to help her. Slipping his arm under her shoulders, he gently lifted her upper body while Harrik quickly moved to the other side.

Harrik held out his hand towards the top end of the bed, and his hand began to glow white. Slowly, the top end of the bed began to rise, and as it rose, Barrie slipped out his arm, allowing Julia to lay back against it.

Julia was so busy taking in her surroundings and the angels that she hadn't even noticed her pregnant belly. Barrie took Julia's hand in his again and asked her gently.

"What do you remember Darlin?" he asked her softly.

She looked into his kind face.

"I think the last thing I remember was you and me driving to my parents' house because they still had some water and a bit of food left," she said, a little less hoarsely.

"Things were very bad, and the last news bulletin I saw said that we were in the last stages," she added.

Barrie had tears running down his face. He gently lifted his hand to stroke her lovely face.

"Yes Darlin, that's exactly what happened," he told her.

"That was the last thing I remember," she said.

Julia looked so confused as she spoke.

"Angels? Are they really angels Barrie?" she asked, as her gaze went from him to the angels.

"Yeah Darlin, they really are what we

believed to be angels," he told her. "They've been coming to our planet since before humans were around," he explained. "But I need to tell you something honey. Do you remember all the animals dying?" he asked.

She looked thoughtful for a moment as she tried to remember, and then she looked into Barrie's eyes,

"Yes, I do remember that," she said.

Her brows furrowed, and her eyes darted as she tried to recollect her memories. "I remember seeing the cow carcasses lying in the dead grass in the fields we drove past."

Barrie nodded his head as she spoke.

"That's right Darlin, we did see that," he told her, "Well; when the angels came to save our planet, they started to clean the water and grow plants. The other thing they had to do, honey, was to repopulate our planet with animals so we could all survive, but they couldn't do it on their own Darlin. They had to impregnate you women, with the animal babies," he said.

I think we all held our breath while we waited for the information to sink in for her. She seemed to take in what Barrie had told her because she looked downwards to look at her stomach.

As her eyes took in the sight of her pregnant

belly, her hand smoothed over her bump.

"I'm pregnant with a baby animal?" she asked Barrie, in a voice that showed her shock and mirrored her face.

She looked from her bump back to Barrie, her face the picture of utter surprise.

"Yeah Darlin you are," he said as he took her hand with the mark in it and showed her the image of a gorilla.

"See," he said, using his thumb to stroke the gorilla marking. "You have a baby gorilla in your belly, but it's only small. You're not too far along, and you don't have to deliver it like you would a human baby," He added.

Barrie then looked at me, so I took that as his cue for me to explain what happened to me with the tiger cub.

"Hi, Julia, my name is, Mel, but the angels call me, Elita; you can call me either," I said smiling. "Please don't worry about being pregnant with the baby gorilla," I told her. "I just recently gave birth to a tiger cub. I was only pregnant for a matter of weeks, and when the Tiger cub was far enough along, Zanika and Harrik removed it and put it into a containment capsule," I explained.

She appeared to be listening without freaking out which was promising, even though her eyes were as big as saucers, so I carried on explaining.

"The angels have powers, and when they removed the Tiger cub, they used their power. It passed through my stomach without me feeling anything or having to be cut," I assured her. "I promise you; it's an amazing experience."

Luckily, Julia seemed to believe every word I said, and I could see her whole demeanor gradually relax. I was very relieved.

"So, what happens now?" she asked as her gaze went to Christik. "I don't want to be stuck in this bed until the gorilla baby is ready to come out!" she declared. "I want to be with my Barrie."

Christik smiled reassuringly at her.

"We can put a mobile monitoring device on your stomach Julia," she told her. "It is very small, and it will cling to your skin. You will not even feel it, I assure you," she added.

Christik looked to Harrik and Zanika who were patiently waiting next to Julia's bed.

"Can you do that now for Julia and then take her and her husband to their room, so that they may reacquaint themselves?" she asked.

Harrik nodded to Christik then walked away, I assumed, to get the monitoring device. Zanika approached the bed and looked at Julia.

"You will be unsteady when you try and walk

for a little while," she told her. "Take your time getting out of the bed; I will get you a drink. When you are ready and steady enough, we will go to your room," she explained.

"Come," Christik said to the rest of us. "We will see if any of the other women can be found, woken, and reunited with their men."

She led the way slowly, so the rest of the men could look at the women to see if any of them were theirs. The men's spirits and banter were a lot more lighthearted, and they were seemingly happier after witnessing Barrie and Julia being reunited.

Within two hours, Harrik and Zanika were back with us after settling Barrie and Julia into their new room. A total of five women were recognized and woken from their peaceful sleep.

Rebecca was the second woman found by her Scottish husband Derek. She was a lovely older lady in her early fifties. Her gorgeous, brunette, curly hair was thick and hung in ringlets around her sweet, round face.

Within minutes of her waking, she threw her arms around Derek's neck; she didn't even notice the IV in her right arm, attached to the monitors next to her bed.

Rebecca or Beccy as Derek called her was

pregnant with a jaguar cub. She took the news really well and, like Julia, she was happy to have the mobile monitor stuck on her stomach until the Jaguar cub was ready to be birthed.

Trudy was a very petite shorter lady with short, brown wavy hair, thirty-ish in age, and was amazing. Even though she couldn't remember her husband Phil, she took the news of her pregnancy brilliantly. In fact, she seemed absolutely thrilled to be pregnant and to be helping to save the animal kingdom; it was amazing to her. She was full of questions too.

"What animal am I carrying? How many animals have I carried before? What animals were they?" The questions were endless.

I liked her a lot instantly, and as she asked her questions, with each answer, she would say "Whoa!" in total awe. We were all smiling and giggling at her enthusiasm; it was contagious.

What was really funny was her husband Phil's face. Trudy seemed to be more excited about the baby animals than getting to know her own husband again. Poor Phil looked very disheartened at first; however, she had him laughing too within minutes.

I think Trudy's reaction actually helped the other women who were already awake to look at it from another perspective. I think we were all impressed with how resilient the women were. All but two of them took the news of what was happening quite well, considering they were all pregnant with baby animals.

The two that freaked out badly were Michelle and Mimi, and my heart hurt at their distress. Their reactions mirrored each other's the moment they saw their small, pregnant abdomens. They both tried to pull out their IVs from their arms while screaming things such as, "Get it out! Get that thing out!"

Both times, Zanika had to use her power to calm them, so we could at least have a chance to talk to them somewhat calmly.

Michelle was so freaked out by the pregnancy and the fact she had no memories—that her boyfriend Jessie begged Harrik to put her back to sleep. Michelle's whole body was shaking with panic and shock. Her eyes were darting in all directions as if she was looking for a way to escape the madness, she'd found herself in.

Harrik glided forward quickly as Jessie tried to comfort Michelle, and Harrik changed the silver buttons back to white on the machines next to her bed.

Slowly, Michelle went limp in Jessie's arms. Her very long, dark brown hair was flowing over

Jessie's arm, and her deep brown wet eyes were closed once again.

With tears in his own eyes, he laid her slight frame back onto the bed where she looked peaceful once again. Jessie turned to Harrik with concern marring his fair complexion.

"What's going to happen now?" he asked, his voice shaky with emotion.

Harrik looked just as upset as Jessie when he answered,

"I am afraid the panda fetus inside Michelle isn't far enough along to birth yet Jessie," he said with regret in his voice, "It will need another three weeks at least before we can remove it," he added.

Jessie was too emotional to say another word; he just nodded his head in understanding. He sat down on the bed next to Michelle, stroking her luscious long hair in complete adoration.

"You know where your room is Jessie," Harrik said, "you may come and go as you please, and spend as much time with your Michelle as you would like, while she is sleeping," he added.

Jessie didn't take his eyes off his girlfriend as we slowly moved away.

Mimi, who luckily had her memories, didn't react quite as badly as Michelle, but it was still bad.

"Now, you know why our women have to

have the choice to do this," James told the angels softly after they had just had to calm down Mimi.

"Not all our women want babies, and some don't even like the thought of being pregnant," He explained.

Andrew, Mimi's husband, nodded his head then turned to Zanika,

"James, is right. She has never wanted children," He told her. "When her sisters tried to show her their baby bumps, it made her feel sick," he explained.

"We are very sorry Andrew," Zanika replied. "We wrongly assumed that all your women would want to help. We will not let this happen again."

Mimi looked up at Andrew with tears streaming down her face.

"I want it out now!" she told him in a sob.

Andrew turned to Zanika again,

"Can you get it out now? Would it survive?" he asked desperately.

Zanika moved right next to Mimi's bed; raised her arm and held her palm over Mimi's pregnant belly. Her hand glowed bright silvery-white for a moment, as did the silvery mark on Mimi's left hand, and then it faded back to normal.

"It is a little early, but yes I believe it will survive," Zanika told him.

Christik stepped forward and looked at Mimi with love and compassion.

"We do not want you emotionally suffering Mimi," she told her reassuringly, "so we will take you now to birth the baby goat. I would like everyone to see how we remove the baby animal. Would you agree to that?" she asked.

"Yes." Mimi whispered, "Just get it out plea-se." she said with another sob.

I think we all felt sad for her as it was such a shame, she was so distraught. However, we were all different, and I had the feeling that maybe Mimi had a different role to play in helping save our planet.

Zanika and Harrik moved quickly and efficiently around Mimi, getting her ready to move to the birthing room.

"Would you like to stay awake for the birthing process Mimi, or would you prefer to go back to sleep until it is over?" Harrik asked her kindly.

"Please put me back to sleep," she answered still very tearful.

Andrew held her hand until she was sleeping peacefully once again, her remaining tears were welled in her eyelashes.

"Come." Christik addressed us all, "we will go to the birthing room now."

Christik moved away from Mimi's bed, so

we all followed suit apart from Zanika and Harrik. They both moved towards the bed. Zanika was at the top end of the bed, and Harrik was at the bottom end.

Using their power, they elevated the bed, and Harrik began to glide in front leading the way. When they had a lead in front of us, we all followed suit.

We walked the long corridor slowly as the other women were still quite wobbly on their legs, but still insistent on making their own way. None of us were in a rush and to be honest; it was lovely hearing the chatter between the men and their women.

"It's heartwarming isn't it, seeing them back together and the happiness between them," I said to James, as we walked hand in hand.

He smiled at me so lovingly.

"Yes, they have a lot of catching up to do and so do we," he replied, and then he winked at me.

I couldn't help the giggle that escaped. I think I knew exactly the kind of catching up he wanted to do, and it wasn't all talking!

While we walked, the men pointed rooms out to the women, telling them what they were for and explaining what the angels were doing to help us and our planet.

It was awesome hearing the women's interest

and their questions. It was just a shame that Barrie, Julia, Michelle, and Jessie weren't with us to enjoy the conversations. Sometimes, one of the angels would answer, if the men weren't sure or didn't know. I seemed to be learning more as I listened too.

Soon, we arrived at the birthing room. Harrik led the bed in with Zanika taking the rear. They glided the bed to the nearest veiled cubicle, placing the machines to the side and then moved away to get what they needed. The men, women, and James all walked straight over to the massive wall where all the baby animals were being stored.

I followed them over, and I was just as fascinated as the first time I'd seen it. The only difference being was that I could actually go right up to it this time and have a really good look.

CHAPTER 8

I was enthralled as I stood at the glistening glass wall. The animals looked so small and peaceful inside their shimmering capsules. They all had their eyes closed and were literally curled up into fetal positions.

I hadn't really grasped before how many were inside the wall, but now I was up close, I could see through the capsules, and there were thousands upon thousands of them all behind each other.

There were so many different creatures in there such as rabbits, deer, hippos, snakes and so many more. It was truly astonishing how much had been accomplished so far.

The others looked inside the wall in absolute amazement, pointing out to each other what they could see.

"Look, there's a leopard." "See there; it's a baby giraffe."

And comments such as.

"I didn't know elephants looked so strange so young!"

And "This bird doesn't have feathers yet, come and see; it looks so weird!"

I was relieved that none of them were freaked out by what they saw and then I remembered, '*They'd seen a lot worse as our planet was coming to an end.*'

Zanika and Harrik re-entered the room; both dressed in their sheer, silvery-white veils and gloves. We all gave them a wide berth, so they could do their thing.

Zanika went to the machines next to Mimi's bed and adjusted some buttons. I assumed it was to stimulate labor and to make sure that Mimi was pain-free like she did for me.

Poor Mimi, it still made me feel so sad at how upset she was. I dreaded to think how her husband must have felt seeing her so distraught. Andrew seemed to have calmed down now and was equally as fascinated with the baby animals as we all were.

Harrik had entered with a capsule hovering between his hands, and as Zanika adjusted the machines, he left it hovering at the end of the bed. We watched as his hand hovered over the capsule, making it temporarily glow white, and as the glow softened, the fluid inside started to give off a shimmer.

My gaze turned to Mimi's left hand, and I saw the marking of the goat glow. I wondered if any of the others had taken note of the marking. I also wondered if the other angels in the room watching had seen any of the births before, considering this wasn't part of their normal roles.

Christik, Livik, Jakiz, and Hulaz all seemed just as fascinated as the rest of us, and it was so quiet in the room with everyone completely entranced; you could have heard a pin drop.

Harrik and Zanika moved positions to either side of the sleeping Mimi. They moved their now glowing hands over her body slowly. Then we watched in awe as they slid the silvery sheet down to her bikini line and rolled her gown to the top of her abdomen. It was always amazing to watch them using their power.

Once her small baby bump was exposed, they raised their hands and moved them into position just above her pregnant stomach.

"I'm not sure I can watch this," Andrew said suddenly, with a shaky voice.

When I turned to face him, I could see that his whole body was shaking like a nervous wreck. It was Hulaz who stepped towards him. Smiling kindly at him, she placed her hand on his forearm, and instantly she began to calm his shaking body. He was visibly relaxing before our eyes.

"Do not worry Andrew," she said softly, "Your Mimi will not feel anything. We do not harm your females in any way; please trust us," she added.

He looked into her beautiful, blue sapphire eyes, and obviously feeling reassured, he nodded his head in agreement.

We all turned our attention back to Mimi and watched avidly. Zanika and Harrik's hands began to glow silvery-white again, as did Mimi's bare pregnant stomach and the goat mark on her left hand.

As the white glow brightened, they both started to raise their hands, and suddenly, we could all see something beginning to appear on top of her smooth, bare skin.

At first, I couldn't make out the baby goat, but as it passed through her unmarked skin, I started to see the top of its head and back through the amniotic sac. As Harrik and Zanika's hands raised higher, more of the baby goat inside its amniotic sack appeared.

There were gasps and sounds of amazement from the women and men around the room when the full form of the baby goat finally rose completely from Mimi's abdomen.

The tiny goat looked so small and vulnerable sleeping in its amniotic fluid. It had sparse pale, sandy-colored fur and tiny little ears and hooves. Its umbilical cord was floating next to its tiny body. Zanika and Harrik moved with ease, the baby goat hovering in its sack between their hands. They moved towards the waiting capsule and just as easily used their power to pass it through the capsule wall until it was safely inside.

We all watched still in awe as the capsule pulsed with light. The baby goat's placenta and umbilical cord started to move towards the side until the placenta made contact with the organic device on the inside wall of the capsule.

We were mesmerized as the capsule pulsed with the bright white light again, and then there was just the rhythmic pulse of the baby goat's heartbeat.

"That was bloody amazing!" Derek said, in total wonderment.

Harrik started to make his way out of the room with the capsule hovering between his hands, and Zanika started covering up Mimi's bare stomach.

"Yeah, I agree that was amazing!" said James, as he turned to look at me. "I'm so glad I got to see for myself how magical that was, and I'm pleased to witness for myself that you didn't suffer baby," he told me softly.

"I want to be awake when I have mine!" Trudy stated as she looked down at her left hand. "Sloth," she added, smiling from ear to ear.

"Me too!" Beccy chipped in, "I think it's totally awesome that we're getting to be a part of this," she declared.

Derek was smiling too as he wrapped an arm around her.

"I think you are awesome!" he told her lovingly.

Andrew turned to Christik with tearful eyes,

"That really was a beautiful thing to see," he told her, "I'm sorry my wife won't be able to help again."

Christik looked at him with heartfelt compassion.

"Your wife has helped us a great deal already Andrew; we are very grateful to her," she told him.

Andrew appeared to be happy with Christik's answer and seemed relieved that his wife's ordeal was now over.

"Can you wake her up now please?" he asked Zanika.

"Yes of course," she said.

She made her way back to the machines next to Mimi's bed. Zanika adjusted the buttons again on the machines next to the bed, and the buttons went from white to silver.

We all stood in anticipation waiting for her wake up again now that the birth was over. Personally, I was hoping that she would be back to her normal self and not the poor panic-stricken lady she was. We all hated seeing her so distraught.

Andrew's body was tense as he stroked her hand, waiting for her to open her eyes. The others began to talk quietly between themselves while they waited.

I could hear Trudy excitedly saying to the others how she couldn't wait to see her baby sloth being born, and that she wondered what the next baby animal would be. If the angels let her do it again.

At that point, Christik spoke to the group.

"We would like you women to help us continue our goal of repopulating the animals of your planet if are willing," she stated. "From now on, you will be able to go with your men and be with the new communities while you are pregnant," she added. "You would only be required to come here to our medical unit for implantation and the birth if you are prepared to do so."

Trudy was softly clapping her hands in glee, her face full of excitement.

"That sounds like the perfect plan to me," she

beamed.

"I agree completely," Beccy said, adding to the conversation. "Now I've seen a birth, which was quite magical and amazing in my opinion, I'd like to do it again after this one," she said, stroking her pregnant stomach affectionately. "As long as I can be active during the pregnancy."

I watched the talking women and noticed that both of them had actually started to gently stroke their animal baby bumps with affection.

It was truly amazing to see the connections forming between us humans and the animals in this way. I wished to myself that we'd all been a lot more respectful and appreciative of the animals before our planet had started to die.

As these thoughts were running through my mind, I heard soft words spoken.

"Is it over?" Mimi asked, still sleepy and calm.

Instantly, everyone stopped talking, with all eyes watching the previously distraught woman.

"Yes darling, it's over," he assured her. "It's gone, and you are a hundred percent back to normal."

She seemed to believe every word I think, but she still clearly wanted to see for herself, or perhaps wanted to check what her stomach looked like. I wasn't sure which. She let go of Andrew's hand and ignoring the rest of us in the room, she quickly slid the silvery sheet down and lifted up the white gown she was wearing.

Looking down she stared at her now empty and flatter stomach. She lifted her left hand and smoothed her small hand over her skin. When she looked back up at us all, there was a smile of pure relief on her beautiful face. Her eyes connected with Christik's.

"Thank you," she whispered.

Christik smiled warmly at her and dipped her head in respect.

"You are welcome, young one; we want you to be happy and whole," she replied.

As Mimi began to lower her gown and pull the sheet back up, she stopped with the sheet still clutched in her hand.

"The mark, it's now gone," she said, as she looked at Andrew,

"Was it okay, the baby goat?" she asked.

I think her curiosity surprised us all. We all seemed to look at each other as if to say, "What the heck?" Andrew took her left hand in his, stroking the top of her hand with his thumb.

"It was fine Darlin, it was perfect," he told her. "It was actually really quite magical seeing it being born. It wasn't anything like I thought it was it was going to be," he said to her gently.

Mimi suddenly looked very embarrassed. She lowered her head and looking up through her long eyelashes, she said softly.

"I'm really sorry I freaked out everyone; I panicked."

I felt so bad for her, especially when any one of us could have panicked the same way. Stepping forward, I smiled at her, hoping it would show the warmth and compassion I felt towards her.

"You have nothing to apologize for Mimi. We are all out of our depth and dealing with a situation that is completely unreal," I told her kindly. "You certainly aren't going to be the last person to panic I'm sure," I added. "but I hope you can help us with the other women and help them through it like we are helping you."

"Yes, I'd like that," she replied a little more confidently. "I think I might like to watch a baby animal being born too," she said with a small smile.

'*Progress,*' I thought to myself, as I returned her lovely smile.

At that moment, Harrik glided back into the room with a stone tray of food and a couple of drinks hovering between his hands which he passed to Andrew. He used his power to raise the top end of the bed higher for Mimi, and he took the tray back from Andrew, placing it softly on her lap.

"We will let you eat, drink and rest for a while with your husband Mimi," he told her, as he moved away from the bed to where we were all standing.

Christik stepped forward, drawing all our attention.

"It has been a very long day for you all," she said warmly. "I know we still have one woman to find; however, you ladies need to eat, drink and rest too," she continued. "So Livik and Hulaz will see you all to your rooms, and in the morning, we will find your other woman," she stated.

She looked directly at the man called John, who had disappointment written all over his face. I think we all felt the dismay radiating from him.

"Is that alright with you John?" she asked, obviously noting the sadness in his features.

"Yes, it's okay," he replied softly, "My angel, Tracy is still sleeping, so I can wait one more night."

James, the warm caring man he was, made his way over to John and put his muscular arm around his shoulders.

"Thank you, John," he told him with such genuine warmth.

John couldn't help the small smile that crept on his rugged face at James' friendly gesture.

"If you would like to follow us," Livik said as she and Hulaz started to glide out of the birthing room.

Zanika and Harrik remained with Mimi and Andrew as they began to eat and quietly talk. When I looked behind me, I could see Christik and Jakiz gliding behind us all.

Everyone was talking about what they'd just experienced in the birthing room. Trudy and Beccy were closest to James and me, with their men Philip and Derek. They were so excited by what they'd just seen. Beccy's ringlet curls were positively bouncing up and down as she walked.

"I seriously can't wait to see my baby jaguar being born," Beccy said,

"I know," replied Trudy, "And I hope we get to do more; I want to be a real part of what the angels are doing," she stated with lots of enthusiasm.

As she said the words, I realized that I felt the same way; it felt like an honor helping to heal and replenish our planet.

I turned to James who was still walking beside me.

"I'd like to do it again too. Would it upset you if I did?" I asked.

I knew as soon as he gave me his sexy smile

what his answer would be.

"No baby, I wouldn't be upset. To be honest with you, gorgeous lady, I would've been surprised if you didn't want to do it again," he stated, smiling like an idiot.

I knew there was a reason why I felt such a bond between us, and with his words, he'd just confirmed it for me. I may not have had my memories all back at that point, but I knew in my heart that I loved him.

Because we were walking at a slower pace, I was able to study our surroundings a lot better this time. When we walked close to the side of the corridor, I ran my fingers along the wall, and I was fascinated. It felt cool and smooth like marble to the touch, and there was an energy coming from the wall as if it was a living thing.

The archways were just as amazing, so decorative and elegant. We stopped at the fourth room we came to.

"This is your room Trudy and Phil," Hulaz said, as she turned to face them.

"I will show you in," she added, and then she glided through the archway with Trudy and Phil following her.

While we waited in the corridor, I looked up

at the archway entrance; the symbols were glowing against the background of the dark archway frame.

"They really do look like Egyptian hieroglyphs," I said aloud.

Everyone looked up to see what I was talking about, and there were many murmurs of agreement.

"We visited the Early Egyptians many times," Christik told us. "They were an advanced race for their time, interested in astronomy, medicine, and social structures," she stated. "We wanted to learn more about your race, so we taught them our written language, so we could communicate with them," she added.

"Well, that makes a lot of sense," James said to the group.

I was staring at the hieroglyphics, in awe of the beautiful intricate symbols softly glowing.

"I wish I could read them," I said quietly.

"You will all get the chance to learn our spoken and written language—if you desire to," Christik told us, "We are going to be here for a long time. Even when we have finished healing your planet, there will still be a lot for us to do," she added warmly.

Hulaz came out through the archway entrance, smiling shyly and looking very embarrassed.

"I do not think we will see them for some

time," she declared with humor in her voice.

We all burst out laughing as Hulaz's whole face glowed a silvery blush.

"Shall we move on?" she asked us all, as her blush began to deepen.

"Yes, let's," James added humorously, leading the way.

I think he was looking forward to us getting back to the privacy of our own room just as much as I was. We had so much catching up to do, and I was desperate to hear more about our children.

My mind kept going back to the images from my dreams. If the images of James were so spot on, then surely the images of our children would be too. My heart ached to be with them and not for the first time; I wondered what they were doing right at that moment.

Soon, we came to another room.

"This room is for you, Beccy and Derek," Hulaz stated.

No sooner had she said it—Derek scooped Beccy up in his arms like a new blushing bride and believe me, she did plenty of blushing. We all burst into laughter as Derek dipped his head to hers.

"I'm going to show you how much I've missed you woman!" he declared. "Ooo—bring it on big man," she replied, giggling like a schoolgirl.

"A passionate race aren't you," Christik said, with a humorous smile on her lips.

"Yes, we sure are," I replied, as I turned to look at James, giving him a cheeky wink that made him raise his eyebrows.

It wasn't long before they were all in their rooms apart from James and me. As we approached my room, Christik touched my arm gently to stop me in stride.

"We would like to thank you, Elita, for all you have done," she said. "If you would consider it, Elita, we would like you to be more involved with our plans," she added.

I was beyond thrilled at being asked and the thought of helping them in a major way was so exciting.

"I'd like that very much Christik," I answered with a smile I hoped showed my excitement.

"Come on wife of mine," James said as he gently tugged my hand in his.

"See you tomorrow," I told the angels with a smile.

We dipped our heads in respect to the angels, and I let James lead the way into our room. The angels were all smiling as we walked away, or should I say when James dragged me away!

No sooner had we entered our room—our

clothes were off, our teeth were brushed, and round three was happening in the shower. I can't even express to you, how whole I felt being in James' arms. When he held me close to his body with the cleansing water cascading down, I felt that I was exactly where I was meant to be.

An hour and a half later, we were in our bed, and James was showing me just how much he'd missed me repeatedly.

I felt so utterly loved while we laid in each other's arms, happy and breathless. We both fell into a deep sleep.

CHAPTER 9

My children are sat down at the dining table that is laden with food. Chips and dip with mini bagels and plates of steaming hot dogs and burgers. James is walking in, carefully holding a birthday cake that is covered with glowing purple candles. I can see all our children: Holly, Anthony, Abigail, and Harrison all sat around the table, and some of Holly's school friends are there too.

They have such happy little faces, with not a care in the world and clearly enjoying themselves. We all start singing Happy Birthday to Holly, and her beautiful little face is lit up with happiness, and she's smiling from ear to ear. The other kids around the table start to cheer and clap.

The memory fades as I mentally try to grasp the images of my kids' faces.

We're in the dining room at the front of the house where all our meager supplies are stored. The kids are huddling in one corner of the room with dirty clothes and their faces are drawn. They are hugging onto their blankets and duvets; the curtains are now closed with the solar lights on dim.

I can hear the screams of people and what sounds like fighting coming from outside, and gun-shots suddenly ring loudly in the air.

James is trying to pack the bottles of water and food we have left while I'm trying to pack sleeping bags and clothes.

I look over at the kids, and their terrified eyes reach straight to my tortured heart. My instincts are telling me that we can't stay here.

"We've got to get out of here, James," I say to my husband, "I've got a real feeling something's coming, and I don't know if it's good or bad."

"Your instincts aren't usually wrong, so we'd better get a move on," he replied, his face looking even more serious.

We finish packing the bags, and then James and I cuddle the kids on the floor. We're trying to reassure them that it's going to be okay while we wait for the fighting outside to stop.

Our plan is to make our way to the army base where James' brother is stationed. If we can make it there, we may stand a chance of surviving.

We can't bring ourselves to end it all with the

kids; this is our only option, and we knew Freddie was alive the week before. Thank god for my husband and his brother's passion for old radio receivers!

It's night time, and the kids have managed to fall asleep in our arms. The fighting has stopped, and we can hear the moans from people dying outside.

"I'm going to check the way is clear baby, so protect the kids," I tell James.

I gently let Holly slide over to James, and I make my way quietly to the front door. Opening it as quietly as possible, I peer out and look in the street.

There are bodies everywhere, and some have obviously been dead longer than others—I'm stood in horror.

We haven't been outside for two weeks, and the noises we'd heard during that time all made sense now. '*There's no way we can let the kids see this,*' I think to myself.

Waking up in our bed, the room was warm with colors of oranges and reds from the rising sun decorating the walls. I'm safe with James' arms wrapped around me, and I let his body's warmth soak through me, letting his closeness chase away the horror of the street outside our house.

I realized that tears were running down the sides of my cheeks, and I let out a sob as I looked into James's handsome face. Instantly, his green eyes connected with mine.

"Why are you crying, baby?" he asked, his face suddenly showing his concern.

"I think I dreamt about Holly's last birthday before the angels came and then we were trying to get to the camp where your brother was stationed," I told him. "One minute I was dreaming about a really happy time, and the kids were full of smiles, and then I dreamt about all the people dying on our road after all the fighting. James, it was horrific. There were bodies everywhere and so much blood," I sobbed. "Please tell me the kids didn't see all those bodies and the people dying or bleeding to death."

James' face was so full of love and warmth when he pressed his lips to mine; it was like his love was healing my heart.

"Don't worry, baby; the kids never saw any of that. We stayed inside the house and protected them. It was just far too dangerous to leave the house," he assured me, "In fact, you're going to be amazed when you see them; they are strong and healthy."

I think I cried then out of pure relief, with huge sobs racking my body like an emotional dam had been broken. I shouldn't have been surprised, considering all the emotions I'd been feeling since I'd woken up in the large sleeping room. James kept me tightly in his arms while I let the emotions flow, occasionally stroking my hair, trying to comfort me.

Eventually, after a few minutes, my sobbing gradually eased, and my tears finally stopped. I felt secure and at ease in James' strong arms.

Looking up at him, I could see my kids reflected in his handsome face, especially my boys' dimples, Holly and Harrison's blue-green eyes, and the dark chocolate brown hair. I was dying to get reacquainted with our children.

"So, what have our kids and you been doing for the last five years while I've been giving birth to animals and helping save the animal kingdom?" I asked him with a small smile, trying to put my bad dreams aside.

"Well hot stuff, the kids and I have been having quite an adventure," he said, smiling and flashing his dimples. "The angels came about two weeks after the night you dreamt about. We'd been rationing our food and water the best we could, but in those last two weeks, we were surviving on next to nothing, and our water had finally gone," he explained. "You decided to try and find whatever you could while I protected the kids.

We'd already had small gangs of desperate people trying to get into the house, so you wouldn't let me leave the kids to go with you. You've always been far too brave for your own good you know," he said, as he stroked the side of my face with his large hand.

"You left me in the house with the kids and left me with the rifle—then you went out with the handgun, and the kids and I fell asleep. I think you came back empty-handed and that was the last thing I remember. Until I woke up in the angels' hospital room," he explained.

"The kids were all in beds next to mine, and we were all on those IV drips. At first, we thought we were all in a hospital, and then we met the angels," he said, and then he smiled. I got the impression that he liked the angels as much as I did.

"The angels explained why they were here when we woke. Then, when we were all a hundred percent healthy, they took us all to the holding structure," he said. "The structures don't look that inviting from the outside, Mel, but you wait until you see the inside of one properly."

James sounded as if he really liked the place. It was a relief to me that he seemed so positive about being there and that he liked the angels.

"So, what happened when you arrived at the

holding structure?" I asked, eager for more information.

"Well I gotta tell ya, baby, these angels are like a well-oiled machine when it comes to organizing," he said with a smirk. "They gave us fresh clothes in the hospital room and then took us to this massive white room. It was full of other people who they'd saved. While I waited there with the kids, the angels would come in and transport the single people and families to the holding structure. Obviously, at the time I didn't know what to expect, but they did explain where we'd be going when I was in recovery, and they seemed well, nice."

James slid his arm out from behind my head, using his arm to prop up his own, making his closed fist a rest against his temple.

"I felt the same way about the angels," I replied, admiring my husband's handsome features as I spoke. "I took to Zanika, and Harrik straight away, especially Zanika. They just seem so calm and peaceful all the time, and it feels refreshing to be around them."

"Exactly," James said, "That's why I felt I could trust them. The kids and I weren't worried while we waited. We were quite fascinated, watching the angels take people to the holding structure. They'd hold the person's hand, then they'd both glow white, and suddenly they'd vanish. The nice thing was that they kept families together. So, when it was our turn, five angels each took one of our hands. We all left at exactly the same time and arrived at the holding structure together."

Suddenly, James slid out of the bed butt naked.

"Wow, I'm thirsty with all this talking," he said, as he walked over to the bathroom area.

I couldn't help but admire his sexy butt as he walked away. I decided to grab a shower and freshen up. So, I climbed out of bed and followed him, giving him a cheeky pat on the butt as I walked past him stood at the sink.

James started to clean his teeth while I stepped into the shower, and I let the water run over my head and down my body.

"So, what was it like inside the holding structure then?" I asked as I washed my body with the cleansing water.

"To be honest, it's like being inside a cruise ship," he replied, "There are rooms for single men or women and rooms for families, so people can stay together. There are stores for everything you could possibly need, a medical center, and there are garden areas. We also have classrooms and not just for the kids, so people can carry on learning. Obviously, there's no money used anywhere as we don't need currency anymore."

"So, why the shops then if no currency is being used?" I asked, confused.

I left the shower and started letting myself dry, walking towards the sink, and passing James as he now headed to the shower area. I started to clean my teeth as he continued to explain.

"Well as I said, baby, the angels do things like a well-oiled machine!" he stated. "Not only do they want us to have a community, but they also want us to have roles in our new community, hence the shops and medical center, etc. Anyone who's in the medical field can work in the medical center alongside angels, any teachers among us can work in the classrooms, and hairdressers can work in a salon and so on," he added.

"The great thing is that we have a choice to do what we did before they came," he continued, "or do something completely different. Accountants are pretty much redundant for example, so one of them is now learning to be a horticulturist; another is learning about green energy sources. Many IT people are busy learning the angels' language, so they can then learn the angels' technology too."

"So, what are you doing now as you're no longer in the motor trade?" I asked while running my fingers through my long blonde hair.

James stepped out of the shower area in all his masculine glory and puffing out his chest, he declared.

"I'm learning to become a vet," he said with pride and a huge grin.

Which made me giggle.

"I've always loved animals, and I don't know if you remember yet, but we had quite the menagerie at home before all this happened," he said, lifting his arms high and out to the sides for emphasis. "We had our dogs, cats, tropical fish, and the girls' rabbits."

Then suddenly his face dropped, and he looked so sad my heart sank.

"Watching our animals die broke my heart, Mel and not being able to save them was horrific. If I can help bring back the world's animals and help them survive, then I'm going to do it. And that's why I'm so proud of you for carrying and giving birth to the baby animals," he declared.

Before I knew what, I was doing, I walked over to him and held him in my arms. We just stood there naked, taking a moment to hold each other, loving each other and physically showing our mutual support.

"I've missed you so much baby," he said as he kissed the top of my head.

Looking up at his handsome face, I lifted myself onto my tiptoes and kissed his soft lips.

"I love you!" I whispered.

After a few more moments, I reluctantly pulled away.

"I suggest we get dressed before anybody comes to our room," I said, smiling at the look of disappointment on his face.

He looked like a kid who'd had his favorite toy taken away. Slipping on a clean dress, I couldn't resist asking more about our kids. I wanted to see them so badly.

"What are our kids doing at the holding structure?" I asked.

My question seemed to bring back his smile and his dimples.

"Ah they're doing so well baby, and they've missed you as much as I have, but they've kept themselves busy," he said. "Anthony's learning the angels' engineering technology, and he's really good at it too. Who'd have thought he'd be able to live without his Xbox," James laughed.

I couldn't help but laugh with him as he appeared truly surprised.

"Holly's learning world history from a university professor who was at Harvard. She has decided she wants to be part of rebuilding society, and she's going to be amazing; Mel!" he stated. "Harrison's doing classes and learning engineering with Anthony. As for Abigail, well she's doing her classes plus she's doing various arts," he went on to explain. "She's very lucky because out of all the survivors, there's a professional artist, a famous singer and a couple of professional dancers. You wait till you see what she can do baby."

He was so full of pride as he talked; it made my heartache for my kids even more. I was so thrilled that they'd all achieved so much while I was away, and I hoped that they wouldn't see me or treat me like a stranger. I wasn't sure if my heart could take that. As the thoughts were running through my mind, there was a tap at the archway entrance.

"Come in," I said, as I began to straighten out our bed.

Christik entered with Livik in tow.

"I thought we could all eat together today and talk on the way to our meeting room if that would be okay with you both," she stated.

"Sounds great," I replied as James walked over to me, taking my hand in his.

"Lead the way," I said, smiling at them both.

We left our room and began our journey to the meeting room, walking at a leisurely pace.

"James, I am sorry, but we need to ask you. Did you and the other men cause the explosion on our water filtration craft as a distraction, so you could get into this vessel?" she asked bluntly, but not unfriendly.

James stopped dead in his tracks, the sheer surprise was written all over his face.

"We pretty much knocked on your front door!" he declared, his surprise showing in his voice, "I don't know why you would think that Christik."

If an angel could be really embarrassed, I think Christik gave the example as she dipped her head and lowered her eyes.

"My apologies, James. In my heart, I knew you did not. However, the thought of our own race doing such an unspeakable thing, hurting their fellow angels is harder to believe," she stated quietly. "We do not want to offend you, James; I am very sorry."

We carried on walking slowly with an awkward silence stretching for a few minutes.

"I do understand why you'd think that way," James stated, his shock gone from his voice and replaced with sympathy.

"I'd never have thought you angels could hurt each other either, but the reason we just showed up here was that the angels who lied to us gave us the impression that they wouldn't help us to come and find our women," he explained. "Even after telling us that they were being hurt. To be honest Christik, the angels who lied to us gave the impression that not only did they not want to be here, but that we were not worth saving."

I couldn't even begin to understand the fear and frustration James and the men must have felt. Being told something like that and being made to feel so helpless and worthless.

"We are truly sorry our angels gave that impression to you and the others, James," she told him with such sadness. "During my long life, I have never encountered any of our race who would behave that way. It is difficult for us to understand why and what has caused this. We have tried to gather the angels you recognized as responsible; however, they have disappeared." she explained. "I have to assume that they had help from someone on this vessel," she added, her voice full of sorrow.

"We will help you any way we can," James told her, and I could tell he meant every word.

As we carried on down the long shimmering corridor, Christik and Livik updated us on how the others were doing. Apparently, the women were doing extremely well and handling all the new information brilliantly.

Mimi was still telling everyone that she'd like to see a birth, now she'd got used to the idea of helping save the planet. I was starting to feel very proud to be human.

"How are you feeling, Mel?" Livik asked, out of the blue.

"I'm feeling wonderful thanks," I replied, giving her my best smile.

Christik stopped in mid-glide and turned to face me,

"That is good," she said, with her own best smile, "as you are going to have the first human baby since we arrived here," she declared.

I looked from her to Livik, to James and then back to her.

"How on earth has that happened?" I asked, utterly dumbfounded, "I've only just given birth to a tiger cub!" I shrieked.

Christik and Livik were both smiling humorously while James stood with his mouth agape, looking exactly how I felt on the inside. I honestly couldn't believe what I was hearing.

"When we deliver the animal babies," Livik said gently, "we use our power to make your body reset, so it's as if you have never had the baby. This way, your body is ready for conception straight away. You and James have been intimate, and your body was ready to have a baby," she added, matter-of-factly.

"Woah," James whispered, as he stood there looking stunned.

If his eyebrows had been raised any higher, they'd have been nestling in his hairline!

"I'm going to be a daddy again!" he said, as he grinned like a Cheshire cat.

Suddenly, he grabbed me and began to kiss me all over my face and neck, taking me by surprise. I couldn't stop myself from giggling as the bloody idiot was thrilled.

"Well I wasn't expecting this," I managed to say between giggles as James lowered me back to the ground.

Christik and Livik began to glide onwards with James and I following alongside, and both of the angels were smiling. I wasn't sure if they were smiling because of the new baby or because of James acting like a lovable fool. I was smiling because he was mine.

"This is going to be a big boost for all of us," James said.

He looked at me with so much love; it was intoxicating.

"You are right, James," Christik said. "You are going to be very important in the healing process for your people and your planet. You, Elita, and all your children."

I was confused but also excited at her words. It sounded as if we were being given an important role to play. I'd always thought that everything happened for a reason and maybe that's why I had woken up on my own. I still couldn't get over the fact that not only was I pregnant, *'God knows what the kids were going to make of that news,'* but also that the angels knew before I did.

"How could you know that I'm pregnant already?" I asked, my curiosity getting the better of me, "I haven't felt any changes."

Christik and Livik both smiled at me.

"We see what you would call auras when we look at you," Christik explained. "All your auras are different. James's aura is mainly red and dark orange, showing great strength and courage. Your aura, Mel, is mainly shades of blue and white, showing peace, love, compassion, and logic. Your aura has got brighter because you have a new life inside you."

I wondered to myself if their auras were white, because they all seemed so pure and innocent. It was intriguing, because I'd always thought an aura was a feeling about someone, how they came across to you, not an actual color emanating from a person's body.

"Do you remember when we were trying to find the angels? Who lied to you?" Livik asked.

James and I both nodded a yes.

"We used our power to enhance those angels' auras, so we could all see. When their auras turned dark grey, we knew they had somehow lost themselves to something dark," she added. "We are going to need your help to find the angel or angels, who have helped them escape from us."

"Of course," I replied.

James gave my hand a little loving squeeze.

"We'll help you any way we can," he told them.

I was very glad we were on the same page. As we kept walking, I couldn't help touching my stomach. A new baby. '*Wow,*' I thought as my hand stroked my stomach through the gown I was wearing.

CHAPTER 10

We arrived at the control room, and everyone was just as busy, as the previous time we were there. Only this time, the men and their partners were all intermingled with the angels. Either looking at what the angels were doing and asking questions or stood talking next to the massive glass window; maybe discussing the water cleaning process.

I could see Mimi was one of the people down by the window, and she appeared to be thoroughly enjoying the conversation.

It was absolutely wonderful seeing their relationships building so quickly, with humans and angels all becoming firm friends.

Christik glided forward and in a louder voice than her usual tone said, “Please follow us, and we shall begin.”

I watched as Mimi and the others thanked their new friends and bid them goodbye, dipping their heads in respect. We all made our way to the meeting room.

When we walked into the room, and I noticed that the table was again laid out with food and drinks. '*These angels know how to layout a feast,*' I thought as I took a seat between James and Christik.

"Please enjoy your morning food; we have a lot to do today," Christik said as she motioned to the food and juice before us.

I was absolutely famished, and I don't think I was the only one as everyone was tucking into the fresh feast on the table. '*Maybe they've been catching up as much and James and I,*' I thought, smiling to myself.

Just as we all started eating and talking, James abruptly stood up and cleared his throat, grabbing everyone's attention.

"Ladies, gentlemen, and angels, can I have your attention for a moment please?" he asked. "I can't contain myself any longer; I've got to share our news!" he declared, turning his head to look at me with that great big grin on his face again.

'*Oh-oh,*' I thought.

"We are having a baby!" he announced.

I didn't think his grin could have got any bigger, but I was wrong!

"It's going to be the first human baby to be born since the angels came," he told them excitedly.

He bent down and kissed me as everyone clapped, erupted with cheers, and shrieked with excitement and genuine joy for us.

"You bugger!" I whispered, "I can't believe you told them all already," I said, giggling at the goofy face he made.

"I couldn't help it, baby, I'm so thrilled," he whispered back.

During our meal, James and I got asked many questions about how we knew, so we explained the conversations we'd had with Christik and Livik before arriving.

We told them everything, including the auras which only the angels could see. We also explained about the angels who'd gone missing, explaining that we needed to help find whoever had helped them flee.

Derek was the most vocal; he stood and looked directly at Christik and the other angels sitting all around the table.

"I think I can speak for all of us when I say that we value and appreciate what you're all doing for our planet and us. None of us would even consider sabotaging what you're doing to save us and our planet," he stated. "We've all lost people and animals we loved, and we would never risk losing anyone else. I think we all feel respect and friendship towards you all, and we'll keep helping you to heal our planet," Derek added.

He spoke with so much passion—he was magnificent, and he said exactly how we were all feeling. We all applauded him and agreed with every word.

Christik dipped her head in respect to Derek and everyone else, as did the other angels. They seemed to believe every word Derek spoke and also appreciated his response.

"We are going to do great things together I believe, for your planet, and for your race," Christik said to everyone at the table.

As we carried on eating and talking, I was pleased to see how everyone was doing. The women were full of life and happy to be with their men again, and the men were all in their element; obviously thrilled to have their women back.

Considering how much had changed for the women, they were handling it all very well. Their men seemed to have totally different demeanors now, compared to when they first arrived at the main craft.

Gone were the anxious faces and the tense postures of their stance. Now they were relaxed and happy; especially now they were with their loved ones. It was wonderful to watch them all talking and laughing together, and as I looked around at the angels, I saw that all the angels were enjoying themselves too.

While we were finishing our food, Christik began to tell us what we were going to do next.

"This morning, we will go to the women's sleeping room, and find the last female," she explained. "We would then appreciate your help in locating the angel or angels who helped the fallen angels. We are eager to find them all and discover their reasons for sabotaging the water filtration craft. As well as hurting their fellow angels, and lying to you all," she said.

I looked across the table to John, and I could see the anxiety in his demeanor. He must have had the patience of a saint, and I wondered if he'd had any decent sleep. I really hoped that we'd find his wife quickly because he obviously loved her very much.

"We need some suggestions, as to how we can identify the helper of the liars," Christik said as we were finishing the last of our meal.

"We have never had this situation before, so this is new to us. Do any of you have any ideas?" she asked.

I should have known that James would be the

first to come up with a strategy; I had a feeling he was a good problem solver.

"I think the best way to trap the angel or angels would be to inform everyone that we've discovered where the angels are hiding," he stated, "Then, maybe you can trace any communications from the helpers to the other fallen angels. Are you able to do something like that?" he asked as he looked at Christik and the others.

Christik looked to the other angels in a silent "What do you think?" kind of way. After a few moments, all the angels nodded to each other.

"We can do that, James; that is an excellent suggestion!" Christik told him.

Everyone around the table nodded in agreement at James' idea, and I felt very proud of him. He leaned over to me and whispered in my ear.

"Who'd have thought watching crime shows would be so useful?"

I giggled at the cheeky grin he was wearing in his gorgeous face.

As we finished up, Harrik entered the meeting room, and Christik told him of our plan; he looked very impressed with the idea. He told Christik that he'd activate the tracers from the control room, and he left the room.

Within moments, we were following suit and

all entering the huge control room. Looking across all the consoles, I saw Harrik standing near the huge glass window. He looked at me, and then he gave Christik a small nod of his head.

I assumed Harrik's nod was confirmation that the tracers were ready to go. Christik stepped forward with all her grace to address all the angels in the room.

"Attention please all angels," she said, her voice loud and strong, "We have good news. We now know the location of the fallen angels who lied to these men," she added, indicating to James and the other men, "and who sabotaged the filtration watercraft, hurting our own," she continued. "We have angels en-route to collect them for questioning. Please carry on."

She then turned back to us.

"Let us see how quickly this works—if it works. Come, let us go to the sleeping room," Christik said, as she began to glide towards the exit leading the way.

We hadn't even got to the other side of the room before Jakiz, and two other angels pounced on an angel who was at one of the control consoles nearest the huge window.

When I say pounced, I actually mean they raised their palms out facing the angel and shot their power at him. He froze on the spot instantly, and it was quite amazing to watch the angels in action.

We could suddenly see the dark grey aura surrounding the fallen angel's body. The diamonds on his wrist markings—darkened to a deep grey as he stood in the angels' white glow of power. The prisoner dipped his head, this time not out of respect, but maybe out of shame or regret that he'd been caught.

When he dipped his head, I noticed something in his hair, a small, round, black ring attached to a lock of it. I was surprised, because I'd never seen any of the angels wearing anything decorative; jewelry or clothes.

"He tried to send a communication," Jakiz said calmly, as her power flowed steadily from her palms.

"Did the communication get out, Jakiz? Did it reach the other fallen ones?" Christik asked.

"No Christik, we stopped the communication before it could reach the source. We will take this fallen one to a holding room for now," Jakiz replied.

Christik nodded to Jakiz and then continued to lead us to the main corridor.

"What did you mean by fallen ones?" I asked.

I'd heard that expression before in movies and books, and I felt intrigued as to what it meant for these angels. Christik looked so sad when she turned to me.

"In my very long life, I have heard tales from the elders of our race—that angels have turned bad before. Although I have not encountered it myself, until now," she said. "If an angel is influenced by wrongdoers, we call it falling, as they fall away from our way of life," she explained. "There are more worlds than we can count with some very evil races, and no race is infallible, Elita."

"I have heard the term fallen angels before," I told her, "What will you do with the fallen angels when you find them all?" I asked.

She smiled kindly at me, and I think it was her way of putting a brave face on it.

"We will find out what caused them to fall, and if we cannot change their auras back, so they are good again, then we will have to seek our elders for help. Our elders are even more ancient than I am," she added with her smile.

"Are your elders here on Earth?" James ask-ed.

"No, they are not, James; they are on our home planet, which is half of your Earth year away," she replied. "I hope we will not have to summon them," she added.

Not wanting to upset the angels, we didn't

ask any more about the topic. We all talked between ourselves about their work as we made our way to the sleeping room.

I still couldn't stop myself from admiring the beautiful corridor, touching the shimmering walls, taking in every detail of the archways and their stunning hieroglyphs.

"I keep seeing repeated hieroglyphs on the archways," I said, more to myself than anyone else.

"That is because you are seeing symbols for your most common words," Christik said.

I was very impressed with her sense of hearing, as well as the symbols.

"Our language does not have an alphabet like yours as many of your scholars believed. The hieroglyphs mean whole words and expressions," Christik added. "We have used the same language since before I existed."

I think we were all fascinated, and I could see everyone else starting to pay a little more attention to the symbols now too. I couldn't wait to be able to read all of the archways and learn their language. The prospect was very exciting, especially because I loved to learn.

John was very quiet while we made our way to find his loved one.

"Are you okay?" I asked him.

His face looked so full of worry and anxiety it made me sad. When he looked at me, he tried to force a smile.

"What if she doesn't remember me or our twins?" he almost whispered, utter pain in his words.

I felt for him with all my heart.

"I don't think you need to worry, John, I didn't remember anything when I woke up, but I did dream about James and our kids the first night," I told him gently. "Also, when I saw James, I felt an instant connection to him, like I knew him but didn't know how. I'm sure you and your wife will be fine John, and at least she's alive with or without memories," I added.

When we arrived at the sleeping room, it was quiet and peaceful, just like before. Not a sound could be heard apart from the machines monitoring the sleeping women. They all looked so good with a healthy glow. I wondered if I still looked that healthy now that I was up and about. The one thing that was missing in my bathroom was a mirror, so I couldn't check even if I wanted to.

John had already started making his way down the rows of women, heading to the rows we hadn't reached the day before.

"I'll go with him," I said, turning to James.

I tried to walk off, but James gripped my hand.

"We'll go together," he replied with a smile.

It seemed we were going to do everything together, and to be honest; I was both relieved and pleased.

We walked after John leaving everyone else behind. The guys and other women were talking and asking the angels more questions about the baby animals.

We caught up to John as he hurriedly scanned the faces of the sleeping women; he was almost power walking. James and I maintained his pace and kept up with him as we walked through the rows.

It struck me just how amazing the human race was. Every woman was different and beautiful in her own way.

While we followed John, I wondered how long it was going to take to reunite all the women with their men and families. We also had to be prepared for the grief that some of these women were going to go through when they remembered that some of their men or family members were dead. The thought broke my heart!

It was as if James could sense my distress. He was just as attuned to my feelings as the angels it seemed.

"What's wrong, baby?" he asked.

When I looked up to his face, I had tears running down mine.

"It's just dawned on me—that some of these women are going to remember that their loved ones are gone," I said, trying not to break down completely.

He stopped me in my stride, pulling me towards his large muscular frame and wrapped his thick arms around me.

Even John had stopped in his tracks at my words, his face looking ashen. James lifted my chin with his hand and kissed my tears away on both cheeks.

"We're all going to help them through it, baby," he said as he used his thumb to catch another tear.

"Yes, we will," John added, his voice wavering slightly.

As he waited for us, tears were running down his own face, and he wiped them away quickly, obviously a little embarrassed.

Taking a deep breath, I wiped away the wetness on my face and looked at John.

"Come on, we have your lovely wife to find," I told him after proverbially putting my big girl pants on.

I smiled at the smug face James was now wearing; it said, ‘That's my girl.’ I grabbed his hand and began walking towards John.

We continued our search for John’s wife, and while we passed the occupied beds, I started to look for the silvery marks on their left hands again.

There were so many different animals being saved; it never ceased to amaze me. A lamb, zebra, shark, a mink, and just as I noticed a silvery manatee mark, John abruptly stopped.

He was completely still, stood at the bottom of the bed where his love was laid.

Tracey had a soft, oval pretty face, a friendly and kind face. Her dark hair was to her shoulders and curly with streaks of silver.

She looked so serene, and John was still; breathless and speechless—looking at her with pure adoration.

I touched his arm to gain his attention,

“John, would you like me to get Zanika and Harrik?” I asked.

He stood blinking at me.

“John?”

“Yes, please, Zanika might have to calm her down,” he replied.

James stayed with John while I went to fetch the angels.

The angels weren't far away, all chatting to each other about the sleeping women and what they were expecting. It seemed the enthusiasm was contagious. It was uplifting and warmed my heart, seeing so much positivity in the group.

I approached Zanika, Harrik, and Christik—who were avidly listening and watching the other couples with smiles on their faces.

"John has found his wife Tracey; could you wake her please?" I asked.

"Yes, of course, Elita," Zanika and Harrik both said, almost in unison.

It was quite comical, and I had to stifle a giggle, as did the other women. I turned away smiling, with the others following behind me. It felt good to smile after a moment of such sadness.

When we reached Tracey's bed, John was sat on it next to her. His hands were cupping hers, his thumbs stroking over the silvery mark.

Zanika and Harrik moved to Tracey's bedside and began to scan her body with their hands, while the others gave her and John a respectful distance.

I stood back next to James and slipped my hand in his, giving it a gentle squeeze, and then we waited anxiously.

Zanika and Harrik started to adjust the

machines, checking the monitors, and watching Tracey carefully.

"It won't be long," Harrik reassured John as he raised the top end of the bed, so Tracey was in more of a sitting position.

We waited only a few minutes and then her hand started twitching in John's.

"She's waking," he said quietly.

Tracey's eyes began to flutter open.

"JOHN!" she screamed.

Her scream went straight through my heart as it was so full of despair and anguish.

"I'm here, my love, I'm here," he soothed.

Tracey turned her head towards his voice, her eyebrows lowering in concentration as her eyes tried to focus.

"John, where am I? Am I dreaming?" she whispered, blinking her eyes rapidly.

"You're in a kind of hospital my love," he soothed her, "you're alright now, and you're not sick anymore."

You could almost tell the moment her eyes were focused enough. Her eyebrows lifted, and her eyes became wide as she looked from John to the rest of us in the room.

"What do you mean John?" She asked, her gaze moving back to her husband,

"What do you mean, I'm not sick anymore?"

We were all looking at each other in confusion, apart from the angels. They obviously knew what John was talking about.

James held my hand a little bit tighter; we could both feel the emotional tension in the air.

"The cancer's gone, my love," John told her.

Lifting his arm from the bed, he pointed at Zanika and Harrik.

"These angels came to save us all my love, and they healed you; you're better, and your cancer has gone," he told her—with so much love—we were all brought to tears.

Tracey looked deeply into John's eyes, tears welling up and escaping down her soft cheeks.

"I don't want to live without my babies John; I want to be with my babies!" She cried out.

It suddenly dawned on me.

John had mentioned their twins, but what he didn't say—was that they'd died.

It felt like my heart was breaking in my chest. No wonder John was so quiet; he was still grieving for his children.

Suddenly, a wave of guilt hit me.

James had declared the news about our new baby, '*oh God!*' I dreaded to think how that must have made John feel, and I couldn't even begin to comprehend their grief.

The angels were just as quiet and as solemn as the rest of us.

"Ashley and Martin would want us to live Tracey," he told her. "These angels came to save us all and Earth. We've all got a fresh start, a new life, and we can be a part of that. The twins would want us to be a part of that!" he implored her.

Tears were streaming down all of our faces; the men were holding their women, just like James was holding me. Even the angels were touching hands, as if they were emotionally supporting each other.

The pain was evident—in both John and Tracey's faces. Tracey turned to look at Zanika, who was standing close by, her face clearly saddened.

"If you're really angels, can you bring my babies back?" she asked.

The look of pure hope was swiftly written all over her pretty face, as she stared into Zanika's sapphire eyes.

"We are very sorry Tracey; we cannot bring back your two children. We are what your people know as angels; however, we cannot bring back the dead," Zanika explained, regret in every one of her words.

"But if you're really angels, surely you can perform miracles?" Tracey asked, her desperation becoming clear.

Zanika looked so apologetic and sympathetic towards Tracey.

"We can do a lot of things Tracey, but we cannot bring back the dead, and we cannot perform miracles. We are very sorry," Zanika stressed softly.

I'm sure I wasn't the only one feeling their loss. I thought the weight of Tracey and John's grief was going to crush me.

"If we had the power to do that for you, we would Tracey," Christik added gently.

Zanika moved closer to the bed, touching Tracey on her arm. When their skin touched, a white glow emanated between them. We could see Tracey visibly relax, her body releasing its tension and sinking deeper into the bed.

John must have seen this as his cue, now that his wife was calmer.

"Tracey, there's something else I need to tell you, my love," he said, "The angels are doing many things to save our planet, and one of those things is saving the animals. Now, I don't want you to panic, my love, but you and some of these ladies here are pregnant with tiny baby animals," he explained gently.

Tracey's eyes went from John to the other women next to me, darting from one bump to another.

"What the fuck! I'm pregnant with a fucking animal, John?" she screeched.

Her eyes were wide with either shock or surprise; I wasn't sure which, maybe both.

"Yes, my love look," John told her, lifting her left hand in his, "see, it's a tiny wolf cub."

Tracey looked at down at her left hand and then to her small baby bump.

"No fucking way!" she gasped.

This time, it was definitely surprise more than shock and horror.

"I can't believe this is fucking happening John!" she declared.

I wasn't sure if her cursing was normal or just due to the surprise of her new situation.

"The wolf cub can be birthed now if you would like, Tracey; it is due in a few days, so it is safe," Harrik told her.

"Would you like to have it now, my love?" John asked "They can all tell you; you won't feel a thing, and you don't have to birth it yourself. These angels use their special magic to get it out. We've seen one birth, and it was amazing," he said, all in a rush of words and probably panic.

Tracey looked at us all—as if assessing whether we could be trusted or not and that John was telling the truth.

"Yes, I'd like to have it now; it doesn't seem right having a baby with my babies gone, even if it is an animal baby John," she told him.

"Would you mind if the others watched the birth, Tracey?" Christik asked, "Not everyone has seen a birth yet, and we would like you all to know what it is like," she added.

"I don't mind as long as John doesn't mind," she replied.

John leaned forward, kissing his wife on her lips and then on her silver-marked hand.

"I don't mind my love; they'll only see your stomach, nothing else," he told her.

"Let's get this show on the fucking road then," she said to everyone.

CHAPTER 11

Tracey sounded emotionally stronger than a moment ago, which I think was a great relief for all of us. Christik smiled at Tracey warmly.

"We will take you to the birthing room now Tracey; do not worry, it will be over very quickly," Christik assured her.

We all moved away from the bed, allowing Zanika and Harrik the room to prepare the monitors and bed for transport. John wouldn't and didn't leave her side, his hand still holding hers.

"How many of you girls have done this?" Tracey asked, looking at me and the other women.

"I gave birth to a baby goat," Trudy told her as her face turned a deep shade of red, "although I was asleep at the time. I was pretty freaked out when I woke up to be honest. I wasn't anywhere near as calm or as brave as you. But now I think I'd like to do it again, only awake next time. Everyone has said it's a beautiful experience, even my husband," she added.

"Thanks for telling me that; I appreciate it…" Tracey told her as her eyebrows raised questioningly.

"Trudy, my name is Trudy," she told her, smiling sweetly.

The angels started to move the bed and monitors, so we all began making our way out of the sleeping room. Stepping forward, I looked Tracy straight in the eyes as I wanted her to know that I was being frank and honest.

"Hi Tracey, I'm, Mel. I just want you to know that you have nothing to worry about. I gave birth to a tiger cub just recently, and I was awake through the whole thing," I explained. "I was shocked at the time because I'd woken on my own, and I pretended to still be sleeping. I didn't give the angels a chance to explain what was going on, but I have to tell you, Tracy, it was an amazing experience," I added. "It really was magical, and there was absolutely no pain or blood. It was truly wonderful. We're playing a very important role; we are saving Earth's animals," I told her, giving her a warm smile.

"When this is over, I'm going to need some time to think about all of this, Mel," Tracey replied.

"I completely understand Tracey; you have been through hell and back from the sounds of it. So, you take all the time you need. We are all here for you," I assured her.

She was a lot calmer when she spoke this time.

"We've only just lost our twins to sickness because of bad water, and I can't handle all this right now," she said, waving one of her arms for emphasis.

John cleared his throat and turned to look at her sheepishly.

"I really don't want to add to your stress, my love, but you've been asleep for five years," he told her.

"What the hell John, are you fucking kidding me right now!" She shrieked, "And the bastard hits keeping fucking coming, don't they!" she said, completely exasperated.

Christik moved to the side, letting the others move in front as we left the room through the arch-way and into the corridor. Tracey was still shaking her head at John and giving him the evil eye as Christik came alongside them.

"We are truly sorry this has all been put upon you Tracey," Christik told her, "we have talked with the others, and we do realize now that letting you all sleep was not the best action. We will, of course—give you all the time you need, to grieve for your children and come to terms with everything that has happened. Elita, who just spoke with you, and the others will help you any way they can, as will we," she assured her.

Tracey nodded and rested her head back on the bed.

The short journey to the birthing room was less exciting than before. I think we were all thinking about Tracey, John, and their lost twins. James and I were very quiet, and it was hard not to put ourselves in their shoes.

We were asking ourselves how we would cope with losing a child, or like Tracey and John, losing two children. My heart ached for them, and I still couldn't comprehend their grief and pain.

We entered the quiet birthing room. Zanika and Harrik moved Tracey's bed into a veiled cubicle and then left the room to get ready. The others went straight to the massive wall of encapsulated baby animals, not able to stop themselves from looking for more different creatures.

"What the hell is that?" Tracey asked John, her eyes wide on her pretty face.

He still hadn't released her hand; it was no different than James constantly holding mine. The men were all very clingy but who could blame them? They'd only just got their women back. I think we were all feeling very needy, but that was to be expected I suppose.

"That's where all the baby animals are kept my love until the Earth is healed enough to put them back into the wild," John explained to Tracey.

Zanika and Harrik returned to the room, wearing their sheer veils and gloves. Zanika had a new empty capsule hovering between her gloved hands.

"Is that what the wolf cub is going in?" Tracey asked Zanika when she reached the bed.

"Yes," Zanika replied, the capsule glowed brightly as she used her power to prepare it.

Harrik adjusted the monitors, the buttons changing color as we all watched, and it appeared that Tracey was just as interested. She watched every move the angels made as they scanned her body again with their hands.

"We are going to remove the wolf cub now Tracey; there will be no cutting and no blood. Please do not be concerned; it will be over very quickly," Harrik assured her.

Tracey nodded for him to continue, so he gently rolled the thin silvery sheet down to her bikini line and then did the same to her gown, taking it up to the bottom of her breasts.

All of us were quiet, including John who stood a short distance away. We were all watching

Tracey who was watching the angels with very wide anxious eyes.

Zanika joined Harrik so they were either side of Tracey, their hands hovering over the top of her small pregnancy bump. The bright glow began between her soft skin and their hands, and when their hands started to rise, the excitement and anticipation grew in the room. More so this time because we all knew what was going to happen next.

When the amniotic sac started to appear—passing through her skin, Tracey's eyes grew even wider.

"Bloody hell, you weren't kidding, were you?" she said, flabbergasted and looking at John. "It is like magic, and I can't feel anything. Fucking weird though isn't it," she added.

There were giggles behind me from the other women. I couldn't tell who it was, but it made me smile.

My eyes were glued to the birth. I didn't think I could get tired of seeing this birthing process as it always felt so special.

The angels lifted their hands higher and quickly we could see wet white fur. As the cub got higher, we could make out its tiny ears and short little legs.

Like the other animals, its tiny eyes were

tightly closed. We couldn't see its tail, so I assumed it was between its legs. Then there were gasps of surprise because there was a second head appearing by the first cub's hind legs, a little head covered in black fur.

The angels raised their hands higher still, and there were whispers of "Wow" and "Oh my god" around the room. Within seconds, we could clearly see another little wolf cub's body covered in wet black fur through the amniotic sac.

"There's two of them!" John declared, his shocked eyes locking with Tracey's.

I could see Tracey's eyes starting to glisten as tears sprung then ran down her cheeks.

"Looks like our twins were brought back after all, just in a different way," she said, quietly and full of emotion.

"We have never had this happen before," Harrik told Tracey and John, "I believe this is very special," he added.

"Yes, I think it is special," Tracey replied, smiling at him and then John through her tears.

We all watched in teary awe as the twin wolf cubs completely rose out of Tracey's abdomen. They were curled tightly together, reminding me of the Yin and Yang Chinese symbol.

Both of their tiny ears were flat to their heads,

and their thin little tails were both hidden between their small bodies. Their legs were mingled together, almost making them appear as if they were hugging each other.

Zanika took ownership of the wolf cubs inside their amniotic sac. They were hovering between her glowing hands while Harrik brought the capsule towards her in his. The twins passed through the capsule with ease, and it glowed brightly once the wolf cubs were fully encapsulated.

We watched avidly as the device inside drew the placenta and umbilical cords to it, giving one last bright, silvery-white pulse as the two things joined.

Harrik glided away with the new wolf twins hovering in their capsule between his gloved hands while Zanika covered Tracey's abdomen again.

"That was nothing like what I was expecting," Tracey told John.

"I know my love," he replied, "I don't think any of us expected you to have twin wolf cubs either."

"It felt very special, didn't it John," Tracey said through more tears, "like it was our babies letting us know that they're okay."

"Yes, my love, I think maybe it was," he replied, leaning over to kiss her as tears ran down his face too.

John was smiling at his wife, maybe out of relief that she seemed emotionally stronger now, or perhaps because the birth was so special and was now over.

"We will leave you alone to eat and drink now. Then Zanika will take you both to your room," Christik told them, just as Harrik returned with a tray full of refreshments for them.

When we started to leave the birthing room, we left Tracey and John holding and comforting each other. Christik addressed us all as we reached the archway entrance.

"If you would all like to eat and rest for now, I will see you all tomorrow. Elita and James, if you could come with me, it would be appreciated," she said.

"Of course," I replied. The others all agreed to meet in the morning while we continued down the corridor.

Gradually, the couples all left the group for their rooms, leaving just James and me with Christik and Jakiz walking and gliding down the corridor.

"Where are we going?" I asked curiously and wondering if we were heading to our room or maybe the control room.

"We are taking you to a holding room where the fallen angel is being kept," Christik told us. "We would like your help to try and find out what made our angel fall," she added.

"What can we do to help?" James asked, obviously just as intrigued as I was.

Christik smiled when she looked at us.

"Not to be unkind, but your race is known to us for being good and bad throughout your history. Your race has had wars over currency, power, land, and religion. We are not that way inclined, so your life experiences will help us greatly," she explained.

I don't think either of us knew quite what to say to that, so we both remained quiet because every word she'd said was completely true.

A few minutes later, we arrived at the holding room. It was the same room where I'd met all the men and James. The memory of seeing James that first time again brought a smile to my face.

My hand went to my stomach as I suddenly remembered that we were going to have a new baby. Somehow, it all felt like fate, like it was all meant to be!

There were guards outside the archway with long purple hair flowing down their backs. I wasn't sure, but it seemed as if their wings were bigger and their shoulders broader than the other angels I'd seen so far. I didn't know why I hadn't noticed the differences before. When I'd seen them the first time, I was feeling nervous about the meeting with the men. So, my mind had probably ignored the differences.

As we approached, the angels moved out of the way letting us pass. James and I held back so Christik and Jakiz could go through first; all of us dipped our heads in respect to the guards.

Christik raised her palm, allowing us to pass through the glistening barrier. When we entered the room, the fallen angel was sitting at the table; animosity was radiating from every inch of him. I felt it the moment we passed through the barrier.

It was a shock to the system to see an angel behaving the total opposite way of what he should be. Again, I noticed the small black ring attached to his long, dark hair. We all sat around the table facing him, and the atmosphere was tense, to say the least.

"Why?" Christik demanded, getting straight to the point.

Her skin was glowing with light, reflecting her frustration and possibly anger.

The animosity radiating from the fallen angel seemed to reach another level.

"This race is not worth saving, Christik; this planet is not worth saving. They have killed each other and have been killing their planet for centuries.

They do not deserve a second chance!" he declared, his voice showing utter contempt and hatred.

Christik and Jakiz appeared to shimmer even brighter with every word the fallen angel said.

"Why are you saying that Nalik? That is not how we think. We do not judge other races or planets; that is not our role to play!" Christik said, confusion in her voice.

Nalik didn't reply; he just glared at her with utter animosity.

Christik took a deep breath and then let it out relaxing her body.

"When did you start feeling this way Nalik?" she asked, a little more gently.

He looked straight at her, his eyes burning angrily into hers.

"Ever since we left the Marilian planet," he spat, his words sounding venomous as he spoke to them.

"Tell me about the Marilian planet?" James asked.

I wasn't sure why James had asked that question, but maybe he was trying to make Nalik relax or something. Instantly, Nalik's whole demeanor changed, and his shoulders moved back as if he was sitting to attention. He held his head higher, making him come across proud or arrogant.

"That was a planet worth saving!" he said with utter conviction. "Inhabited by a far superior race. The Marilians know how to live and rule," he added.

"How can you judge the human race and not the Marilians?" Christik asked. "They are a race that takes over other planets and races, enslaves them just because they can Nalik," she declared.

Again, he looked at her straight in the eyes.

"They are superior to the human race, and when they arrive here, they will do what Marilians do best; they will conquer!" he spat out.

I was absolutely stunned by this fallen angel. The hatred coming from him was a stench in the air. James leaned forward, resting his elbows and forearms on the table-top.

"Where did you get that decorative ring that's in your hair Nalik?" he asked.

Christik looked from James to Nalik, confusion on her face as if she hadn't noticed the hair ring. Nalik looked at James with sheer disgust writen all over his angry face as if James wasn't worthy to converse with him.

"It was a gift from the Marilian ruler for saving them and their planet," he stated, as his hand reached up to touch the small metal ring.

"We do not usually accept gifts from other

races," Christik told James and me. "It is very unusual for one of our angels to accept one—very unusual," she added.

James looked thoughtfully at Nalik, his eyes kind and his demeanor patient.

"Did anyone else accept a special gift from the Marilians ruler Nalik?" he asked.

"A number of us did, yes," Nalik snapped.

"And are those angels who accepted these gifts the same angels that have also fallen and gone missing?"

"Yes," Nalik responded with hatred pouring off him in waves.

It was a miracle that he was talking to us at all, considering his hatred towards James and I was so strong.

James turned to Christik with concern in his eyes.

"I think the Marilian gifts have something to do with this; we need to remove it, so we can find out for sure," he told her quietly.

Nalik completely ignored us, as if we weren't even worth listening to.

"I would like to see this ring, Nalik. Can you remove it, so that I can admire this special gift from the Great Marilian ruler?" Christik asked him calmly.

Her words seem to appease him and some–

how massaged his ego. I didn't realize that angels had egos, but obviously, the bad ones did.

He looked at her with approval in his eyes as he raised his hand and removed the small black metal ring.

It slid down his hair with ease. The moment he placed it on the table in front of Christik and his fingers lost contact; his dark grey aura faded away. We watched in amazement as he dimly glowed white. The diamonds on his markings slightly glowed too and then dimmed to a low glimmer.

Nalik's eyes abruptly widened as he looked at James and me; then his eyes connected with Christik's.

"I do not understand what has happened Christik; I feel like myself again," he said softly.

Christik smiled at him with kindness.

"It seems that the Marilians tricked you and the others into accepting these gifts so that they could influence you all," she told him, "We do not hold you responsible for this situation Nalik; it is the Marilians who are to blame," she added.

"Would you like me to dispose of this evil trinket, Christik?" Jakiz asked as she stood from her seat.

"Yes, if you would Jakiz. We need it secured safely before anyone else gets hurt," she replied.

Jakiz raised her hand with her palm up, facing the ceiling. There was a white glow emanating from it, and then a small bubble of fluid began to appear. When it grew to the size of a large orange, she turned her hand over and positioned it over the top of the black metal hair ring.

The bubble acted like a magnet, drawing the hair ring inside its center. Jakiz then turned her hand palm up again, and the hair ring was floating inside the fluid.

As we watched, the bubble began to solidify until it was a solid glass ball the color of amber.

"I will contain this evil gift in the secure holding room," she said, as she gracefully left the room.

There was a moment of silence after Jakiz left with the evil hair ring. I think we were all taking a moment to process the information we'd gained from Nalik, and I think he was still in shock himself.

"I do not know why I accepted the gift Christik," Nalik suddenly said. "We have visited and saved so many worlds. I have been offered gifts from so many races, and I have never accepted them. So, why did I accept this one?" he added.

Christik, gracious as always, smiled at him in reassurance.

"The Marilians are not just vicious Nalik; you know this," she told him, "They have powers too, some of which they did not let us see. I believe they have ways of making other beings comply to their will."

Nalik's expression showed that Christik's words weren't making him feel any better. He still looked like someone who had been given a slap around the face.

"Nalik, you would not have been able to stop Drakron the Marilians ruler, from compelling you into taking the gifts. Again, I tell you, you are not to blame." Christik assured him.

I think James and I both felt sorry for the poor angel in front of us, knowing that he'd unwittingly been a part of hurting so many of his fellow angels. It must have been a heavy weight to bear.

I wondered if he'd felt their pain the same as the Angels did while he'd been under the power of the ring, as the rig angels were being burned alive.

"Why would the Marilians do this Christik?" James asked, just as confused as I was.

"The Marilian race is very old and powerful. I would imagine the slow death of their planet was a deflation to their collective ego," she said. "They like to give other races the impression that they are all-powerful. Unfortunately, they were not willing to save their planet and themselves until it was too late, and then they were unable to," she explained. "They have spent thousands of years proving to other races how undefeatable they are. I would imagine that they did not want to even admit to each other that they had failed themselves and their planet," she continued. "I believe they may feel they have something to prove to the other races in their solar system now. I also believe that we have unwillingly given them their next target by us coming to Earth. I think they will use Earth to try and regain their reputation with the other races. They have tried to use my angels to make it easier for themselves to conquer your planet, which is unforgivable!" she informed us all.

"How on Earth are we going to be able to stop them Christik?" I asked, feeling totally panic-stricken.

Instantly, I started thinking of our children and our new baby. '*How could we possibly protect them now?*'

"Christik, there is no way we can defend Earth against these creatures. There are hardly any humans left, and we're spread out all over the wor-ld," James stated. "If they arrived today, tomorrow or a month from now, they could probably wipe out humanity in a day," He added.

Christik looked thoughtful for a moment, and then her demeanor changed. She suddenly looked very determined.

"Luckily, their technology is not as advanced as ours," she said, "so we will have time to heal the Earth and prepare to defend it. This is going to be a very new experience for us. We have never been in a battle before, but we cannot allow your planet to be destroyed and your race enslaved!" she declared.

"Well, I'd never have believed I'd hear something like that said in the real world," I declared.

I could not quite believe what I was hearing. The whole situation just didn't seem real. I thought this kind of stuff only happened in movies and books.

"We need to find the other fallen ones asap," I told Christik.

She looked at me with confusion.

"ASAP means as soon as possible," I explained.

"Ah," she said, smiling. "I am still adjusting to your language, Elita; it has changed greatly since we last visited, and Tracey's words are very confusing to us," she added.

I knew instantly what Christik was referring to. She was talking about Tracey dropping the F-bomb in nearly every sentence.

"I'll explain about that later," I told her.

I was feeling a little less frightened now, knowing the angels were going to help us against the Marilians.

James put his hand back on mine, stroking the top of it with his thumb. When I looked up at him, he was smiling his sexy smile, dimples and all. '*God, I love this man,*' I thought to myself.

We turned back to Nalik; his body had lost all its tension and his aura no longer malevolent. I hoped that he felt our sympathy and understanding!

"Do you know where the fallen ones are hiding now, Nalik?" I asked.

His head dipped, and when he raised it again to look at me, his sadness was clear to see.

"They are hiding in an empty building, not far from the holding structure. They wanted to be close enough to cause more damage," Nalik explained. "They do not have control of themselves Christik. I did not have control of myself," he added.

Guilt or maybe shame was getting to him. He lowered his head, resting it on the tops of his arms. Christik leaned forward and placed her hand on his head, the contact glowing a brilliant white for a moment.

This time when he looked up, his sadness, guilt, and every other negative emotion he was feeling had gone from his eyes and face.

"Thank you Christik," he said quietly to her, giving her a lovely smile.

"We know this was not your fault Nalik. We

also know that none of you are responsible for anything that has happened. We do need your help, however," Christik replied. "We will walk, Elita, back to her room and then you, James, and myself will take a team to collect the other fallen ones," she stated.

I felt very put out that I wasn't invited to go along until I reminded myself that I was now pregnant and taking part in a sorté was probably not a good idea.

I was full of emotions, and I didn't know whether it was because everything was happening so fast, or if it was pregnancy hormones running rife through my system.

Either way, I was feeling pissed off, and I was struggling to keep my emotions in check.

We all left the holding room, and as we exited the archway, Christik tilted her head at the guards, indicating for them to follow us. It wasn't long before we reached our room. I stopped with James at the archway entrance and wrapped my arms around his waist.

"Please be careful, baby," I said against his chest.

I could hear his heart beating quickly against my ear.

"Don't worry, baby, I think I'm in good hands," he replied, kissing the top of my head.

"See you soon," I said, looking up into his eyes.

James kissed me again, this time on my lips, and I released him from my arms, watching him walk and the angels glide away.

I walked into my room, desperately needing a shower and a rest. My whole body felt exhausted, but I wasn't surprised. How much excitement could one person take?

Within an hour, I was clean, fresh, and relaxing on our bed. It felt wonderful just laying still and feeling my body relax while my mind went over what had happened since waking up in the sleeping room. I was obviously more tired than I realized and soon drifted off into a deep, restful sleep.

CHAPTER 12

The next thing I knew, James was trying to gently wake me up.

"Mel, baby, wake up gorgeous; I'm back," he said quietly.

"Are you okay, James?" I asked, through my grogginess and feeling confused.

"I'm good, baby. We have the other fallen angels. Will you come with me now to meet the others and talk to them?" he asked. "I have some food and juice for you before we go," he added, pointing to the small table.

There was a mini-feast waiting for me and fresh coffee which smelled heavenly.

"How long were you gone for?" I asked.

Not for the first time, I wished that I had a watch on.

"We were gone for about three hours, baby. Do you feel better for having had a sleep?" he asked.

"Mmm, I sure do and I'm now starving, plus I have a mouth like a surfer's flip-flop," I replied, sliding off the bed. James chuckled at me, patting my backside as I walked away.

I quickly brushed my teeth, ran my fingers through my hair, and splashed some water on my face. Feeling human again, I made my way to James who was pouring me some coffee at the table.

"So, what happened?" I asked as I sat down on one of the chairs, keen to get all the information from him.

James went on to explain that Nalik had led them to the empty building where the fallen angels were hiding. It had previously been a medical center before Earth had started to die.

Luckily, because it wasn't in their nature to be evil or deceptive, the fallen angels hadn't thought to leave any traps or ambushes of any kind.

They were, however, preparing to sabotage more of the water cleaning crafts and also planning to attack the holding structure. They were hoping to create as much chaos as possible. Apparently, there were makeshift bombs at the ready in one of the treatment rooms.

James and the other angels were able to take them by surprise using the angels' power. It seemed that all the action movies and crime shows James said he'd watched for all those years had come in very handy.

"I was like Bruce Willis in the Die-Hard movies, baby," James told me, showing me the biggest smile and his dimples.

I couldn't help but giggle at his enthusiasm and pride.

"Sounds like you showed the angels some of your badass skills muscle man," I told him, through my giggles.

"Where are they now?" I asked, taking some of the mouth-watering food from the stone tray between us.

"They're in the holding room. Christik and Jakiz are going to come here for us soon," he replied.

"Did the other fallen angels have Marilian gifts like Nalik had in his hair?" I asked.

"One of them had another of those hair rings, one had some sort of bracelet on, and the others had necklaces with pendants attached," James explained.

"We managed to get all of them, and Jakiz has put them all in secure bubbles with the first one. She's put them in the secure holding room. We need to talk with all the fallen ones, Mel. They're all very distressed at being deceived and used," he added. "Also, they're all feeling as guilty as hell over the explosions on the rig craft."

While we finished our meal, my mind processed all the information which only brought up more questions than I wanted answers to. Just as I was going to ask James, there was a knock on the archway and Christik appeared with Jakiz at the entrance to our room.

"Are you ready?" Christik asked.

"We were born ready," I answered, giving them both a smile.

They both looked so comical with confusion written all over their faces.

"It's another human expression, meaning more than ready," I told them with a giggle.

"You'll get used to us eventually," James added, with his cheeky smile.

James indicated for the angels to lead the way, and together we made our way to the large meeting room next to the control room.

Everyone was in the meeting room except for Michelle, who was still in her sleeping state. I was surprised to see Jessie in attendance. I didn't think he'd leave Michelle's bedside, but I was pleased that he was there talking with the angels and the others. He seemed a lot more relaxed and happy to be back with his friends.

We were greeted with smiles and hellos from

everyone, apart from the ex-fallen angels who were all looking at the floor and still looked forlorn.

Their hair and markings were all back to normal colors, but they weren't shimmering properly like Christik and the others as yet. They all looked dimmer than they should.

"Please all take a seat," Christik asked.

The humans and angels all took a place around the table. Everyone was intermingled this time. Angels and humans blended together, and it was good to see.

"Welcome back Keiz, Nalik, Hazik, Franz, Anglik, and Toniz," Christik declared, indicating to each angel, so we'd know, who was who.

"Before we discuss the danger, we all face, I need you all to understand that these angels were corrupted by the Marilian race, whose planet and race we recently saved," she stated. "They were deceived into accepting gifts, which held the power to corrupt them and force them to turn against their own kind and your race," she explained. "These angels did not act willingly, and they also did not have free will while wearing those evil gifts. Now that the gifts have been removed, our angels are free once again," She added.

Jakiz stood up from her seat, and the other angels followed suit.

"Please hold out your hands," she asked the ex-fallen ones.

As we all watched in fascination, the solemn ex-fallen angels all raised their hands above the table. Jakiz and the others placed their hands on top of the other angels' hands. Instantly, we all saw and felt the bright white glow of power flowing through the contact between them and through the room. The ex-fallen angels glowed brightly and sparkled before our eyes; it was breathtaking.

When Jakiz and her colleagues broke the contact; the white glow dimmed. The ex-fallen angels were shimmering in their natural beauty once again.

All sadness and guilt were gone from their beautiful faces, and they all seemed happier and at peace. One by one, they all dipped their heads in gratitude and respect to their fellow angels.

"Let us get this show on the road," Christik said, looking at me with a smile on her face.

I couldn't stop the giggle that escaped me, and I was glad. It seemed to liven up the room with giggles from the other men and women too.

"Let us all be seated again," Christik said, giving all the angels a beautiful smile.

The ex-fallen angels took their seats again, and they all looked visibly relaxed. In fact, everyone had relaxed now including James and me.

"We spent a long time on the Marilian planet before coming here," Christik told us all. "Like your planet, Marilia was dying. Unfortunately, the Marilians did not care about saving their planet's wildlife or saving themselves, lest it makes them look weak and vulnerable. We arrived on their planet in time before all of their wildlife was lost, and their race demised into extinction," Christik added. "As I have explained to, Elita and James, the Marilians only care about and thrive on two things: power and enslaving other races. Now that their planet is healed but their numbers greatly reduced, it seems they want to follow us here and take Earth."

"What will happen if they manage to conquer us?" Derek asked.

He had concern firmly fixed on his face, mirroring everyone else's including mine, I'm sure. Harrik leaned forward addressing everyone.

"If they conquer this planet, they will drain Earth of every resource it has, including your planet's core. They will leave your planet an empty shell by the time they are finished. While they are doing that, they will be changing you all into one of them which would be a slow agony and would result in your deaths," he explained.

"Why the hell did you save them then and their bloody planet, if they're so fucking evil?"

Tracey demanded, in her usual blunt way.

Christik smiled at her with genuine warmth and understanding,

"It is not our way to judge whether a race or a planet is worth saving Tracey. We cannot as you would say, play God," Christik said. "We had hoped that having been on the brink of extinction and coming close to losing their planet, it would change them or change their ways. Unfortunately, it obviously did not," she added.

"But they're fucking monsters from what you're saying. So, what good was to come of saving them if they're that bad?" Tracey demanded.

She was probably asking what most people in the room were thinking, including me. Everyone around the room was tense, their faces showing their worry and stress now.

"If we were to allow a planet to die, it could impact other planets in their solar system, killing millions of other races," Christik explained. "We also cannot stop races from being good or evil. However, we can and will protect an innocent race from being wiped out," Christik told us.

"How long before they get here?" John asked.

"Before we answer your question, John, let us show you what we will be up against," Christik told him.

Anglik stood from her seat and then she outstretched her arm, with her palm facing outward towards the center of the table. Her hand began to glow brightly, and an image started to appear in front of us all.

It was a planet, a turbulent, harsh-looking planet. We could see what looked like massive hurricanes on its surface, but they were fiery red and orange. As the image zoomed in on the planet's surface, Nalik began to explain what we were being shown.

"The Marilian planet is hostile, and that is how the Marilian race like it," he said, "It is your race's definition of Hell, full of fire and death. They fight against each other to the death constantly, which is why they have a constant need to replace their numbers by enslaving other races. Once someone has been changed, there is no changing back; you become one of them in body and personality with the same bloodthirsty traits. They are an intelligent species; they have spacecraft and the technologies needed to drain any planet of all resources," he stated.

The imagine zoomed in even closer this time showing a village. The sky above was fiery and thunderous. The Marilians were living in domed stone structures similar to igloos but made of a dark, burnt-orange stone. These were arranged in a circle with a ring of black stones in the middle.

To me, the Marilians looked very much like sloths. They were covered in thick long and shaggy grey-looking fur, which was covering hard, muscular bodies.

Their aggressive-looking faces had large red evil-looking eyes. As I looked down their furry bodies, I saw they had massive long talons. The talons looked as nasty and sharp as any decent knife blade.

I couldn't stop the shudder that ran through my body. My blood ran cold, and I could feel the hairs on the back of my neck stand to attention and prickle.

They looked like huge creatures, but it was hard to gauge from the images before us. There were Marilians fighting inside the black stone ring, and it was barbaric.

They were slicing at each other with their vicious long talons, causing deep slices through each other's bodies. There were sprays of black blood appearing with every wound, and they were so fast; it was almost a blur of action.

While I sat there watching the Marilians trying to kill each other, I couldn't help but think that we didn't stand a chance against these monsters.

"It only took us a matter of months to reach

Earth from their planet; however, their technology is thankfully not as advanced as our own," Nalik explained. "Depending on how quickly they can fix their crafts, they could be here in one of your Earth years," Nalik said.

Anglik closed her palm, making the image disappear. She sat back down in her seat looking very worried and somewhat shaken. The room was now in a stunned silence.

The women were suddenly trying to get closer to their men, and the men were wrapping their arms around their women or taking a hand in theirs as the information and the images sunk in; the men felt even more protective.

"How the hell can we stop them?" Mimi asked in a small voice showing her shock.

James squeezed my hand gently under the table.

"I have spoken with Christik and the other angels," Harrik said, "From what I understand, the only thing the Marilians understand and respect is dominance. So, we need to make sure that we are all more dominant and better at fighting than they are," he explained to our worried friends.

"We will begin preparations immediately, and we will need all your help to organize training and weaponry," Christik said as she stood to address everyone." Our race has no experience in war, so you will all need to help us to find people of your race with the skills we will need so that they may teach and train others. Are you all willing to fight for your planet and your race?" She asked.

Tracey suddenly stood from her seat, "Abso-fucking-lutely!" She said, bringing a smile to all our faces.

There were many shouts of "Amen, Hell Yeah!" and agreements from everyone around the table. I could see the sheer determination appearing in all their faces.

"Please get some rest; we will begin tomorrow," Christik told us all.

Slowly, everyone got up to leave, talking between themselves about what they had just seen and what they'd like to do to the Marilians when they arrived. Especially the men, who obviously felt very protective of their women who'd they'd just got back and their families at the holding structure. The angels who were leaving with them didn't say a word, but they appeared to be listening thoughtfully.

"Can you and James stay for a moment please?" she asked as we also began to rise from our seats.

"Yes, of course," I replied, sitting back down with James.

After everyone had left, Christik and Harrik moved to the seats closest to James and me. I couldn't tell whether Christik and Harrik were nervous or excited; maybe a little of both.

"We have something important to tell you both," she said in her usual calm manner. "Sometimes, when a planet begins to die, it starts an evolutionary event; nature has a way of trying to survive. We believe that it was an evolutionary event that made us who we are because we know our own home planet at one point nearly died," she explained. "We believe, Elita and James, that your new baby will be the first to be born with new evolutionary effects."

It took a few moments for her words to sink in.

"Our baby isn't going to be normal?" I asked in a whisper, looking up into Christik's sapphire, peacock eyes.

"Your new baby is going to be the new normal, Elita," she replied with a warm smile.

James was just as stunned as I was. He tried to speak but then cleared his throat to try again.

"So, what is our baby going to be like?" he asked, probably displaying the same shocked expression that I had on my face.

"Your new baby girl will be a little more like us," Christik said, "Your baby will be born with wings, beautiful wings, and she will be more angelic in appearance," she added.

"Wow, another little girl," I said under my breath, sounding more like Mimi.

"That's amazing!" James uttered next to me.

"Will she have power like you as well?" I asked, my mind still trying to wrap around this new revelation.

I couldn't help but place my hand on my pregnant stomach. James leaned forward, placing his large hand over mine.

"She will not have the power we hold, but we do believe she will have special gifts. She will be completely human, and she will be the first of a new generation of humans," Christik explained.

I didn't know about James, but my mind was reeling. We were going to have a new daughter, and she was going to be the first of her kind. The first new kind of human, and she was going to have wings. '*I have to be dreaming surely!*'

"How do you know this for sure?" I asked Christik, my hand not moving from my pregnant stomach.

Christik leaned towards me, placing her hand on top of James' and mine. She raised her other arm with her palm facing towards the center of the long table and instantly an image appeared.

"This is what your baby will look like in five months' time, Elita." she said.

There, above the middle of the table, was our baby girl, and everything was there. We could clearly see her little arms and legs, her tiny eyes, nose, and mouth and there on her back were tiny little wings covered in little white feathers.

She was absolutely beautiful!

"I don't know what to say," I whispered.

My brain was not only shocked but also in awe. I couldn't take my eyes off our new baby.

"Say you will give her the same love and care you give to your other children," Christik pleaded gently.

"Of course," I replied, still glued to the sight of our baby girl, "that goes without saying, she's going to be extremely loved by our children and us."

Christik lowered her arm making the image vanish just as quickly as it appeared.

"I could have watched her for hours," James said, smiling and flashing his dimples.

Christik rose up from her seat and looked at both of us with love.

"Yes, I could have watched her for hours too. We are very much looking forward to meeting your new daughter," she said.

Harrik stood from his seat, smiling and

pointing towards the exit.

"We also have a surprise for you, Elita," he said.

I whipped my head around at the same time as James and there approaching the glass doors were our children. Instantly, I could feel the tears welling up in my eyes and then slowly running down my cheeks.

Their faces were glowing with nervous excitement, and they made my heart melt. James and I both hurriedly rose up to greet them as they entered the meeting room. My heart was pounding in my chest.

I was suddenly really nervous, wondering if they were just excited to see their dad, who'd been in their lives constantly for the last five years, or whether they were excited to see me too? I immediately felt like a nervous wreck. '*Were they going to treat me like a stranger? Were they going to feel awkward around me?*' So many questions were suddenly rushing through my mind.

I didn't need to worry because when the kids burst through the glass archway doors, they ran straight up to me, all of them wrapping their arms around me.

They were hugging me so tightly I could barely breathe. It was the best feeling in the world, and

I could feel their love all around me.

I tried to hug them all back, desperately trying to gather them up in my arms and bring them even closer. I could feel my tears falling freely down my cheeks; the love and the bond I felt for my children was overwhelming.

I looked up through my tears to see Christik and Harrik, gracefully making their way out of the meeting room doors. Christik looked back at us all with happiness.

"Thank you," I mouthed to her.

Her responding smile made it clear that she understood how much that moment meant to me.

I don't know how long our kids and I were stood there hugging. They were all clinging to me just as much as I was clinging to them. I do know that I didn't want to let go of them, and I don't think our kids wanted to let go of me either.

It took James suggesting that we all sit down to talk for us to finally let go of each other; the kids and I reluctantly releasing our hold.

Before the kids all sat at the meeting room table, they all gave me a kiss and a final squeeze. It was the best feeling in the world, and my heartfelt, so full of love for them.

We all began to take our seats, all sitting at one end of the table, so we could all still see each other clearly. Hulaz arrived with a large black stone tray of food, juice, and coffee.

"Welcome children, we are very pleased to have you back with your parents. I am Hulaz," she told them with a lovely warm smile on her beautiful face.

The kids all responded to Hulaz with warm smiles of their own, all thanking her for the refreshments and dipping their heads in respect.

"Thank you for bringing us here; we've all missed our mom probably more than she realizes," Anthony replied in a very deep voice that shocked me.

He turned to look at me and gave me his dad's lovely smile. His words went straight to my heart, and it suddenly struck me just how much the kids had grown up. They weren't kids anymore; they were young adults.

Hulaz dipped her head in respect to all the kids, and then her gaze turned to James and me.

"We have added more beds for your children in your room for you. We have also extended your room by opening the adjoining room. We thought you would all like to stay together," she explained.

"Thank you so much Hulaz, we really appreciate that and everything you've done for us," I replied, hoping she could feel my utter gratitude.

She dipped her head again but this time to all of us and went to leave. As I watched her glide out of the glass doors, I thought again how lucky we all were to not only have the angels there but also lucky to have them as friends.

The moment she left, James and the kids began to tuck into the food from the tray. There was a selection of various salad leaves, vegetables, and fruits. '*Some things don't change!*' I thought to myself; kids love to eat and are generally always hungry. It all looked delicious, but I was still feeling far too nervous to eat anything.

"Your dad has told me how well you've all been doing while I was sleeping," I told them.

I kept looking from one face to another, trying to take in every detail such as Anthony's height and his long curly hair. Holly's womanly figure and her long, brunette hair like James' and the maturity that showed in her green-blue eyes. Harrison and Abigail had changed greatly too.

Harrison had become a man-mountain full of muscle, and Abigail was now a proper young lady. Her figure was more athletic, and both of them had darker hair, which was now a dark blond instead of the white blonde from my dreams. My heart was aching to hold them close to me again.

"I am so proud of you all. You have really

shown just how resilient and strong you all are and determined, from what your dads told me," I told them, with pride swelling in my chest.

"I'm so amazed at how well you've coped with everything that's happened. Not only what was happening to our planet, but also with the angels coming and then settling into the holding structure with your dad. I'm so grateful that you didn't let things get to you and that you all took the chance to learn new things as well as supporting each other," I added.

I could tell how much my words meant to them as I could see it in their faces. Anthony leaned forward and put his hand on mine.

"Are you really okay Mom?" he asked, concern appearing in his green eyes which were so much like his dads.

"I'm more than okay darling!" I replied, re-aching out to take his hand in mine.

I made eye contact with all our children, trying to give them a reassuring smile, and I began to explain everything to them.

I told them about waking up in the sleeping room, stressing to them that I wasn't in any dis-comfort while asleep. Then I told them about giving birth to the baby tiger cub, explaining the whole process from beginning to end. I felt that I needed them to understand that the lies they were told were just that, lies!

James helped me to explain about the fallen angels too. Also, what happened when they caused the explosion on the rig craft and about the Marilians coming to conquer Earth.

Even though they'd been through so much already, we needed them to understand the serious threat the Marilians posed. Their sweet faces mirrored each other's, a mixture of emotions showing as they absorbed each bit of new information.

I was saddened, and it made my heartache in my chest to be having to put so much on their young shoulders, especially when our reunion was supposed to be a happy time.

However, I was so impressed with their questions because it showed just how mature they'd become.

Our children had lost so much of their childhood; they'd had to grow up so quickly over the last seven years. Coping with the end of our planet and all the trauma that came with that and then the surprising arrival of the angels.

Our children were truly amazing people and suddenly the pride I felt was all-consuming. I felt as if I was going to explode.

I didn't realize that I'd started swaying in my

seat until Holly stood up suddenly.

"Mom are you alright?" she asked, her voice full of concern.

James took one look at me and stood quickly, grabbing me by my shoulders to stop me falling to the floor.

"Baby what's wrong?" he asked, worry prominent in his husky voice.

"I'm okay. Just a little light-headed; too much excitement from seeing the kids probably," I replied, smiling at my beautiful children.

"I know what it is," James said, to our now worried kids. "We've got something to tell you."

CHAPTER 13

James looked at our kids with his happiness shining through his bright eyes.

"Your mom and I are having a new baby!" James told them a ridiculous grin on his face showing how thrilled he was.

The kids went from shocked to ecstatic in a matter of seconds.

"Good grief Dad, you two have only just got back together; you didn't waste any time!" Harrison said, laughing and grinning from ear to ear.

He obviously had his dad's wicked sense of humor! Holly and Abigail giggled at James who was wiggling his eyebrows at them all.

"It's meant to be!" James told them. "Your new baby sister is going to be the first of her kind for the human race."

When the kids' faces turned to confusion, James explained what the angels had told us about nature's way of surviving and evolution accelerating to help our race survive.

"So, our new baby sister is going to be born with wings, like real wings?" Abigail asked her dad, in absolute awe.

"Yep, she sure is, and she may have special gifts too, although we don't have any idea of what they could be," James replied.

"She's going to be amazing just like you all are!" I told them with pride ringing through my words.

"I can't wait to meet her," Abigail said as she bounced up and down in her seat. "I can't wait to see her fly too; she's going to be awesome!"

When I looked at my kids, I was again staggered by how grown up they were; they really were a sight to behold. I could see Holly's mind ticking over as she processed the news.

"Hang on a minute Mom, you've only just given birth to a tiger cub, so you couldn't have possibly had a period already. So, how have you managed to get pregnant so quickly?" she asked.

I could tell she was probably going over the timeline in her head, '*My girl was so sharp!*', I thought. James sat back down next to me, sliding his arm around my waist. I think for emotional support, or maybe he was just worried I was going to keel over.

I couldn't help but smile at Holly.

"Do you remember when the angels found you all, took you to their hospital room, and healed you?" I asked.

They all nodded their heads.

"Well, part of their birthing process is re-setting our bodies straight after delivery using their power. That way, we stay ultra-healthy and are ready to conceive straight away," I explained.

"Ahh," Holly said softly.

Anthony, Harrison, and Abigail were all nodding with her, obviously understanding everything I'd said.

"So, getting back to these Marilians; they are vicious monsters who will kill us by changing us into one of them," Anthony clarified.

All their demeanors changed again rapidly. Anthony was obviously wanting to get to the really serious issue at hand. James held Anthony's gaze.

"Yes, I'm afraid so son," James replied. "It seems that because of what happened to their planet and the way they live, their population numbers are down drastically. So, to continue their way of life..."

"You mean killing each other," Holly interrupted.

James looked at her warmly.

"Yes, and because they want to carry on

killing each other, they have to replace those they've lost. To do that, they'll try to conquer other planets and races and change them into more Marilians," he explained.

I could tell the kids were totally mortified at the idea.

"They're no better than a disease, spreading and changing other cells, destroying and infecting everything else!" Anthony stated almost shouting.

We could all tell how disgusted he was, and we all felt the same way. James stroked his head in sympathy, ruffling his dark, curly hair.

"We've spoken with the angels, and we do have a plan," James told them. "While our planet is being healed, we'll find out who among us are skilled in combat, air, land, and sea. We must have servicemen and woman among us survivors with different skill sets. We just need to find them and ask them if they're willing to help train the others in everything they know. We also need to find volunteer delegates from every holding structure around the world, so we can plan, organize, and execute our defense.

Everyone old enough will be needed I think, including you guys. I'm afraid there aren't enough of us to be able to not include you all," James declared.

When James said that they would all be

needed, subconsciously, our kids abruptly sat up straight pulling their shoulders back, lifting their heads higher as if they were ready for anything. While I sat there admiring our children, I thought to myself, '*Yes they really are ready for what we're all about to face.*'

"We're all meeting with the angels tomorrow to start putting things in motion," I said, grabbing a juice from the tray. "So, let's talk about you kids while we finish our meal," I added, placing the juice in front of Holly and grabbing the next one to hand out.

While we ate our meal, the kids told me all about life at the holding structure. They even had a nickname for it, calling it the cruiser. I wondered if they'd got that idea from their Dad; he'd already told me that it was similar to a cruise ship inside.

I found this funny, considering the only cruise ship we'd been on was a Disney cruise liner after a decent win on a scratch card.

They were full of enthusiasm as they described the different shops and which ones were their favorites. Holly's favorite apparently was the craft shop.

She explained that there were many people of all ages who had craft hobbies. They would make their arts and crafts such as jewelry, paintings, and decor, give them to the shop caretaker and anyone could select what they wanted for their cabin.

She also explained that people thought differently now because of what they'd been through and that because money wasn't used anymore, people just took joy in the fact that others loved their work. It seemed from what she said that everyone was settled into their new home and were making the place their own.

Holly also told me all about a social group she'd set up for everyone, where they could discuss any topic and plan community events. She was so proud of what she'd accomplished and how many people had started to attend. I wasn't surprised that Holly wanted to be involved in rebuilding society; she really did have the skills for it.

Thomas and Harrison told me all about the engineering work they'd been learning and doing, both clearly very proud of themselves. Not only were they learning from the angels and their technology, but also from the surviving human engineers too.

One of the communities had set up a workshop where they were learning to convert human machinery, technology, and devices to clean, green energies.

They were already preparing for when the angels would leave. From what they both told me, I didn't think we would need any fossil fuels ever again, and that was a wonderful piece of news.

As for Abigail, she was so full of enthusiasm while telling me about the amazing artists she'd been working with. I remembered what James had said about it, but I didn't realize that she was learning so many different art forms. I was surprised she found time to sleep with all the classes and activities she was doing.

She was apparently learning dance routines and being taught various painting styles. Abigail was thrilled to tell me that quite a few people had taken her art for their cabins from the shop.

I was beyond thrilled that the kids had been doing so well and doing so much while I was sleeping. I couldn't wait until I could go to the cruiser myself and see what it was like, but I had a feeling it was going to be a while before that was going to happen.

"I am so very proud of you all," I told them.

My heart was so full of love for them.

"Come on, let's go to our room and get some sleep because we've got a big day tomorrow," I added.

After putting everything back on the stone tray, we made our way out of the meeting room. We walked through the bustling control room and headed for the corridor.

As we passed all the angels busily working at their consoles, we were greeted with lots of dipped heads and many more smiles. The kids were so used to being around the angels that they automatically did the same in return.

We were soon in the long corridor and making our leisurely way to our room. The kids being curious were looking everywhere. Abigail reached out, and as we walked, she ran her fingers against the wall just like I had.

"This isn't made of the same material as the cruiser," she said, her eyes wide with awe.

I was intrigued.

"What's the cruiser made of?" I asked.

She looked thrilled to be able to tell me more, her sweet face full of smiles.

"It's made of a white kind of stone, similar to the stone tray that Hulaz brought the food on," she explained. "We have archways like these though," she added as we passed one.

"But the Hieroglyphs aren't the same color as these or quite as big. Did Dad tell you that we also have a natural pool for swimming at the cruiser, Mom?" she asked.

“No,” I replied, shaking my head.

“It’s amazing, Mom, and it’s one of my favorite places. It's like a mini tropical paradise with different water lilies, fish, and birds,” she said with so much happiness. “We love swimming with the fish and the birds, and they don’t mind us doing it. Lots of the birds will eat from our hands now,” she added.

Listening to her made me realize that our kids had a great and wondrous appreciation for nature. It was heartwarming, and I couldn't wait to see it all for myself.

We all talked quietly among ourselves as we walked down the corridor. The kids telling me about all the things I’d missed while I was asleep. I was enjoying our conversations with our kids so much that we were back at our room in no time.

When we entered our room, I was amazed at what the angels had done for us, especially in such a short space of time. They’d somehow removed the side wall of the room, replacing it with an archway and making the two rooms into one. So, the kids had one side, and we had the other.

The other side had four beds with added decorative partitions for privacy and a table with comfortable chairs in the center. When I got closer to the archway, I noticed a symbol on the side of the frame. I touched it gently with my finger and inst-antly a silver barrier appeared.

"Told you, baby, these angels are like a well-oiled machine, and they think of everything," James said, flashing his cheeky dimples.

'*That man always makes me giggle,*' I thought to myself, chuckling.

In less than an hour, we were all showered and in our beds. The excitement of the day was mak-ing us all tired. The kids had each given me a massive cuddle before closing the archway and climbing into their beds.

Once the barrier was up between our rooms, James and I couldn't hear a thing.

"You've done an amazing job with the kids," I told him as I laid in his arms all warm and sleepy in our bed.

"They're amazing kids, Mel," he replied, nuz-zling his face into the back of my neck. "They've really missed you, and they seem really excited about the new baby too," he added.

His hand slid down to my pregnant stomach, and slowly he started to stroke my bare skin, making goosebumps appear all over my body. I could feel his arousal pressing against me as he gently pulled me closer.

A couple of hours later, after repeatedly reminding each other of our love for one another again, we both fell asleep. As I drifted off into my slumber, it was as if the floodgates had opened up on my memories.

Dream after dream was full of my memories coming back to me. Memories of James and I, the kids, and our house. Remembering the kids' first steps, all of our Christmases together and the kids, birthdays, as well as holidays we'd shared. Then I dreamt about what had happened just before the angels came.

Snippets appeared in my dream of the news alerts, Earth's animals dying and the oceans dying. James and I stocking up on food and water, stashing it all in the house. The noises outside from the people fighting and killing each other.

So many cries of pain from adults and children haunted my dreams. Images of James crying because he'd had to put our last dog Diesel to sleep to end his suffering. So many happy memories and then so much pain and suffering all came flooding back to me.

By the time I finally woke up, I felt like I hadn't had any sleep at all. My mind was still reeling from the bombardment of all the memories and the good and bad emotions that came with them. My heart was beating wildly in my chest, and my skin felt damp and clammy all over.

"Mel, are you ok?" James asked, his voice still sounding sleepy.

"Yes, I'm fine; all my memories came back last night, so I still feel really tired. I'm going to get a shower to wake myself up, I told him, still feeling quite shaken but kissing him on his soft lips to reassure him.

"Are you sure you're okay, baby? he asked. "That's a lot of memories to mentally digest."

I could see James was concerned, and I loved him for it.

"I promise I'm okay," I told him, "it's great to have my memories back of us and the kids; I'm just worn out from it all," I replied, making my way to the bathroom.

After my very long shower and cleaning my teeth, I felt like my old self again. Even though it had been a tough night, I was grateful to have all my memories back. Especially all my memories of James and the kids.

They were all waiting for me when I came out of the bedroom area, all dressed and ready to go. Even James was ready which surprised me. My face must have shown my surprise because James was giving me his dimpled smile.

"You were in the shower so long baby that I decided to jump into the kids' shower," he said laughing.

Coming over to me, he wrapped his muscular arms around me, pulling me in close to his body.

"Are you ready to get the show on the road fair lady?" he asked.

"Oh, husband of mine, I was born ready," I replied, giving him a cheeky smile.

"Get a room!" The twins called out in unison, both of them rolling their eyes at us and making both of us laugh.

"I missed that," I whispered into his chest, as I gave him one last cuddle before we had to start dealing with the serious things.

Nearly everyone was already in the meeting room when we all arrived. There was a formidable feast spread in the center of the table too, courtesy of our hosts. As always, we were greeted by smiles and dipped heads from our fellow humans and angels alike.

I felt so proud as I introduced our kids to everyone, and the kids weren't intimidated whatsoever, meeting so many new people. They were quickly shaking hands with everyone and joining into conversations.

Again, pride began to swell in my chest as I watched them.

We ate and talked with the others, and it gave me a chance to talk with Nalik and the other ex-fallen angels. They seemed to be doing well since their corruption and were very eager to share their thoughts about the Marilians.

They appeared just as worried as we were, or maybe even more so. Which wasn't surprising considering what they'd seen on the Marilian planet and what they'd been through on our planet.

We were all sat down at the table finishing our food when Christik and Harrik entered, determination and seriousness written all over their expressions. Two other angels followed through after them and began to clear the table of food, replacing it all with juice, coffee, and water. Much to my delight!

Just as the two angels began to leave again, Christik began to address us all, standing up from her seat.

"Thank you all for coming this morning, I hope you all had a good night's sleep."

'*I wish I had,*' I thought to myself.

Christik continued.

"From today, I am afraid things are going to become very busy. We have absolutely no time to waste before the Marilians arrive here. Not only do you all need to be trained in combat but so do we," Christik added. "We need to find anyone who may have skills in weaponry and combat. Any ideas on how to do that quickly?" She asked.

"Dad?" Anthony said, looking at James with a look that said, 'Go on then.' James cleared his throat, obviously feeling a little nervous with all eyes on him suddenly, then he took a deep breath and pulled his shoulders back.

"I think the easiest way of coordinating our efforts is to make contact with each main angel craft. We can ask them to reach out to every holding craft and get them to hold meetings with our people," he explained. "The angels and humans need to work very closely with each other like we are because that will make us more effective in our defense," James added.

Everyone seemed to be agreeing with everything he'd said so far, either nodding their heads or saying "Yes" or "I agree" as he spoke, angels and humans alike. James reached for a cup of water with a slightly shaking hand, speaking and maybe nerves making his throat dry.

"Can I please have some paper and something to write with Harrik?" Holly asked during the pause.

"Of course," Harrik replied, dipping his head and gliding swiftly out of the room.

When I looked at Holly, she seemed thoughtful.

"Why do you need paper, etc. darling?" I asked.

She broke out in a confident and beautiful smile.

"I want to make notes and do a plan of action, and I'm going to give everyone a copy. So, everyone knows what we're doing, and they can refer back to it," Holly answered, very matter of factly.

'*Wow,*' I thought to myself; our girl was very impressive!

As James placed his water down on the table, Harrik glided back into the room with Holly's paper and a writing instrument. It looked like a twig to me, but Holly began to write her notes down quickly and with ease.

When James spoke again, he came across a lot calmer with his nerves now settled. I think the distraction of Holly talking, receiving the paper and pencil probably helped.

"Okay," he said, "So when the people in the holding crafts have their meetings, we need key people to gather information about who has what skills. You'd be surprised at what skills are going to come in handy. For example, we have a body painting artist called Ann at our holding craft, and she could paint and disguise your angels to blend into any surroundings. The Marilians wouldn't see you or know you were there, even if they were standing right next to you," He explained.

"That would give us a great advantage," Harrik responded, looking seriously impressed.

"Yes, especially if the Marilians are made to think that you've already left. They'd think we were defenseless, and it could make them overconfident, less on guard and hopefully less defensive when they attack," Derek added.

"Very good point Derek!" James replied. "We also have talented engineers, including my boys here. Plus, we have IT people who are proficient at using your technology now and plenty of ex-service people who survived because they used their combat and survival skills. We'll have to make it clear to everyone what we're about to face because we aren't going to force anyone to help. We want people to volunteer to help," he added.

"What about the women who are still sleeping?" Tracey asked, "There's bound to be many women with useful skills who'd want to volunteer. I actually want to volunteer myself," she said, straightening her back to appear more formidable.

Her husband John looked very shocked and surprised.

"You're not an ex-service woman or engineer my love," he told her gently.

Tracey's face said it all. She was very unimpressed by her husband's comment and was seriously giving him the evil eye again.

"Maybe not," she said defiantly, "I'm a real estate agent, commercial and residential. That means I know the best locations for setting traps, ambushes, and the best buildings to store weapons in," she continued. "I can be a fucking badass to John!" she said, with eyebrows raised as if to say, "Bite me."

I looked at my kids when Tracey dropped the "F-bomb" word again, thinking I was going to see shocked faces. Instead, I saw them all giggling and trying to be quiet. Holly looked right at me with humor written all over her face.

"I like her," she mouthed, making me giggle too.

James cleared his throat again getting everyone's attention,

"Tracey is spot on; we'll need people with all sorts of different skills, and this is why we need to act fast to see who we have," he stated.

James then turned to Christik and Harrik who'd been listening intently—nodding their heads in agreement throughout.

"Tracey's also right about the women who are sleeping. We need to find their families as soon as possible, so we can start waking them up," he told them.

Christik and Harrik both nodded in agreement. Christik then paused a moment, as if going over something in her mind, and then she looked back at James as if she'd made her mind up.

"Yes, James, we do need to wake them as quickly as possible," she told him. "When we do wake them, we will need to gently explain everything. First, tell them about how they are helping repopulate your planet and then explain about the Marilians. We will ask them if they would like to volunteer to fight the Marilians, and if any women do not want to, then we will ask them if they would like to carry on helping your animal kingdom. They will all have the choice to help or not," she explained, looking at Derek by the end of her sentence.

She'd obviously thought a lot about what Derek had said, with regards to giving all women the choice to help or not and decided it was the right thing to do. I knew that was going to make the men and women in the room very happy.

"We need to move fast, so let us contact the Viziers, the heads of the smaller main control crafts, and start putting things in motion," Christik declared to the room.

She then turned to Harrik and gave him a nod of her head.

Harrik stood from his seat, raising his arm with his palm facing the middle of the table. His hand began to glow, but instead of a flat image this time, it was a silvery-white sphere.

We all watched in fascination as square images began to appear within the sphere. Images of other angels appeared one after another until the sphere was completely covered.

"Welcome Viziers," Christik greeted, as the sphere slowly turned. "I have called on you as we have a deadly threat to contend with. Some of our angels fell to corruption by the Marilians while we were saving their race and their planet. The Fallen ones are now back to normal; however, it seems the Marilians want to replace their numbers by following us here. They want to conquer Earth, consume everything on it, and inside it as well as take the humans for their own. Viziers, we cannot let this happen!" she declared.

The slowly turning sphere above the table gently stopped, and one of the angels in the sphere placed his hand on his throat, making it glow.

"Are you suggesting we go to war against the

Marilians Christik?" he asked respectfully.

Christik stood from her seat.

"Yes, I am Mickiz," she said firmly. "The humans have warred against each other during their history, I do not deny that fact; however, as they developed, their warring lessened. The humans who have survived are good people, innocent people. We must save them and their planet; that is our way and our role in the universe, to save others." she stressed.

Her compassion and determination were shining through. Mickiz dipped his head in respect and then he met Christik's sapphire eyes.

"Yes, you are correct Christik, that is our role. My angels and I will fight for the humans and Earth," he told her.

All at once, all the other angels in the sphere began to touch their throats and then stated their agreement to fight and defend our planet. Christik sat back down in her seat. I could tell she was relieved at the response from the Vizier's.

I think all of us in the room were just as relieved, when they'd all agreed to fight the Marilians. Once the room was quiet again, Christik went on to explain the plan. She told them that we needed to be reaching out to people in the holding structures.

Finding the families of the sleeping women and waking them up was to be the first step. She then asked the Viziers to arrange the meetings and co-llection of information to help us defend our planet.

When Christik had finished explaining to th-em everything that we'd discussed, she stood again, only this time she seemed full of pride.

"The people and angels you see in this room have been key in helping us to formulate this plan, especially James," she said as she pointed to my husband.

James suddenly became quite bashful, dipp-ing his head in respect to Christik and the angels in the sphere.

"James seems to have defense and organ-izational skills he didn't realize he had," she stated with a smile. "James and everyone here will be working closely with us, and they have already pro-ven to be invaluable as colleagues and friends. Please find humans to help you and build relation-ships with them."

Harrik stood from his seat, getting everyone's attention in the process.

"I believe we should activate the Earth's an-cient defenses; it may slow the Marilians down as they try to enter the planets orbit," he stated.

I don't think I was the only person in the room who was utterly confused at his statement. All the men and women in the room were looking at each other in bewilderment, which the angels picked up on straight away.

"I assume most of you here are familiar with some of Earth's ancient structures such as the Pyramids in Egypt, the Mayan temples, and Stonehenge in England," Christik said.

Most of us were thinking of the ancient structures she'd just mentioned as well as others that we were aware of. All of us nodded or acknowledged that we understood.

"There are many ancient structures around your planet which we helped your ancient people build. They are positioned on what you would call ley lines, which are Earth's natural power lines. Or they are aligned with the stars, and our home planet Anunaki," she explained. "Some of the structures are buried, due to time and natural events. We are able to resurrect them and connect all the structures. Together, when they're reconnected, they will again be able to help protect your planet," she added.

Christik looked to the Sphere and the waiting angels.

"Viziers send out teams of angels to locate and repair all monoliths, please. Also, prepare the star passages in case we need help from the elders," she requested. "I will activate the main Star passage myself."

The Viziers acknowledged her requests with dips of their heads.

"What are star passages?" I asked, more than curious.

The others all looked expectantly at Christik, clearly just as intrigued. Christik smiled warmly at our interest.

"Star passages are planetary gateways. We used them in the past to visit your planet and your ancient civilizations without having to bring our ships," she explained. "Once we activate them, we can summon our Elders if we need to. We can also use them to escape Earth in the event of a defeat," she added.

I didn't know about everyone else, but I was feeling truly overwhelmed by all the new information. I had no idea our planet held so many secrets, and to be honest; I was blown away.

Christik faced the waiting Viziers.

"We will speak again very soon; farewell Viziers," she said calmly.

Christik dipped her head to the angels in the sphere showing her respect.

Harrik closed his hand, making the sphere disappear and sat back down.

Christik looked at everyone in the room.

"Let us begin" ......

CHAPTER 14

As our meeting came to a close, everyone began to slowly leave the room. Everyone seemed to be discussing all the new information and what we were going to do next. Humans and angels alike wore concern and worry on their faces. As James and I were about to leave with our kids, Christik approached with Harrik and Hulaz following behind her.

"Would you mind coming with us to activate the main star passage? I would like you to see it," she asked.

My eyes widened with excitement, and when I looked at James, he appeared to have the same expression.

"We'd love to," I replied, maybe a little too keenly. "Can the kids come too?"

As always, Christik's demeanor was warm when she answered.

"Of course, they may. We will take a small

craft to Peru," she stated.

Abigail was nearly jumping up and down with excitement with her face full of glee.

"We're going to Peru?" she asked, almost shrieking.

"It seems so little one," Hulaz told her with a smile.

While we made our way to the smaller craft in the lower deck of the ship, Christik explained more about the ancient monoliths and star passages. We were all totally fascinated.

"Your early ancestors were very open to communication and were eager to learn," she explained. "We taught them some of our architectural and healing techniques, as well as astrology, so they could grasp where in the solar system we came from. Your ancient civilizations did not have words for us, so they used the words that they knew, such as angels and gods to describe us."

Everything she was telling us made sense. I remembered learning a little in school about the ancient civilizations, and I was always fascinated with the ancient Egyptians.

"Your race has no idea just how many monoliths there are on your planet. So many of them are buried beneath the surface. Many were broken by later civilizations as memories of us were lost," Christik added. "I believe there has been a lot of confusion as to how your ancient civilizations were able to build such large and precise structures. Now you know."

Before too long, we arrived at the smaller craft. It was the same as those I'd seen repairing the destroyed water filtration craft out at sea. Inside, it was the same as the inside of the main craft.

The craft walls were smooth and pearlescent, and there was plenty of room for all of us inside. We all sat in smooth bucket-like seats which seemed to suck you gently in, making you feel secure.

We watched as Hulaz glided to the front of the craft, but rather than sitting in a captain's chair or pilot's seat, she stood facing the front glass shield.

Hulaz began to give off a strong glow, and she began to raise her arms out to her sides. It was as if her power was reaching to the craft, and the craft was starting to reach out to her.

Just like the earth healing crafts had the vines appearing beneath them, this craft had silvery, white vines growing out from the craft walls.

When the vines reached Hulaz's fingertips, they wrapped around her finger, hands, and arms. A bright shimmering light flashed as Hulaz and the craft became one.

I turned to look at James and our kids who had also been watching. James looked as if he was catching flies with his mouth agape. The kids were all looking seriously impressed and in absolute awe. When Harrison made eye contact with me, he mouthed the word '*Wow,*' making me smile.

When the craft began to rise, it made me jump even though it was a smooth ascent. Before long, we were cruising gently and slowly towards a large opening that had appeared on the side of the main craft.

Once we were outside, the ship flashed forward at great speed. I was half expecting to feel my body being pushed back into the seat I was in, just like human astronauts and fighter pilots were, but it didn't happen.

With no way of telling time, I had no idea how long we had been traveling for, but in less than an hour approximately, we had reached our destination. The craft gently landed on the ground, and the vines detached from Hulaz's body.

Unwinding from her hands and arms, they melted back into the craft walls. When she stopped glowing, she turned around and used her power to open a door at the back of the craft.

Feeling our seats release their holds, we

stepped out into the middle of nowhere; the earth beneath our feet was dust and stones.

"Ouch!" I gasped, as I felt the heat of the ground on the soles of my feet.

Suddenly, we were all leaping back into the craft and breathing a sigh of relief. For a moment, Christik appeared confused, and then realization showed on her face.

"I am sorry everyone; we do not feel heat and cold like you do," she said, raising a palm towards us.

With a bright light from her hand, we were all instantly wearing shoes that were as comfortable as my favorite pair of sketchers. One by one, we stepped out of the craft again, only this time we were comfortable enough in the heat to be able to look around.

As far as my eyes could see, there was nothing but dry dirt and rocks. Some rocks were standing in odd-looking circles, and some were partly buried in the dusty earth. I couldn't see any signs of civilization anywhere. There were, however, huge collections of stones that looked man-made.

Christik started to glide forward towards some pink stone monoliths, and we all followed behind. Harrik and Hulaz moved towards the smaller stones that were scattered around—while we followed

Christik.

We kept our eyes on the two angels, curious as to what they were going to do while being careful not to bump into each other. Harrik stopped next to one large cluster of stones, and Hulaz stopped at another further on.

Both angels started to glow as they raised their arms slowly up at their sides. I could feel a vibration in my feet as the stones began to move before our eyes. The stones which were buried rose from the earth, moving into place alongside the others effortlessly, forming perfect circles. Some stones moved above the top of the arid soil until they were in place, and then they sunk in the earth as if the ground were as soft as butter.

"We are here; if you could stand back a little please," Christik said.

She stopped in front of a massive slab of pink stone, which looked as if it had been carved into the side of a natural rock face.

There was a deep groove down either side of what seemed to be a stone door. At the bottom was an alcove, large enough for a human to stand inside easily.

As we watched with intrigue, Christik raised her arms out and began to glow brightly. I could feel not only a vibration in my feet this time but also a strong breeze forming, blowing through my hair and thin gown.

The ground started to vibrate more strongly, and tiny glittering specks began to rise up from the ground. In a matter of minutes, we were all surrounded by a swirling and glittering wind; it was like something out of a fairy tale.

“This is so magical,” Holly shouted above the noise of the wind.

I felt a hand on my arm, and I turned to see Anthony next to me.

“What do you think she’s doing, Mom?” he asked above the din.

I was just as confused as he was and shrugged my shoulders.

“I have no idea son,” I replied loudly, but I wasn’t sure if he’d heard me.

When I looked back to Christik, she was turning her palms up towards the sky, and the glittering wind was beginning to swirl above them. She then turned her hands again, so they were facing the stone door, deflecting the glittering flecks until they started to collect in the deep grooves on the sides of the door.

As more and more flecks collected, I realized that it was gold coming up from the ground. The gold glowed as it became hotter until it was molten in the grooves.

By the time the deep grooves were full of molten gold, Harrik and Hulaz were back with us and were now standing a small distance away from Christik. Both had their glowing palms out as if waiting for something.

Christik turned her palms towards them, redirecting the gold to both waiting angels. While the gold being was transferred to the two angels, I noticed that hieroglyphs were appearing on the gold inside the grooves.

Soon Hulaz and Harrik had a massive amount of gold swirling between their hands, and in the next second, they were gone. The wind gradually died down, and Christik was no longer glowing.

We all looked windswept apart from Christik who looked immaculate as always. The girls and I had hair all over the place as if we'd been dragged through a bush.

"Where have they gone?" I asked while sweeping my hair out of my face and trying to get it under control again.

Holly and Abigail were trying to do the same thing.

"They have gone to activate the other six-star passages that are here on Earth. We will know when they are all active. This one is called, Amaru Muru or Gate of the gods, as the Inca people called it. It is one of many here and around your world," Christik told us. "There is a sacred lake between all the star passage gateways, and beneath the water is an ancient city called Titicaca, which we helped the Inca tribes build. The Inca tribes tried to protect our gateways for a very long time," she added.

"Christik look," Abigail said, pointing to the gateway.

We turned to look at what she was pointing at, and the stone door was beginning to glow. Small glowing tendrils of gold were forming and moving downwards towards the alcove at the bottom. I hadn't noticed before, but there seemed to be a circular indentation in the gateway alcove too.

The gold started to collect and swirl in the circle, and abruptly the pink stone door vanished. What replaced the stone was some kind of energy barrier, similar to the barriers the angels used at the holding room on the main craft.

When I looked behind me to see if James and the kids were watching what I was seeing, I realized that the stone circles Harrick and Hulaz created were all glowing with energy too.

I was just about to speak when Harrik and Hulaz suddenly reappeared.

"It is done Christik, and the Viziers are activating the last one now," Harrik told her with a dip of his head. Christik dipped her head in response, and all three of the angels looked up to the sky.

I didn't know what they were looking for, but automatically we all followed suit, staring up into the clouds. I looked for anything unusual, but it all looked normal to me.

A couple of minutes later, I could feel an energy in the air; the hairs on my arms prickled and stood to attention on my skin. James and the kids ran their hands down their arms too, mirroring my own actions.

A thrum behind—us made us all look around to the gateway. Lightning shot out from the top of the now open star passage, it spread up and outwards in huge arcs.

We all quickly turned to face where it was heading, and in the distance, we could see more lightning coming to meet it.

In absolute wonderment, we all watched the lightning connect and spread out across the sky. In between the streaks of energy, a golden barrier was forming, encasing our planet.

Who'd have thought or believed that the earth had this technology and defense system the whole time, without us even knowing? It was blowing my mind.

"It is done; we may return to the main craft,"

Christik said as she began to glide back towards the smaller craft.

I think we were all still quite stunned by what we'd just witnessed, as we embarked on the small craft. We took our seats again, and Hulaz began to fly us back.

"I still can't believe this was all here for that purpose, and we didn't have a clue," James said as he reached out a hand to mine.

When I turned to face him, he wore the same astonished look that the kids wore.

Harrik smiled at James' statement.

"The evidence has been here for thousands of your earth years. Some of your people discovered what we had built with your ancestors, but, unfortunately, the majority of your people would not believe their theories," he told us.

"It was a great loss to us, discovering that so much knowledge was lost over time," Christik said softly. "We taught your ancient civilizations methods of healing the body, how to use green energies, and agricultural techniques. All of which were natural, and in harmony with your planet," she added.

"I don't understand why all that knowledge was lost," I told them, feeling very confused and honestly, frustrated as hell.

"You are not the only race who has erased

natural knowledge for power and greed," Christik said without judgement. "Many races we have encountered have ignored what is natural and free to procure wealth and power from others. Unfortunately, they didn't realize how damaging it was to their planets until it was too late either."

Christik and Harrik were definitely giving us all food for thought.

"Are you using all this knowledge to heal our planet?" James asked them.

"Yes, we can show you our natural agricultural methods when we return to our main craft, if you would like, James," Harrik replied enthusiastically.

All of us showed an interest in learning how they were healing the Earth. The angels seemed to appreciate our eagerness to learn from them.

The rest of the journey back to the main craft was full of light conversations and banter between James and the kids. It filled my heart with happiness watching my family enjoy each other's company.

It was very different from seven years ago when the kids were so engrossed with their phones, gadgets, and social media. Back then, we had to prise them away from their gadgets and ask them to put their phones away to appreciate what was around them. Now our kids were engaged in life and eager to learn as well as willing to try new things.

As sad as it was that our planet had begun to die, the silver-lining was the new appreciation our younger generation now had for each other and their planet. I felt even more hopeful that our race wouldn't make the same mistakes again.

When we arrived at the main craft, the angels arranged to collect us from our rooms after we'd eaten and freshened up. It was bliss having a shower after our trip. As I washed my body in the cleansing water, I felt as if I was washing away half of Peru.

The dry, dusty soil had apparently got into every orifice, especially after Christik had generated the wind.

After we'd all freshened up and sat down for the meal the angels had provided for us, the kids and James were full of conversation, excitedly discussing what we'd learned earlier and how they'd all like to use the ancient techniques.

Before long, Harrik and Hulaz arrived, and on our way to the agricultural section of the craft, the kids asked a lot more questions. As I watched the kids interacting with the two angels, I was again aware of a strong connection between Harrik and Hulaz.

Harrik appeared mesmerized by Hulaz when she spoke to the kids, and she was in awe of him when he spoke.

Walking down the long main corridor, we soon arrived at the section where all the large rooms were for the plants. We'd walked past them a number of times before, but this was going to be our first time actually going inside.

Hulaz approached one of the large archways; the big, glass doors were wet on the inside with water droplets slowly running down. We were all excited to enter. She used her power to open the doors, and as the doors opened, I felt a small gust of moist air wash over me.

Hulaz led the way, and as we walked into the room, the scene before me took my breath away. The room was massive and extremely long, filled with various plants as far as my eyes could see.

What surprised me the most was the large tanks of water that were there, which were filled with large fish leisurely swimming around. On top of the tanks were flourishing plants with their long roots swaying in the water amongst the fish.

"Wow, Zanika told me about this?" I said to Harrik, who was following closely behind us.

He smiled at my surprise and amazement.

"This is an agricultural technique which we

taught the Aztecs and Mayan civilizations. They used natural bodies of water, and man-made canals to grow their food. Unfortunately, we cannot do that until your planet has healed more."

"How does this system work?" James asked, completely in awe.

Out of the two of us, James had always been the gardener with the green thumbs. We'd had a beautiful garden, and it was all through James' hard work. As for me, I'd kill anything green. Not on purpose of course, but I was the only person I knew who could kill a cactus.

"It is a very simple method, with the plants and fish thriving together in harmony," Harrik told us. "We call it the Chinampas technique. The fish feed from the algae which grows on the roots and the plants feed off the waste from the fish."

"So, the fish and the plants nourish the other?" James asked, in total awe with his eyes nearly popping out of his head.

"That is exactly how it works," Hulaz added to the conversation.

She smiled at Harrik with so much love I just had to finally ask.

"Are you two married?" I questioned curiously, smiling at them both.

Both of the angels smiled back at me with

their eyes sparkling, as they then looked adoringly at each other.

"Yes, we are what you class as married," Hulaz said softly. "We call it pairing because we are all halves, and when we find our other half, the pair becomes a whole," she explained.

"That's beautiful," Holly said, letting out a sigh.

"You are definitely my other half, my lady," James said as he took my hand in his, lifting it to his lips and kissing the back of my hand.

"Get a room!" The kids all said in unison, making us all laugh including the angels.

"Come, we will show you around," Hulaz said proudly, once we'd all composed ourselves again.

The angels gave us a fabulous tour of the growing room, and it was much larger than we'd first thought. There were plants from all over the world in the room, some of which were very strange.

"Many plants are not native to our country. Are you going to plant them here too?" James asked.

"Some of them, yes James. We plant what will make your planet thrive, not just the plants that are native to your specific regions," Hulaz replied.

We carried on with the tour for another hour or so, all asking questions about their techniques and how we could learn them. By the time we got back to our rooms, we were completely worn out. We must have walked miles throughout the day, and I was personally feeling exhausted.

After eating the waiting meal, the angels had provided, and talking with the children about the strange but amazing day we'd all had, I showered and fell into bed. Within minutes, I was asleep with James cuddling me from behind.

The Marilians are here in their thousands, their blood-red eyes darting here and there, searching for their next victim to cut and turn into one of them.

I'm frozen in shock as I witness people laying on the ground, writhing in agony as they begin to turn.

Their bodies are jolting as the blood in their vein's changes; their skin is starting to turn a dark brown, and their eyes change to blood-red.

I turn to our kids behind us.

"RUN !!" I scream into their terrified faces.

I didn't know that I'd screamed out loud until James woke me, with his hands on my shoulders trying to shake me awake.

Pushing him away from me, I sat bolt upright in the bed trying to catch my breath. For a moment, I felt as if I couldn't breathe, my lungs struggling to take in any air. I felt a panic all through making me shake all over.

"Slow deep breaths, baby, slow and deep; it's okay; you're safe," James soothed.

When my breathing started to get under control, and my heart slowed to a more regular rhythm, James wrapped his arms around me. I clung to my husband as if my life depended on it.

"They are definitely coming, James; I saw them," I whispered. "I don't understand how I know—but they are coming for us James—in their thousands."

The look on James' face said it all!

CHAPTER 15

Two months had passed, and it was the big day. The first big meeting at the angels' holding structure, the residence of our fellow humans where we were going to find out who among the new community had what skills that we could use to help defend our planet.

It had been a very busy couple of months. The viziers had been busy building relationships with the humans in their care. Also, we had all been busy finding the families of the sleeping women in preparation of waking them up.

I should have been feeling thrilled and excited about seeing the holding structure, or the Cruiser as the kids called it for the first time. Instead, I was feeling as sick as a pig with morning sickness. '*Oh, deep joy!*' I thought.

I'd honestly forgotten how bad the morning sickness was with my other kids, but it was suddenly all coming back to me.

I didn't just get morning sickness; I got morning, noon, and night sickness.

There was nothing the angels could do about it either, because I was not ill, just pregnant. Although they were very kindly providing foods that didn't turn my stomach.

I supposed it was a small price to pay for having another beautiful daughter, especially when she was going to be so special and unique. Wiping my mouth, I decided to give my teeth another clean. My mouth suddenly felt as dry as Gandhi's old flip-flop.

"Are you finished hugging the toilet yet, Mel?" James called from the bedroom.

"Yeah almost, just cleaning myself up, yet again," I called back with a mouth full of foamy toothpaste and feeling exasperated.

I was excited about the day really, especially seeing the cruiser after what James and the kids had told me about it.

The kids all wanted to show me the large cabin they'd shared with their dad. Abigail was desperate to show me the natural pool they swam in with all the fish, birds, and exotic plants.

When I thought about all the help the kids had been, it made me feel so proud of them. As young as they were, they were well-respected by the angels and the humans in our group.

Feeling all refreshed again, I walked into our main room and saw James and the kids were all ready to go.

"Wow, you all look ready for some action today," I told them.

I was greeted by smiles all around, the kids all standing up from the comfy chairs and standing proud.

Holly was at the ready and was armed with her folder containing her paper and pencils. She seemed to have a gift for making very useful notes and action plans which had been a big benefit for all of us.

"Let's get this show on the road shall we!" James declared, taking me by the hand and grinning at the kids.

Leaving our room, we started to make our way down the main pearlescent corridor, which always seemed to impress me. The shimmering walls that looked like mother of pearl and the beautiful archways with their stunning hieroglyphs that led to rooms were impressive. I was starting to recognize some of the hieroglyphic images now and some of the shorter words such as plants and seeds.

We talked among ourselves as we walked, occasionally passing angels who were gliding gracefully past us. All of them giving us a nod of their head in respect. My admiration for the angels had certainly grown the more I got to know them.

There was a good reason why humans had revered the angels for centuries; it was because they seemed to be a race full of peace, love, and compassion.

"Are all our group going to the cruiser?" Holly asked, distracting me from my thoughts.

"No, I don't think so, honey," James replied, "Some of them are already busy with the defense projects."

Holly looked very thoughtful; she seemed to have taken quite a shine to Mimi and Tracey, especially Tracey. John and Tracey were going to be coming with us for the meeting, as well as Julia and Barrie. Derek and Rebecca were already at the holding structure.

It made sense to make all our group the human council for our zone, as we were already working closely together. Things were starting to really get going. The Viziers had their own groups of humans to work with and from what Christik had told us, they were getting along brilliantly.

Soon enough, we all arrived at the control

room which, as always, was a hive of activity. The angels were busy working at their curved shaped consoles, but they still all greeted us with smiles, waves, and dips of their heads.

We greeted them with nods and smiles as we walked through to the large meeting room and, as we approached, I could already see through the glass doors that everyone was there.

Seeing the angels and humans all mingling and talking together still put a huge smile on my face.

"Good morning everyone," I said with a happy heart as we entered.

We were welcomed with smiles and hugs from our new friends. Even the angels had started to hug us when they saw us now too. Taking our seats around the large table, we all started to eat the amazing feast before us. There were three large black stone trays full of fresh fruits and vegetables and like always, some I recognized and some I didn't.

I must admit, I did enjoy trying the new foods, and dragon fruit was my new favorite. The angels gave the impression that they enjoyed us all eating together every day, and it was a great time for us all to catch up on any news.

"I had a meeting with the Viziers earlier this morning," Christik said to us all. "I am pleased to tell you that our air regulator crafts are finally getting to a point where we can now see a major difference in your air quality," she added.

"I didn't realize you had air regulator crafts," I told her.

"We have crafts that clean your air and crafts that are repairing your ozone too," Christik said with a smile. "Your air quality was very bad, compared to what it was when you had dinosaurs on earth, and compared to when we were visiting during the early Egyptian times," she stated.

"Why such a difference?" Abigail asked, always so inquisitive.

"There is a big difference for many reasons, Abigail. Your race has used fossil fuels since early man discovered coal and oil," Christik explained. "As your planet's population grew and developed, so did your usage. A growing population also meant more natural habitats being destroyed, on land, and in your oceans. It is your trees and plants that create your oxygen," she added, giving Holly a warm smile.

"Wow, I didn't realize that we'd had such a negative effect on our planet," Abigail replied, her face showing her sadness.

"Don't worry darling," I told her as I reached for her hand, giving it a gentle squeeze of affection.

"We aren't going to make the same mistakes this time, especially now our friends the angels are showing us how to really use green energies," I added with a reassuring smile.

"I think we've all got a greater sense of appreciation for our planet and a new determination not to do anything to sabotage it again," Tracey said.

There were plenty of agreements from everyone and nods of heads. Tracey was so right. We all had a new dedication to the health of our planet, and all of us were adamant not to take anything for granted ever again.

As we continued eating and drinking, we all discussed how the other crafts were doing. Christik and Harrik told us that our wild lands were repairing nicely too, and there were some areas of land that were healed enough to start introducing small amounts of animals. This news was so exciting for all of us, especially James, as he was still learning to become a vet.

Within moments of us finishing our food, three angels entered the meeting room to clear away the table. After they'd finished, and we'd thanked them, Christik stood from her seat.

"Let us make our way to the holding structure," she said. "Please all take the hand of the nearest angel."

Soon we were all paired with an angel. I was holding Christik's hand, James held Zanika's, and everyone else had a partner to travel with. The men and my kids looked very relaxed and raring to go. On the other hand, I was not relaxed whatsoever.

"I'm actually nervous about doing this," I said to no one in particular.

"Me too!" Tracey replied.

As I looked at Tracey and Julia, they both looked as nervous as I was feeling inside.

"Don't worry, Mum," Harrison told me, giving me a reassuring smile. "You'll just get a really warm feeling and then when we arrive at the cruiser, you'll feel a little shivery, but it soon wears off," he assured me.

"Okay, I'm ready!" I declared, not feeling ready at all.

"Let's get it over with before I lose my nerve please," Julia added, giving me a nervous smile.

"Shall we?" Christik asked, giving the other angels a nod of her head.

Suddenly, I felt a warmth spread through me starting in my hand that Christik held, spreading up my arm and rapidly dispersing throughout my body. For a matter of seconds, all I could see was a bright, white light, and the heat in my body was getting hotter and hotter.

Then, abruptly the bright white light vanished, and we appeared at the entrance of the holding structure. Instantly, a coldness spread through my body as soon as Christik released my hand. As I stood there shivering, the others quickly arrived, appearing all around me. For a moment or two, my teeth actually chattered, and I wasn't the only one. When I looked around, nearly all of us humans were shivering.

James walked straight over to me just as the other men went to their women, wrapping each other in their arms to warm each other up. Even Anthony and Harrison were hugging their sisters to warm them while the angels waited patiently, smiling at the scene before them.

Being in James' strong arms warmed me up very well, and it didn't take long at all before my body felt like it was back to a more normal temperature. James kissed my neck softly and whispered in my ear, giving me goosebumps.

"Are you okay, baby?" he asked, concern written all over his handsome face.

He was even more protective over me since we'd found out that I was pregnant again. I didn't blame him for being overprotective; the oncoming threat of the Marilians had all the men behaving in the same way.

"I'm fine James honestly, I'm really okay," I assured him as I stroked the side of his face.

While everyone was collecting themselves, I took a moment to look around my new surroundings. We appeared to be very close to a beach; I could see the golden sandy beach a short distance away. The seawater was gently and a little too slowly lapping at the shoreline. From that distance, I could even see that the seawater still wasn't the right color, but it was definitely improving.

The water cleaning crafts, which still reminded me of white oil rigs, were dotted in the seawater, all working hard to clean the pollution from our oceans. As my eyes scanned the area, I could just about see the angels' main craft in the distance, and I was amazed at the size of it. The main craft was huge from what I could make out.

Most of the lower part was hidden by beautiful, now healthy trees. So, I assumed that the angels had the Earth healing crafts in the area, changing the dry, dead earth, and dead vegetation back to the healthy landscape I was now admiring.

"Wow what a difference!" I declared.

"You're so right," Tracey added, just as amazed as I was.

My mind went back to my memories of the trees and numerous shrubs around our house. They'd all died quickly, turning brown and dry due to the relentless heat and lack of water. I wondered what they looked like now and if we would ever live there again? All of the women were looking around as well, suitably impressed.

"Shall we enter?" Christik asked, indicating the entrance of the holding structure.

"Yes, let's go; I want to show my mom around," Abigail said excitedly, grinning from ear to ear.

The holding structure was a massive, white stone curved structure with curved balconies in rows along the sides and big circular windows. Not only was I impressed with its size but also how pleasant it looked.

I could see the occasional person on their balcony, either sitting and relaxing or standing and admiring the views.

We started to walk towards the entrance; all of the women were looking around taking everything in. All of us curious as it was our first time there.

The entrance was a large archway, just like the big archways on the main craft with hieroglyphs above, softly glowing against the dark frame. The doors were made of dark wood, so solid and heavy; they looked as if they could withstand anything.

As we approached, Christik raised her arm with her palm facing towards the door, and instantly her palm began to glow as she used her inner power to open the heavy, wooden doors with ease.

Approaching the now open entrance, we could hear the sounds of activity. People were busy moving around and talking. Children's laughter and squeals of play could be clearly heard, and it was music to our ears.

We walked into a stunning foyer that could have been in the middle of a tropical rainforest with beautiful flowers, shrubs, trees, and vines everywhere. All of the women including myself were in awe of the place. I don't think I was the only one that breathed out a '*WOW.*'

As Christik lead the way, my eyes were darting this way and that, trying to absorb the sights before us. All the plants and trees seemed to be growing up through patterned cracks in the floor, which were obviously made to be that way. The smell of all the flowers was truly amazing, and I definitely wasn't the only one to breathe in the floral scents that were drifting in the air.

James gently tugged my hand, breaking my serene moment. When I scowled at him for spoiling it for me, he just giggled and nodded towards where everyone was waiting. I let him lead me to our group, and I could feel my cheeks burning from embarrassment.

"Don't worry, Mel," Julia said with a grin.

"Barrie had to snap me out of gawking too."

I rolled my eyes making her laugh. We carried on walking, and as I looked around, I could see the shops that James and the kids had described. There was a gardening shop with more exotic flowers and plants, another shop with hand-made mats and rugs, and a gallery shop too. I wondered if Abigail's art pieces were in there.

The shops were obviously very popular with the community as many people were going in and out, either socializing or getting something.

I loved the fact that money wasn't used anymore. There wasn't a need or use for money anymore, removing all power, conflict, and greed. If there was something in one of the shops that somebody liked, and they wanted it for their cabin, then they could have it for free.

People got joy from others liking what they made or the service they offered. It was a whole new way of life.

The cruiser was a very busy place, and as we strolled through, many adults and kids passed us by with smiles and nodding their heads at us in respect.

I soon realized we were approaching a decorative seating area in the center of the main promenade. As we got closer, I saw that some of our friends were already there waiting for us.

Beccy was waving happily to us with her husband Derek by her side. He was engaged in conversation with another couple, smiling and obviously happy to see his friends. When we approached, all four of them gave us smiles and dipped their heads.

"Good morning everyone. I'd like you to meet Luiza and Shawn," Derek said, indicating the couple next to him.

Luiza was the same height as Beccy, with stunning golden hair and a mischievous beautiful face, while Shawn was tall like James and just as stocky.

"Luiza is a highly trained nurse, and Shawn's an engineer; both of them are sharpshooters," Derek added. "There ain't nothing Shawn doesn't know about guns, and he's got a massive collection back at his house," he stated.

"Well, that's very good to know," I told them, shaking Luiza and Shawn's hands. "It's a pleasure to meet you both, and it's awesome to have you on our team," I added.

"Maybe you can both give us all some weapons training," James suggested. "I think we're going to need all the help we can get," he chuckled.

Christik came over to us and dipped her head in greeting; as always, she was friendly and warm.

"Hello, I am Christik, the head of the angels;

it is a great pleasure to meet you both, Luiza and Shawn," she told them, "Is everyone ready for our meeting?" she asked as she looked to Derek.

"Ready and keen to get the show on the road, Christik," he replied, indicating for us to follow him.

As we followed Derek, Beccy, and the others, I was in awe of how huge the Cruiser was. There were so many shops, workshops, and classrooms. The place was buzzing with activities.

Above the shops, were what I assumed to be the cabins with smaller archway entrances, like the ones on the main craft. Flowered vines twined around the banister rails—in keeping with the rest of the natural design of the structure.

We walked for a few minutes passing men women and children of all ages. It was wonderful to see women from the main craft who'd been sleeping now back with their families, and they looked so happy.

Some of them were still carrying baby animals, as I could see their small baby bumps. Some didn't have baby bumps, obviously deciding to either help fight, or they just wanted to be left alone to be with their loved ones.

Just as I was thinking about all the happy

families, I saw what looked like a tropical oasis, and then I remembered what Abigail had told me. She'd said there was a natural pool for them all to swim in, and she was right about how beautiful it was.

Surrounded by various flowering trees, plants, and rocks was a stunning pool with different kinds of water lilies floating on top. Tropical birds were perched in the trees, and some were swimming with the children who were thoroughly enjoying themselves.

"Amazing isn't it, Mom?" Abigail said, taking my hand in hers. "Let me show you the fish," she added, her young face full of delight.

"Okay," I said in complete wonderment.

Abigail led me to the pool until we were stood at its edge; the kids made me smile with their carefree laughter and water antics. The birds didn't seem to mind them at all and carried on paddling around in the blue, green water.

When I looked down into the water, I could clearly see fish of different sizes, lazily swimming around the pool, and just like the birds, they didn't mind the children either.

"It's wonderful isn't it, Mom?" Abigail said with a beautiful smile on her sweet face.

"Yes, it really is wonderful," I replied, hoping that soon I'd get to swim in it with our kids.

"Mel, Abigail, we need to go," James called to us, beckoning us with his hand.

When I turned around, everyone was stood there patiently, waiting for us with smiles and knowing looks that said, "Yep, we could stand there all day too." I felt myself blushing again as I walked back to James with Abigail giggling next to me.

We carried on walking for another couple of minutes and approached a large meeting room on our left. It was very similar to the meeting room on the main craft with large glass doors; only this room was a lot bigger inside.

In the center of the room was a massive round table with at least fifty chairs all the way around, so everyone sitting down was able to see each other.

CHAPTER 16

I could see that most of the seats were already taken as we entered, and I couldn't help but think of King Arthur, and the knights of the roundtable. Butterflies started to flutter in my stomach as we entered our first defensive meeting.

"Welcome to you all," Christik said to them, as they all dipped their heads in welcome. "I am Christik, head of the angels here on Earth, and these are my angels Zanika, Harrik, Hulaz, Livik, Jakiz, Anglik, Toniz, and Nalik," she added, indicating the angels who were taking seats around the table. "I would also like you to meet our friends who are part of our team: Mel, James, Anthony, Holly, Harrison, Abigail, Julia, Barrie, John, Tracey, Derek, and Beccy. Some of who you may already know," she told them as we also took our seats.

The people around the table all seemed friendly, and some were apparently a little nervous. I noticed tapping fingers on the wooden table, and one lady was nervously twirling her hair around her finger.

As soon as Holly sat down, she placed her folder and pencils on the table and began to prepare to take her notes. None of our kids appeared nervous or uncomfortable, even though they were the only teens in the room.

"You know why we are having this meeting," Christik announced. "We believe the Marilians are on their way to conquer your planet. We angels will not allow them to succeed," she stated.

"Do you have the list of people who have usable skills?" she asked, her eyes scanning everyone around the table.

Her sapphire blue eyes stopped on a stunning lady whose dark, curly hair framed her beautiful complexion. She looked a few years younger than me, and she seemed shy as she raised a hand that held a piece of paper.

"Hello everyone, I'm Emily, and this is my husband Nick," she said softly, indicating to the dark-haired man sitting next to her. "I have the list of people and their skills. I'll go through the list and introduce them to you," she added as her pale cheeks began to turn a delicate pink.

"First I'd like to introduce Ann," she said,

indicating a young lady at the table. She had rich, dark skin and eyes that almost sparkled.

"Hi everyone," Ann greeted nervously.

"Ann is a special effects artist and a very talented body painter. She's very gifted and has won many body painting competitions," Emily explained. "Ann will be able to paint any building to disguise any ambushes we set. Plus, she'll be able to body paint the angels to disguise them, so we can hide them from the Marilians until we're ready to fight. As Christik has already mentioned, this will give us a great advantage because the Marilians will think that the angels have already left. This will hopefully give them a false sense of security, making them less defensive and hopefully sloppy."

There were smiles all around for Ann, who nodded to everyone as a mild blush appeared on her face. Her skills were going to come in very useful in deceiving the Marilians.

"Next on the list we have Scott," Emily said, indicating an older man.

He was sitting next to Jakiz, his frame broad and muscular with a complexion that showed he'd worked outside in the sun for many years.

"Hello all," he said, his face rugged and serious.

"Scott was a very well-known builder before

everything turned to shit," Emily stated with a smirk. "He used to build houses of all sizes as well as massive commercial buildings and schools. So, he's more than capable of building anything we need," she added.

James leaned forward in his seat, resting both of his arms on the table top.

"That's very good to know because something occurred to me last night," James said.

I could tell by the look on his face that he was mulling something over.

"If I were the Marilian ruler, and I wanted to conquer earth, take all the resources, and change the human race to Marilians, the first thing I'd do is find the humans. That way, I'd be able to change all the humans and have even more Marilians to take what we want quickly and efficiently," James explained. "So, if I were the Marilian ruler Drakron, I'd seek out the holding structures where the humans are located and attack them first," he added. "We need fake targets to draw them away from our people."

All of a sudden, the room went deathly quiet as everyone absorbed the weight of what James had just said. He was absolutely right, and we all knew it; it made perfect sense.

"I think we all agree with you James," Christik said softly. "We are very pleased that you are on our side," she added, with a warm smile. "So, Holly, I believe our first item on our action plan list is to gather human and angel volunteers to help Scott build fake holding structures. It would be quicker and easier to convert existing buildings I believe," she added. "Tracey, can you help us to locate suitable buildings for this purpose?" Christik asked. "Also, are you able to find buildings for us to store weapons and any locations suitable for ambushes?"

Tracey looked absolutely thrilled to be asked, and she looked at her husband John with a look that said, 'See I can be a badass and useful.' John rolled his eyes and chuckled, then he wrapped an arm around his playful wife.

"Yes, of course," Tracey replied, grinning like an idiot.

Christik seemed pleased that Tracey and Scott were both going to be working on something so important. As our Earth was dying, we'd already lost around eighty percent of the population, so we definitely couldn't afford any more human loss. Harrison held up his hand, probably by force of habit from school.

"I'd like to add something," he said, nervously. "I think we need to get Abigail and the other people who are good at painting to camouflage the holding structures so that they're hidden in the landscape," he explained. "The Marilians will be coming from above in their crafts, so we don't want to make it easy for them to find us, and Ann is already going to have her hands full. If we camouflage the real holding structures, they'll be automatically drawn to the fake ones."

"Agreed Harrison, and thank you for those very important points," Christik told him.

"I think we need to go to the nearest army bases too," Anthony added. "Not only can we get camouflage netting that would help save us a lot of time and energy, but we can also get some top-grade weapons and body armor. From what my dad has told us, we're going to need the body armor if we have to do hand to talon combat, and I don't fancy getting sliced open," he stated with eyes as wide as saucers.

As I looked around the table, all the adults were nodding in agreement, and all seemed extremely impressed with our son's contributions to the meeting. I felt so proud of my kids.

"Another good point Anthony," Christik said, just as impressed. "We angels are able to use our power to deflect an attack, but we want you to have some protection too."

Holly was busily writing everything down. She had a habit of poking out her tongue to the side of her mouth and watching her do that while concentrating made me smile. It reminded me of when she was really young coloring in her art books.

As I continued to scan the people around the table, I noticed Nalik's eyes were glued to Holly, and he was mesmerized.

I nudged James and tilted my head in Nalik's direction. James' eyes widened in surprise, and he was smirking when he looked back at me. '*Thank goodness he's not being the over-protective father,'* I thought to myself, just as the door to the meeting room opened.

Two angels entered with drinks and food on stone trays hovering between their hands.

"Let us take a break," Christik said to the ro-om.

No sooner had the angels placed the large stone trays of food down on the table than everyone began to tuck into the fruits, vegetables, and drinks. I think all the talk about the Marilians had notched up everyone's stress levels. So, the food and distraction were very much needed.

During our break, I tried to keep up with the conversations around the table. Derek and Beccy were catching up with Derek's friends Luiza and Shawn, and I think Beccy was trying to get to know them better.

The angels looked like they were enjoying

the conversations, and James was in deep conversation with Christik and Harrik. Tracey was busy talking with Holly, giving her details for buildings she already knew about, which were ideal for storing backup weapons. She also gave Holly locations that she thought would be good for some ambushes and traps.

I was keeping to myself because just the sight of the food on the table was making me turn green. '*Please don't let me throw up in front of everyone,*' I kept thinking to myself, hoping my sheer willpower could stop it.

My eyes were flicking between Holly and Nalik. I was extremely curious, as he really did seem besotted with her. I wished I could read his mind. '*What was he thinking?*' '*Was he just curious about her or was he attracted to her?*' My mind was deliberating both with questions.

Before long, the food and drinks were nearly all gone, and as if on cue, the angels who'd brought the food in came back in to clear away the trays. We all thanked them and watched as they gracefully glided away.

"Let us get back to business, shall we?" Christik declared.

There were nods from everyone and many "Thank you's" to the angels who were taking the trays away. As Holly looked up from her papers, her eyes connected with Nalik's.

Suddenly, Nalik began to glow brighter. '*Oh shit,*' I knew instantly what it meant.

Everyone around the table seemed to hold their breath, and Holly was transfixed, gazing into Nalik's peacock multi-colored eyes. It looked as if his bright shimmer was pulsing, almost like a rhythmic heartbeat.

"Oh No!" Christik exclaimed.

"Holy Shit," Tracey added, loudly.

Holly turned to Tracey with a stunned look on her face, her cheeks beginning to glow a deep pink from her blush. Tracey pursed her lips as if she was trying to keep her mouth shut.

When Holly glanced at James and me, my heart dropped for her. She looked so confused and embarrassed. James took my hand in his, giving it a soft squeeze of reassurance.

"Don't worry," I mouthed to Holly.

Nalik looked just as embarrassed as Holly, and I felt bad for him too.

"Right, let's get back to business, shall we?" Christik declared.

"Yes, let's get on," I added, giving Holly and Nalik a reassuring smile each.

James was very quiet, probably trying to

process what had just happened, exactly the same thing as I was doing. My mind was racing. '*How could this happen?*' And what the hell is going to happen now? were just some of the questions I was going over in my mind.

"Okay," Emily said, interrupting my thoughts. "Next on my list is actually Derek who was in the Special Reconnaissance Regiment. This is a special reconnaissance unit of the British Army, and I have to say that there's not much this man doesn't know about battle and weapons, etc. We also have quite a few ex-servicemen and women on the list who are all willing to help us," she added.

"I've already spoken with the other ex-service people, and we will work closely with the other volunteers to get what we need, such as the weapons, body armor, camouflage, netting and clothing for us," Derek informed us, "We'd like an area for weapons training too, Christik, if possible?" he said as he faced her.

"We can arrange that for you Derek; it will be ready in two days' time," Christik replied. "Emily, thank you for creating the list and speaking with everyone," Christik told her warmly.

Christik looked back to everyone around the table, her face showing subtle signs of stress and concern, but also a real determination. The other angels mirrored the same look. It wasn't surprising, considering they'd all witnessed what the Marilians were capable of first-hand.

"I believe we are making good progress so far; however, we have a long way to go before we are ready," she stated. "We have the ability on our main craft to detect incoming crafts from across your galaxy, so we are now monitoring that closely. We should have time to position ourselves in the correct places before the Marilians arrive," Christik added. "Derek and James, I would like you both to create our plan of action please, with the help of the servicemen and women," she told them, smiling kindly. "Holly is doing an amazing job of writing everything down," she said as she gave Holly her beautiful smile.

"We're going to need vehicles too," James said, "We can't just flit from one place to another like you angels, so we're going to need reliable vehicles for combat and speed. Maybe John and I can go with Derek and the others to find what we need because we'll have to check them out before bringing them back here," he added.

"That is a great suggestion, James," Harrik re-plied. "I will arrange for angels to flit you as you call it," he said with a smile on his face, "to the bases to retrieve the vehicles you need."

Christik looked very thoughtful for a moment, and no one said a word, all waiting for the next person or angel to speak.

"I will organize angels to help us in the air; however, our crafts do not have weapons, only the ability to freeze another craft in mid-air. We will need some of your ex-service people to fly your aircraft, so that they can shoot down the Marilian crafts as we freeze them," Christik explained. "Holly would you be willing, to work with the key members of our team to organize the sorties and training please?" she asked.

Holly still looked somewhat shell-shocked from her moment with Nalik. Her beautiful face was blushing once again now that all eyes were on her, especially Nalik's. She cleared her throat and looked into Christik's eyes.

"Yes, of course, I'll stay behind and start arranging everything," she replied with a bashful smile.

Christik seemed very pleased, her face showing a lot more optimism and confidence. She then turned her gaze to me.

"How are things progressing with the women on our main craft, Elita, sorry, Mel?" she asked, a slight glow appearing on her cheeks.

"It's going very well. Zanika and Harrik have

been working with us ladies on the team to wake them and explain everything to them," I told her. "I believe we've been able to wake around sixty percent so far. I'm thrilled to say that most of them still had their memories, which has made things a lot easier," I added.

"Most of the women who have birthed their baby animals have opted to help fight the Marilians," Zanika added to the conversation. "Once the battle is over, the majority would like to continue our efforts to repopulate the animal kingdom," she stated.

"That is wonderful news," Christik declared. "Let us meet here again in five days' time to check our progress. In the meantime, we have something for you all, to enable us all to communicate with each other."

Harrik rose from his seat and raised his arm with the palm of his hand facing the center of the table. We all watched in anticipation as his palm began to glow a shimmering white.

Suddenly, a white stone tray appeared on the table with what looked like necklaces and bracelets. They looked exactly the same as the markings on the male and female angels.

The necklaces were beautiful with sparkling diamonds spaced out along what appeared to be thin, dark-grey ribbons, and the bracelets were two thin, dark-grey ribbon bands with hieroglyphs in between.

Harrik's palm continued to glow, and just as we were all admiring the angel jewelry, they began to glow and rise from the tray. We were all fascinated watching the jewelry move gently floating through the air.

The necklaces glided towards each woman around the table, while the bracelets glided towards the men. Just as they landed on the table in front of us, Harrik lowered his hand.

"These are your communication devices; pl-ease adorn yourselves," he said.

I was intrigued because the angels' markings looked as if they were part of them, actually in their skin like tattoos. The others were just as intrigued as I was, picking up the communication devices in their hands and examining them first.

Beccy, who was sitting across from me, was the first to put hers on. We all stopped to see what would happen. She slipped the necklace over her head and let it slip into place around her neck. For a split second, there was a slight glow around her, and then it was as if her skin absorbed the necklace. It went from laying on her skin to being in her skin, and just like the angels, it now looked like a stunning tattoo.

"I didn't feel a thing!" Beccy exclaimed as

she ran her fingers along the line of the communication device.

"Yes, I can hear you clearly," She told Christik.

A little confused, we all looked at Christik who was smiling at Beccy.

"Angels can communicate mind to mind. Our communication devices enable us to talk to each other from any distance, enhancing our ability. They will now help you all to communicate with each other and us, by using your minds," she explained. "All you have to do is think of the person's name you wish to talk to, and they will hear you."

Happy with Beccy's reaction and Christik's explanation, we all began to put on the communication devices.

I placed the necklace around my neck, letting it slip down under my dress. When I looked down, I could see it glow momentarily as my skin instantly absorbed it. I ran my fingers over my new markings.

I glanced at James and watched him slip the bracelets over his hands, sliding them to his wrists. Again, they glowed for a second or two, and then they were absorbed.

The new markings looked kind of hot on my handsome husband. When I looked at him and saw that he was looking back at me, I couldn't help but give him a cheeky smile.

'*I can't wait to get you naked again, woman,*' I suddenly heard in my head. I looked around, instantly worried that the others had heard what he'd said. And as my cheeks began to glow bright red,

I scanned our friends and was very relieved to see them all chatting quietly to each other. I could hear James chuckling in my mind.

"You're an ass," I said, giggling at him as he gave me a cheeky wink.

"You dirty bad man!" Tracey abruptly said, clipping John around the head playfully.

John started laughing hard, making all of us giggle including my kids.

"Well I have to assume that the communication devices are working," Christik said, with a big smile on her face. "Now that we can all communicate; my angels will take any of you who aren't staying here back to the main craft. James and Mel, if you could stay behind with Holly, I would like to talk with you," she added.

The angels and our friends all rose from their seats, nodding their heads and saying goodbye as they left the room.

"I'm going to take Abigail and Harrison for a swim at the pool," Anthony said as he walked past Holly, gently giving her shoulder a squeeze.

Harrison and Abigail both gave her a supportive hug, obviously picking up on her nervousness.

Within a few minutes, it was just the four of us left, and I had a feeling I knew what Christik wanted to discuss.

CHAPTER 17

As we sat with Christik at the large meeting room table, I was feeling half intrigued and half worried. Holly looked like a small rabbit staring at a car's oncoming headlights.

"Thank you for staying behind," she said, giving Holly a warm smile. "We have a very unusual situation. We have been to and saved thousands of planets since I have been in charge, and I have never had an angel attracted to another race, until now," she explained. "As you saw Nalik glowed when he was looking at Holly. What Nalik was feeling in his heart caused that to happen. I believe you are his other half, and he is in love with you Holly. How do you feel about that?" she asked our daughter.

Poor Holly couldn't have blushed any harder if she'd tried. I just wanted to hug her at that point as I could see how uncomfortable she was, my darling girl.

"I do feel drawn to Nalik," Holly answered quietly and honestly.

She didn't lift her head but looked at Christik through her lashes.

"You haven't done anything wrong, Holly. Just because he is an angel does not mean that he is more important than you, or more sacred," Christik told her warmly.

Christik placed her hand on Holly's, and instantly there was a glow between their touching hands. Holly visibly relaxed with all her tension and anxiety melting away. She looked up into Christik's eyes more confidently this time with her head up and her shoulders back.

"I do have feelings for Nalik," she told Christik in a much stronger voice. "But I don't know if it's love, and I don't know if I am his other half," she added again, honestly.

"I see," Christik responded gently, "Would you like to get to know Nalik better and find out Holly?" she asked our daughter.

"Yes, I think I would," Holly replied, this time a little more nervously, her eyes darting from mine to James'.

Christik removed her hand from Holly's and looked at James and me. I wasn't sure about James, but I was feeling very apprehensive about the whole situation.

"Would this be okay with you both?" Christik asked.

James looked at me questioningly, and I was stuck for words for a few moments, quickly trying to gather my thoughts.

"Well I suppose on the bright side, he's not a hormone-driven teenager with only one thing on his mind," I said, thinking out loud.

"I guess I won't be needing the t-shirt I've been saving," James added, giggling.

Holly looked at her dad with total confusion, and Christik had the same comical look.

"It says on the front, I have a shovel and a gun, and I'm not afraid to use them," James explained, laughing at Holly's look of sheer horror.

"Dad!" Holly exclaimed, looking totally exasperated.

I couldn't help cracking up, and my laughter was infectious. Within seconds, we were all giggling around the table.

One of the angels from earlier walked in the room with juice and coffee on a tray, looking very bemused.

"Thank you Jennik," Christik told her as she placed the tray down on the table.

"So, I believe the best way for Holly and

Nalik to get to know each other, without Holly feeling uncomfortable, is for Nalik to help her coordinate with the team members," Christik stated. This way it is more formal, and Holly receives the help she will need."

"Yes, I think that's a great idea," I told her. "What do you think Holly? Would you like that?" I asked her gently.

Holly's face was again flushed with pink, but she still looked a lot more relaxed than before.

"Yes, I'd like that Mom," she replied. "You and Dad started as friends, so I think that would be best," she added.

"That is settled then," Christik said rising from her chair. "Your children are still swimming at the pool. I will see you all soon," she added, nodding at the three of us and gracefully leaving the large meeting room.

James, Holly, and I all rose from our seats. Holly still seemed somewhat overwhelmed with the whole situation.

Walking over to her, I wrapped her in my arms, giving her a motherly hug. As she rested her head on my shoulder, James came up to us and wrapped his arms around us both.

"Everything happens for a reason, Holly. Who knows what our future holds, what's going to happen, and who with," James told her.

"Thanks, Dad, Mom, I think I needed that," Holly replied as she lifted her head, giving us a beautiful smile.

"Come on; I want to go swimming with my family and the fish!" I declared, not wanting to wait any longer.

We left the meeting room, and I felt so much more lighthearted, especially now we had more of an idea as to how many people could help us defend Earth.

James took my hand, and we headed towards the natural pool where our other kids were. As we turned a corner, Nalik was stood there waiting and leaning against a vine-covered pillar. The moment he clapped eyes on Holly, he straightened himself, and his eyes and body literally lit up.

All three of us stopped in our tracks, absolutely surprised to see Nalik there. He dipped his head at James and me; then he moved forward, so he was right in front of our daughter.

"I hope you do not mind. I would like to swim with you and your family," he told her gently. "Would that be okay with you, Holly?" he asked, his voice quiet but masculine.

Holly turned to James and me, and she raised her eyebrows questioningly. I nodded my head, giving her the go-ahead.

Smiling sweetly, she looked back at Nalik who hadn't taken his eyes off her.

"Sure, that's okay with me," she told him, sharing her sweet smile with him.

Just for a second, his already glowing shimmer got brighter as he smiled back at her. Relief showed on his face.

"Shall we?" he asked, indicating the way.

We continued towards the pool. James and I were completely intrigued listening to Nalik, and Holly make small talk. He was genuinely interested in what Holly did and didn't like. What she liked to do in her spare time, and what she wanted to do after we battle the Marilians. Holly seemed confident, telling him about herself and appeared just as keen to find out more about him.

"What is your role among the angels Nalik?" Holly asked him.

Nalik gave her another of his affectionate smiles.

'*Good grief, he's totally smitten with her!*' I thought to myself '*Shit, Fuck, and Balls, this isn't going to end well.*' I couldn't help but worry about

Holly after everything we'd already been through. The last thing I wanted was her heart being broken if it didn't work out.

"I am a Sky angel," Nalik told her proudly. "I help to heal your ozone layer and remove the poisons from the air you breathe," he added.

Holly certainly looked impressed by the look on her face.

"I like being here on your Earth, Holly; it is the only planet I've visited where there are beautiful sunsets and sunrises," he told her. "I wake early to watch them, and when I have the opportunity, I sit by the ocean and watch the sunsets too."

My daughter's eyes were looking more and more dreamily at Nalik.

Luckily, we were arriving at the pool, and I could see Abigail and our boys in the water having fun. I could feel my heart soar with love as I watched the boys splashing each other, while Abigail was trying to swim like a mermaid.

"Are you ready to go in?" James asked, snapping me out of my reverie.

"Yes, I'm ready. Where do we get the swimwear?" I asked as I looked around the pool area, trying to spot a pile of swimsuits and towels.

"I've said it before baby, but I'll say it again,"

he said, giving me his cheeky grin. "These angels are like a well-oiled machine."

Taking me by the hand, he led me to some steps, leading down into the glistening water. I was so confused. What the heck was I supposed to wear after swimming when my dress got soaked?

Going with the flow, I started going down the steps, and just as the hem of my dress touched the water, it began to shrink. My gown was actually shrinking and reshaping to my body.

The bottom of it shrank up to my butt, and the middle of the hem slid between my thighs joining together, as the top began to cling to my breasts.

Within moments, I went from wearing a go-wn to wearing a swimsuit. I was amazed.

"See, well-oiled machine, baby!" James said, laughing at my expression as he led me further into the water.

The water felt amazing on my legs, and it was just cool enough to be refreshing. As our kids started to swim towards us, I was expecting the fish and birds to swim away, but instead, they followed the kids.

There was no fear from them, and I watched in fascination as some colorful fish swam behind Abigail, as if they were racing.

"Fantastic isn't it, Mom," Harrison said as he

reached James and me.

His trousers and tunic had shrunk just like my gown, clinging to all his muscles. '*Bloody hell, my son is a muscle man.*' I was blown away by how manly both my boys had become.

Both of them were now over six feet tall and good looking like their dad. No wonder there were so many eyes on them from the teenage girls in and around the pool.

I was instantly aware of just how many young ladies there were, and my boys both appeared completely oblivious to them.

"It's truly amazing," I told Harrison.

I could feel my heart swelling with love for my kids as I admired their happy faces. I suddenly wished that I hadn't got all my memories back.

The awful memories of all the animals dying and rotting, people and kids dying on the streets, and the horror on our children's faces. Those mental images were ingrained in my mind. However, if I hadn't have gotten my memories back, I wouldn't have had a stronger appreciation of my family and our planet.

The glistening water felt cool on my skin as I continued down the steps. I could see tiny, red fish swimming around my feet. Nalik passed me and gracefully dove into the water without even a splash, with Holly following behind.

Once I was fully submerged up to my neck, I swam toward James, Abigail, and the boys, enjoying the sheer happiness emanating from them.

Every now and then, I could smell the scents from the tropical flowers that surrounded the pool.

All of a sudden, I realized that James and Abigail had become animal magnets. It seemed that all the birds and fish in the pool were making a beeline for my husband and daughter, as they were both swimming towards me.

However, I was wrong.

When the birds and fish reached James and Abigail, they kept going, swimming past them and heading for me. I stopped swimming and began to tread water, as did Anthony, Harrison, Holly, and Nalik. They all watched, entranced at what they were witnessing.

"Dad, Abigail stop a minute!" Anthony called out.

James and Abigail stopped and started to tread water too, with confusion on their faces as they watched the birds and fish swim towards me.

I felt something brush past my waist and when I looked down, I couldn't believe what I was seeing.

Fish of all colors and sizes were swimming

around me, circling my body and moving gracefully around my legs, torso, arms, and even around my neck.

"Woah, what the heck," I said, breathlessly.

Every so often, I could feel one of the fish brush against my stomach, not an aggressive bump but almost affectionately. I felt something brush against my hair and ear, so I looked up quickly and turned my head to see what it was.

There, right next to my head, was a bird similar to a stork. It was big and quite impressive; its body was black and white while its beak was black and a vivid red.

While I looked at it in complete surprise, it gave a small squawk and then rubbed its beak against my head again affectionately. I couldn't help the giggle that escaped me. Abigail and the others all began to laugh with me.

"I don't understand what's going on," I declared, amused but very confused.

"They seem to have all taken quite a shine to you, baby," James said as he swam up next to me.

We were both in awe as all the various birds and fish surrounded me, circling around, and brushing against me in a very loving manner.

"I've never seen anything like this," James exclaimed.

"Neither have I," I told him, still giggling.

"They are drawn to you, because of your baby," Nalik said as he reached us with Holly.

"Why are they drawn to the baby Nalik?" Holly asked.

Nalik raised an arm with his palm facing towards me, using his other arm to keep himself afloat. His raised palm began to glow white. He closed his blue peacock eyes for a moment with concentration on his face.

"I believe there is a connection, between the baby and the creatures. I can feel it coming from your baby; the creatures can feel it too," Nalik explained. "I think the animals want to protect you Mel, and the baby," he added.

"Well, that's unexpected!" I stated, feeling a bit overwhelmed.

"Do you think that's going to be one of her gifts, Nalik?" Harrison asked, extremely impressed with the whole situation.

"I believe so, yes," Nalik replied, "she may be able to communicate with animals when she has been born. We will have to wait to find out," he answered.

It was absolutely wonderful, swimming with my family, the birds and fish. Wherever I swam, the creatures would follow, protectively swimming around me and brushing against me.

Trying to make the most of our special time together, I tried to ignore the growing crowd that was forming around the pool area. Adults and children were sitting on the rocks or coming into the pool. All eyes staring at the strange woman and her creature followers. James and the kids thought it was hilarious!

Abigail swam over to me after playing diving challenges with Harrison.

"I know you're enjoying your swim, and I am too, but can I show you our cabin now Mom?" Abigail asked.

"Yes, of course, darling," I told her, "Let's go and see it."

While we made our way to James and the kids' cabin, I mulled over just how strange the pool experience was. I hadn't felt any pull towards the birds and fish, but our baby obviously did. The explanation that Nalik had given us made a weird kind of sense.

When I'd tried to leave the pool, the birds and fish had followed me right up to the start of the steps. The fish had all gathered at the bottom while the birds attempted to follow me up the steps.

The whole situation must have looked so

comical. Nalik had to use his power to gently move them away while I stood in amazement as my swimsuit changed back into a dry gown once again.

Something I did notice while trying to leave the pool—were all the young ladies admiring our sons as they got out of the water; they seemed to have many admirers.

Within minutes, we were walking down a long walkway with cabin doors on one side of us and a banister rail on the other. The spaces between the doors varied depending on the size of the cabin. I could smell the tropical scents from the flowering vines that wound around the railing, and when I looked over the side of the railing, I was in awe of the holding structure's beauty.

Just like the main craft, everything was so natural, and the trees and plants blended seamlessly with the cruiser. I could even see colorful hummingbirds feeding from the tall, flowering trees.

"Here we are," James said as he opened one of the larger cabin doors.

"After you my ladies," he said, gesturing for Abigail, Holly, and I to enter.

"Why thank you, kind sir," I replied as I followed the girls into the cabin, with the boys and Nalik following behind.

A “Wow” escaped me as I scanned the large living area. The main family area was spacious and bright, the walls and furniture were a light sandy color.

James and the kids had made it homely with colorful material draping the chairs and hanging from the large glass doors that faced outside. There were colorful works of art on the walls: paintings and pencil drawings of animals, flowers, and angels that were stunning.

“Did you do all these?” I asked Abigail, with pride starting to fill my heart.

“Yes, I did,” She replied gleefully.

James walked up to her, putting an arm around her shoulders with his face full of pride also.

“Totally amazing isn’t she!” he declared, looking down at her and giving her a huge grin.

“Yes, you certainly are Abigail, these are amazing. No wonder people here are taking your work for their cabins,” I told her sincerely.

Abigail was brimming with pride as she showed me around their current home. The cabin was stunning, and I was in awe of the natural beauty which complemented the accessories James and the kids had made.

When we entered the main family area again, I walked to the large glass doors and opened them, so I could look outside. Standing on the balcony, I surveyed the scenery before me, and as far as I could see, there were beautiful trees and wild fields.

Any buildings in the distance were surrounded by trees and shrubs and various climbing plants growing up the sides.

Nature was reclaiming the land; now the Earth was healing, and it was all because of the angels.

As I stood there admiring what the angels had done, I felt my husband's strong muscular arms slide around my waist. James pulled me into his body, nuzzling his face into my neck.

"It's really quite amazing what the angels have achieved already, isn't it?" he said, kissing my ear softly.

I could feel a pleasant shiver go down my spine, and goosebumps began appearing on my skin. Even after all those years, James still had that effect on me.

"Yes, it's amazing all right," I replied. "I can't believe how green and alive everything looks."

"It's not all like this, Mel, I'm afraid," he added, "When us guys headed to the main craft, we passed through areas that the angels haven't got to yet; it was heartbreaking to see. It won't be long before our planet is fully healed, and then we can concentrate on healing each other. After we fight the Marilians, of course."

"I'm terrified for the kids, James," I told him as tears welled in my eyes. "They've been through more than any kids should have to go through already, and now they're getting ready to fight an alien race who are freaking terrifying. How can we protect them, James?

"We'll protect them the best we can, baby; that's all we can do," he soothed, hugging me tighter. "There's so few of us left; we haven't got a choice whether we let them fight or not, Mel. We're not just fighting for each other; we're fighting for the whole world, baby."

"I know," I replied, trying to control the despair I was feeling.

"We'd better get back to the main craft," James said. "You've got to wake up some more women, and I've got to meet with John about the vehicles, etc., plus the boys need to start the ball rolling with Scott on the holding craft projects."

Taking my hand, James led me back to the living room of the cabin where the kids and Nalik were waiting and talking.

"Nalik, could you please take us all back to the main craft?" he asked.

Nalik stood immediately and dipped his head

to James and me.

"Yes, of course, I can only do one at a time," he told us politely.

Nalik took Holly's hand in his and disappeared. I wasn't surprised he took her first. His eyes hadn't left her since the big meeting earlier.

Within moments, he was back for the rest of us and ten minutes later, we were all back in our room on the main craft. I had to assume that Nalik had told someone we were coming back because there in the family area was food and drink for everyone.

"Thank you Nalik," I told him warmly.

My stomach was finally feeling back to normal, and I was so hungry. Truth be told, I was now craving bacon very badly!

"You are very welcome, Mel, I could sense that you were not feeling so sick now," he answered, indicating towards the waiting food.

"This one's a keeper Holly," I said with a giggle and giving her a wink.

"Mom!" Holly said as her young cheeks started to glow a pretty pink.

'Sorry' I mouthed as we all began to take seats around the low table. Nalik was actually smirking, enjoying the banter, and as I watched Nalik interact with us all, I couldn't help but think that having our daughter possibly date an angel wouldn't be such a bad thing.

After all, didn't all parents want their daughter to settle down with a proverbial angel or a saint?

CHAPTER 18

We finished our refreshments with lighthearted conversation about the cruiser. The children asked me what I thought of it and what I liked most. I told them how impressed I was and how amazing the pool was with all the plants, birds, and fish. Then the conversation moved to the event in the pool with the creatures.

"I wonder if our sister is going to be able to really talk with animals," Abigail said, clearly thoughtful.

"Wouldn't that be the coolest thing ever!" Harrison declared. "Especially when you become a vet, Dad; she'll be able to ask a sick animal what's wrong and then tell you," he added, obviously impressed with himself that he'd thought of it. James got up from the table with a big smile on his handsome face.

"Absolutely son," he told Harrison, ruffling

his hair. “Okay, back to business family; you all know what we have to do. So, we’ll see you back here later to eat and catch up. Please keep in contact using the communication devices,” James told us all.

We all left our rooms going in different directions. Nalik followed Holly of course, and the boys went off together to meet with Scott.

Abigail set off to meet with Ann and the other artists while I made my way to the sleeping room to meet with Zanika and Harrik.

The sleeping room was as peaceful as always when I entered; the monitors were humming in a soothing rhythm, and all the women were lying peacefully in their beds. I could see Zanika down the end of one row, scanning one of the pregnant women with her hands.

As I made my way down to her, I began to look at the women’s left hands to see what they were pregnant with. Some of the silvery marks were clear to see, and others weren’t, depending on the women’s skin tone.

It always fascinated me to see all the various animal marks; a donkey, badger and a leopard were only a few different animal markings I saw as I walked past.

There were always a few animals that I

wouldn't recognize, and these were usually animals from places such as Madagascar or the depths of the Amazon rainforest.

"Hi Zanika," I said, when I reached the angel, "I see you are already busy."

"Hello, Mel," she replied, "Yes, Harrik and I have made good progress today. We have eight more women, who we can wake today. We have already checked them, and they are ready to birth," she added.

"That's wonderful, Zanika," I responded, and then a thought occurred to me. "Zanika, because we have so much to do preparing for the Marilian arrival, I think it may be wise to talk and debrief the women in groups. Not only would it speed up the process, but I think it would help the woman if they had each other's support, as the girls and I had," I explained. "What do you think?"

Zanika took a moment to ponder my suggestion and then she smiled. "I think that is a great idea, Mel," she said. "Come, Harrik has the first two women in the birthing room and is waiting for us."

She turned away and began to gracefully glide towards the exit archway, so I followed after her.

Before long, we were in the long, pearlescent corridor and on our way to the birthing room.

"We have had two women come back today as they want to continue, to help us repopulate your animal kingdom, Mel," Zanika said, seemingly impressed.

"Wow, that's fantastic news Zanika," I replied, feeling impressed as well. "That's quite a few women who want to continue."

Zanika smiled and appeared very happy.

"Yes, it will mean we can carry on with our task while everyone else is preparing for the battle," she continued. "We have ceased releasing the animals who were ready. We do not want them hurt during the battle. The creatures who have already been released will hopefully hide when the Marilians arrive."

When we arrived at the birthing room, Harrik was just entering through the other archway, and a shimmering glass capsule was hovering between his hands.

Zanika and I both dipped our heads in greeting, and Harrik reciprocated as he walked to one of the occupied beds, leaving the capsule floating at the end by the woman's feet.

"I will fetch the other capsule," he said, gliding back through the archway he'd entered.

While he went to get it, I walked over to the

massive glistening wall on the other side of the room, always amazed at the baby animals who were stored there.

Every time I looked, I always noticed diff-erent animals, all asleep in their capsules and looking so peaceful.

My eyes landed on a baby dolphin. It was dark beige with splashes of a blueish-grey on its face, back, tail and fins. It looked so cute.

"Are we ready?" Zanika asked as Harrik glid-ed back into the room with another capsule.

"Yes, I believe we are," he replied, placing the capsule at the end of the second bed where it hovered in place just like the other.

I walked over to the bed and reached for the woman's left hand while the angels went to get ready.

The woman was in her early fifties with dark blonde hair; a stunning English rose face and a slim figure. There on her hand was the silvery marking of a sea otter.

The woman looked very peaceful in her slumbering state and not even a flutter of her eyes could be seen. Only the gentle rise and fall of her chest.

The angels returned gloved and veiled. Zanika moved to the right side of the bed and began to use her power to roll the silvery sheet down that was covering the woman's slim body and pregnant belly. Next, she rolled up the gown that the woman was wearing until it rested just underneath her breasts.

Harrik came and stood next to me, and I watched as both angels hovered their hands over the woman's stomach. Instantly, their hands and her pregnancy bump started to glow a bright white.

A moment later I stared in awe as the amniotic sac began to appear with the sea otter inside—passing through her skin as if her skin was a magical barrier.

Its fur was sleek and the darkest brown with a lighter brown under its face. Tiny eyes were visible along with its ears which were flush to its head. The sea otter's tail was tucked between its hind legs and was curling against its body.

Once it rose fully from the sleeping woman's form, the angels moved over to the waiting capsule with the shimmering fluid inside.

The bright white light glowed brighter as the sea otter, floating in its amniotic sac, passed through into the capsule. There was one more pulse of light as the placenta and umbilical cord were drawn to the organic device inside.

While Harrik took the capsule for storage in

the glass wall, I took the chance to look again at the woman's hand I was still holding, while Zanika replaced her sheet and gown, covering her body.

The silvery mark was almost gone, and I watched as the last of the otter's tail vanished. Zanika moved towards the machine, pressing the buttons so the woman would be able to wake.

"I'll greet this lady while you and Harrik birth the other woman," I told her, giving her a warm smile.

Zanika smiled back, dipped her head, and glided over to the next veiled cubicle. As Harrik returned with a tray between his hands of fruits and juice, letting it hover beside the bed. It was only a matter of minutes before the woman's hand twitched in mine. Suddenly, she sat bolt upright, pushing my hands down onto the bed.

She sat with her eyes open wide, and when I tried to move my stuck hands away, she looked right at me with our level eyes connecting.

"Hi, I'm Mel," I said quietly, "Don't worry, you are safe."

"Where am I?" she asked with a lovely English accent, her eyes blinking rapidly as she tried to focus.

"You're in a kind of hospital unit. What's your name?" I asked gently.

"I'm Joanne," she replied shakily, "Has the world ended? Am I dead?"

I understood her confusion; she obviously remembered our planet dying, but I didn't want to tell her too much until the other woman was awake.

I quickly grabbed the tray of fruits and juice, placing it on her lap.

"You aren't dead Joanne; in fact, you're now in perfect health. Please eat and drink something; it will give you time to focus," I told her warmly.

I looked through the sheer veil beside us to check on the other woman. The angels were just placing a curled-up pangolin into the waiting capsule. I knew it wouldn't be long before the other woman was awake too, so I turned back to Joanne who was drinking some juice.

"Joanne, you obviously remember that our planet was dying, so what was the last thing you actually remember?" I asked.

She looked up, trying to concentrate, and that's when she noticed the glistening wall of encapsulated animals on the other side of the room.

"What the holy hell is that!" she exclaimed, her eyes nearly popping out of her head.

'*Shit,*' I thought, closing my eyes for a second and trying to brace myself for any panic that was about to erupt. Opening my eyes, I placed my hand her upper arm.

"Joanne, remember what I said; you are safe, so please take deep breaths, and I will tell you everything," I assured her.

I casually touched the communication device around my neck, '*Zanika, please move the veils, so the glass wall is out of sight,*' I said in my mind.

'*Of course, Mel,*' Zanika's reply entered my mind, '*Harrik and I will take this capsule to the wall. Call for us when you are ready. Mel, this woman will wake any time now,*' she added.

Joanne looked at me with concentration on her lovely face. Her eyebrows furrowing and her eyes darting from me to the veil as it closed silently behind us.

"The last thing I remember is being stuck in a hotel with my husband and my two toddlers," she said, as tears welled up in her eyes. "Where are my husband and children? Are they safe too?" she asked earnestly.

"I will find out for you, Joanne, as soon as I can, just bear with me for a moment, okay," I told her as I turned around to the other woman.

Sliding back the dividing sheer veil, I could see that the other woman was beginning to wake. Joanne watched me as I moved over to the waking lady who was now trying to focus her eyes, her head turning from side to side.

I placed my hand on her startling her which wasn't my intention. The look of fear in her eyes wrenched my heart.

"It's okay, you're safe," I told her as gently as I could. "What's your name?"

Tears were running down her cheeks when she turned to look at me.

"April, my name is April. Where's my girlfriend? Where is she?" She asked desperately.

"I don't know where she is yet April, but I will find out for you, okay," I assured her. "My name is, Mel, and this is Joanne," I said, indicating to the woman behind me. "What do you remember, April?"

The tears were still flowing down her cheeks, and her body started to shake.

"Ashley was hurt; our neighbor stabbed her when we tried to stop him from taking our water," she said quietly. "I remember holding her in my arms while the bastard ran off with some of our bottles. She still had the knife stuck in her chest. I can't remember anything else," she sobbed.

I wrapped my arms around her, bringing her close to my body while trying to comfort her. She sobbed and sobbed, her small frame shaking against me. I held her until her crying eased, and Joanne waited patiently behind us.

Releasing April as her sobs eased and letting her lay back on the bed, I moved behind her and lifted the top of the bed to let her sit up.

"I know you are both confused and scared," I told them. "I was the same when I woke up too. I have a lot to tell you, but there are six more women I have to wake, and I'd like to tell you all together. Is that okay with you both?" I asked.

"Yes, that's okay with me," Joanne stated. "Is that okay with you April?" she asked the still trembling younger woman.

April nodded at Joanne with tears still trickling down her puffy cheeks.

"Okay, there's two things I need to tell you both now, before we go any further," I told them. "While the Earth was dying, an alien race came and saved all of us survivors. They are what we know to be angels."

Both of them suddenly had eyes wide with disbelief, looking at me as if I was the town's, crazy lady.

"I know it sounds absurd, but it's true," I added. "They arrived to save us, our planet and also our animals. However, to save our animal kingdom, they needed our help." I explained.

Both women appeared to be fairly calm and were taking it all in, so I continued.

"I recently gave birth to a tiny tiger cub, and the angels magically removed it. I felt nothing and was not hurt in any way," I stated.

Joanne was very quick to process this new information.

"Does that mean that we have given birth to animals too?" she asked.

"Yes, you both did, and as you can see, you are both in perfect physical condition. The angels aren't here to harm us, only to heal our planet and everything on it," I assured them. "Would you like to meet two of the angels?" I asked.

They both nodded in stunned silence. Touching the com device just above my breasts, I spoke aloud, so the two women could hear me too. "Zanika, Harrik, you can come back in now with the next women," I said.

Within moments, the two angels arrived, both gliding gracefully with two more sleeping women behind them in their beds. The women and the beds were softly glowing white as they followed behind. Using their power, the angels guided the women's beds into the two nearest empty cubicles while April and Joanne watched in silent awe.

The angels glided over towards us, and when the veils moved away from the ends of the beds, both angels dipped their heads in respect to April and

Joanne.

"Hello, my name is Zanika, and this is Harrik. We are very pleased to meet you," Zanika said gently, giving both women a warm and genuine smile.

"You, you have wings!" April exclaimed, her eyes running over the angels' bodies, taking in every detail.

"Yes, we do," Harrik replied.

He stepped forward, placing a hand on April's trembling foot, and I watched in awe also as he opened his beautiful wings and bowed his upper body. His wings seemed to suddenly fill the room. He was magnificent and appeared all the more angelic. It was the first time I'd seen the angels' wings in all their glory too.

"Amazing," Joanne whispered.

"Yes, they are, aren't they," I said quietly in agreement.

Harrik lowered his wings, effortlessly folding them behind his back.

"Joanne, April, we need to birth two more animals. Would you like to watch so you may see for yourselves how we are helping to heal your Earth?" Harrik asked.

"Yes please," April said instantly, her body no longer shaking so badly.

'*Harrik must have calmed her with his power*

when he touched her foot,' I thought to myself.

"I would like to see it too, please," Joanne added.

Zanika and Harrik dipped their heads to both women, and as Harrik glided away, Zanika began to use her power to slide back the dividing veils between the other two sleeping women and us.

"Are those all the baby animals?" April asked, pointing to the glistening glass wall now that Zanika and Harrik were no longer blocking their view.

"Yes," I replied, "the baby animals are placed into containment capsules. So once our planet is healed enough, they can be released when they're ready," I explained.

Just as I was explaining, Harrik returned with two more capsules, both hovering above his outstretched palms. '*Show off,*' I thought, smiling to myself.

Zanika began to prepare the first woman, adjusting her sheet and gown as Harrik positioned the shimmering capsules at the ends of the beds. While Joanne started to share the tray of food and juice with April, Harrik joined Zanika on the other side of the bed.

"Zanika, do you know what the women are carrying?" Joanne asked politely.

Zanika looked up and smiled at Joanne, and then she took the sleeping woman's hand and lifted it to show them the silvery mark.

"She is carrying a lynx kitten," she replied.

"That is amazing," April said between mouthfuls of fruit.

While April and Joanne watched transfixed as the angels birthed the new animal babies, I took the opportunity to speak with Trudy and Mimi.

Touching the com at the top of my cleavage, I mentally reached out.

'*Mimi, Trudy, are you both at the cruiser?*' I asked. Within seconds they both responded.

'*Yes,*' Trudy answered.

'*I'm still here too, are you okay?*' Mimi asked.

'*I'm fine. We have two women awake, one called April who's missing her girlfriend Ashley, who was stabbed just before the angels arrived,*' I told her, '*The other woman, Joanne, is English and has a husband and two children who were very young. Can you see if you can find them all and bring them here, please? It's definitely going to make things easier,*' I added.

'*Will do; we'll tell you when we're ready with them,*' Trudy replied.

'*See you soon, Mel. Oh, and we heard about*

the fish and birds at the pool; it must have been so weird, but amazing at the same time,' added Mimi, and then they were gone.

By the time we'd finished our mental conversation, Zanika and Harrik were already working on the fourth woman, and the lynx kitten was in its shimmering capsule.

April and Joanne were still mesmerized, watching the angels every move.

"So, what do you think?" I asked both of the women.

"It is incredible," Joanne said quietly.

"It's magical isn't it!" April added. "I didn't think I could get pregnant because I've always had major problems with my ovaries," she confessed.

"Well, your ovaries are perfect now. When the angels came, you were all healed, so you've never been in more perfect health.

One of the women here called Tracey had cancer before all of this, and she's healed now too," I explained.

"That's incredible," April exclaimed, now smiling and appearing genuinely happier.

Before long, the other two women were both awake, and after introductions between us ladies and introducing the angels, the women were talking and eating between themselves.

I took a moment to reach out again to Mimi and Trudy, who apparently were just about to leave with Joanne's husband and two children.

Trudy sounded quite choked when she delivered the bad news that April's girlfriend was already dead when the angels arrived.

My heart ached in my chest at the thought of having to tell her. I was grateful that she was getting on so well with the women before me. She was going to need her new friends to help her through her grief.

I told Mimi and Trudy about the other two women, explaining who they were missing and asked them to meet us in the smaller meeting room with Hulaz. We were going to need the angel to show them what the angels had shown me.

"Ladies, I'm going to take you now to a meeting room, so that we can explain everything to you. Is that okay?" I asked.

After all agreeing, Zanika, Harrik, and myself led the women to the meeting room. As the angels walked in front of the women, I walked behind them and watched them taking everything in. All four were looking this way and that, admiring and studying the corridors, archways, and the hieroglyphs.

When we arrived at the meeting room, the women's family members were there waiting for them, minus April's girlfriend. Joanne's husband and children rushed to her with open arms, sandwiching her between them all, with tears of relief and joy streaming down their faces.

Hulaz and I made a beeline for April, and as I looked into her eyes, I knew she was preparing herself for the worst. Hulaz reached for her, placing her hand on April's in preparation for the heartbreak she was about to endure.

The other women were so wrapped up in their sheer happiness that they were oblivious.

"April I'm so sorry, but Ashley didn't make it," I told her as gently as I could. "She had already passed away before the angels arrived," I explained.

April's eyes were wide with disbelief and shock as her body began to tremble. Hulaz started to let her power flow between her hand and April's.

April glanced at Hulaz and then back to me as if waiting for us to say that we were mistaken. We waited for her to absorb the reality.

"She lost a lot of blood, and I couldn't stop it," she said, with a sob.

"It wasn't your fault April; things were so bad before the angels came, and many lives were lost through similar circumstances," I told her softly. "We will help and support you through this, okay."

"Thank you," she answered as a huge sob

escaped her.

She moved towards me and laid her head on my shoulder. I couldn't fathom one so young, losing the one they loved. My heart broke for her as I wrapped my arms around her, giving her the comfort, she so desperately needed.

CHAPTER 19

By the time I arrived back at our rooms, I was utterly drained, and my emotions were all over the place. My heart was still so heavy with April's grief, but the joy felt by Joanne and the other ladies helped to balance the emotions out.

Waking the women in groups was definitely working a lot better than before and was more productive in helping the women to acclimatize to their new situation and surroundings.

Zanika or Harrik had arranged food and drink, including coffee, so I grabbed a cup and made my way to the large, round window.

Looking out to the ocean, I watched the rig crafts in action. I was reminded again how amazing the angels were in all aspects of healing our planet.

Our freshwater and seawater were nearly cleaned completely; our land was getting there now too. Also due to all the women, there were now thousands upon thousands of infant animals ready to put in the wild. I sighed at the accomplishments we'd already made and the wonder of it all.

Hearing voices behind me, I turned to see Harrison and Anthony walking in, and they seemed to be full of enthusiasm.

"I still can't believe the plans that Scott's drawn up so quickly," Anthony said in awe.

"Well, now we know why he was such a successful builder don't we," Harrison replied, his eyes brows rising. "Hi, Mom."

"Hi boys, are you hungry?" I asked, pointing at the food-laden tray on the table.

Both boys raised their eyebrows as they tilted their heads as if to say, 'Really, Mom, that's a silly question; we're always hungry.' I laughed aloud at their comical faces.

They joined me in the seating area, and we began to snack on the food and talk while we waited for James and the girls to arrive back.

Harrison and Anthony had had a great day with Scott and a few of the other men and women. They'd been making action plans for the fake holding structures and had been making the architectural plans too. They'd really enjoyed learning from the others and being a part of it.

"Turns out Scott has a daughter who's about

the same age as Anthony," Harrison said, with a smirk on his face. "Doesn't he Anthony," he added while wriggling his eyebrows at his brother.

Poor Anthony was embarrassed at his younger brother's statement.

"Don't tease your brother, Harrison," I chided. "There are so few of us left, that if you all find love and happiness with someone, it will be a true blessing," I added, giving my eldest a wink. "What's she like Anthony?" I asked curiously.

I was relieved and pleased to be able to talk about something so positive after the morning I'd had. Anthony took a deep breath trying to relax.

"She's awesome Mom, and she's called Christine. She's smart, funny, and she knows how to build houses like her dad," he answered. "She's been on building sites with her dad since she was young."

"Wow, she sounds very impressive," I replied, genuinely pleased for him.

"Yeah, she is, and I'm going to meet her later at the lagoon pool," he added, obviously very keen.

I was thrilled that the kids seemed to be making connections with others, especially possible partners.

Life felt even more precious now, and I desperately wanted our kids to find happiness.

About half an hour later, the girls came back

and, of course, Nalik was still with Holly. I felt that I needed to have a quiet chat with Holly about Nalik to make sure he wasn't being too full on and over-crowding her. She came across happy enough, but I wanted to check.

The girls had had a great day just like the boys, and with just as much enthusiasm, they told us all about it. Abigail explained that she loved working with Ann and the other artists. They already had ideas for camouflaging the holding structures and the angels.

Holly couldn't wait to talk about all the things she was organizing too. As she was describing her day, Nalik sat silently looking at her with pride and adoration on his face. 'My goodness, he's smitten with her,' I thought to myself.

As I listened to the kids sharing the details of their day, I began to wonder where James was, and then I remembered the com around my neck. Not wanting to disturb the kids from talking between themselves, I discreetly touched it and reached out to him.

'*James, how are you doing?*' I mentally asked.

I didn't get a reply,

'*James are you okay!*' I asked a little more anxiously.

'*I can't talk right now, babe; we've got a situation right now,*' he answered breathlessly.

Worry flowed through me instantly. It sounded like something very bad was happening just from the tone of his voice. My heart was instantly racing ten to the dozen, making it feel like it was pounding in my throat.

'*James, where are you?*' I desperately asked in my mind.

'*Outside the cruiser,*' he replied in a rush of words.

My mind was made up.

"Nalik, could you please take me to the holding structure?" I asked, trying to sound much calmer than I felt.

Nalik looked at me surprised and then concerned. However, fair play to him, he didn't let on to my kids what he was obviously sensing from me.

"Of course, Mel," he said, getting straight up from his seat.

Before the kids had a chance to ask what was going on, Nalik touched my arm, and we vanished from the room.

When we reappeared, I suddenly felt icy cold, and we were in the small meeting room and not at the holding structure.

"What the hell Nalik? I said the holding structure; James is outside it!" I shouted, feeling so pissed and panic-stricken.

Nalik held up both of his hands, as if in surrender.

"Mel, before I place you in any danger, I need to know what's happening," he told me gently.

I started to tremble with anxiety and anger.

"I don't know what's happening Nalik, but I think James is in danger, and if you don't take me there right now, you will be the first dead angel of your fucking race!" I shouted.

I couldn't help myself from letting my panic spill out; I just knew that James needed me. Nalik didn't argue; instead, he touched my hand, and we disappeared again.

When we arrived outside the cruiser, all hell was breaking loose, and I wasn't quite believing what I was seeing before us.

Nalik instantly moved in front of me protectively and was suddenly glowing brightly. I peered around the side of him with my heart racing even faster.

There were eight angels and James in a near circle, and they were surrounding a Marilian, '*How the hell is this possible?*'

The Marilian was so fast, zapping from one place to another within the circle, dodging the angels' light beams of power.

It looked to me as if he was repeatedly trying to get to James, '*Maybe he wanted to try and change him.*'

The angels were desperately trying to trap him, but he was so fast, with his razor-sharp talons slicing through the air every time he got close to James.

Panic rose sharply in my chest, and I touched my com. '*Nalik, tell the angels they need to cross their power beams like this,*' I told him, showing him the Star of David in my mind. '*Then, tell them to bring their power towards the center. One of the beams will trap him,*' I added.

I felt Nalik in my mind, '*Yes, Mel.*'

Within mere seconds, the angels had changed their tactic, instantaneously redirecting their power beams into the shape I'd shown Nalik.

Abruptly the Marilians movements changed too, his zapping from one place to the next becoming more hesitant, his eyes darting in all directions, trying to find a weak spot.

When I looked at James, his eyes were wide with fear, not for himself, but for me.

Something blinded me suddenly as if a

camera flash had gone off right in front of my face. Nalik moved his arm around my back, placing his hand on my wrist.

'Don't worry, Mel, one of the power beams hit the Marilian; just keep blinking your eyes, it will pass,' he told me calmly.

As I rapidly started to blink my eyes, hating the fact that I was momentarily blinded, I felt large, strong arms wrapping around my waist. Instantly, I knew it was James.

"Are you alright, baby?" he asked, desperately needing reassurance.

I turned around in his arms while still blinking away the flash of light. James began to come into focus before me, his furrowed brows and thinned lips showing his worry.

"I'm fine, James, honestly. I thought that bastard was trying to get you," I told him, my shaky voice taking me by surprise.

"He was trying to get me, Mel, but he's contained now, look," he said, pointing behind me.

When I turned around, all the angels had the Marilian within their beams in the center of their circle. He was frozen on the spot, unable to move his thickly haired muscular body.

His face was full of rage. Razor-sharp teeth were clearly visible as he snarled his fury, and his blood-red eyes flickered as if they were wild flames. A shudder ran through my whole body as I felt the evil flowing from him.

Without warning, Christik abruptly appeared right next to us, her silvery-white power emanating from every inch of her body. She was obviously very angry.

"Enough!" Her voice boomed over the sou-nds of rage coming from the Marilian.

All the angels turned to look at her in all her fierce glory as she lifted her arms with both palms facing the monster.

I watched in awe as the Marilian began to lift off the ground. Under his feet, silvery vines started to burst through the earth, winding around his ankles, slowly moving upwards and around his thick body.

The other angels reined in their own power, three of them disappearing. I realized that the vines were metal as they wound around his body.

Before long, the Marilian was encased in silvery vines, from his feet to his muscular shoulders.

The Marilians snarls and rage made my skin crawl as did his fiery eyes. James' arms around me made me feel safe, but the hatred and murderous feelings that I felt from the monster were so strong, it was as if they were my own.

Christik glided towards the Marilian while

lowering her palms to face the earth. Her palms began to glow brighter and, like before, I felt the earth tremble beneath my feet. A strong breeze was beginning to form around us, my hair starting to whip around in the increasingly strong air currents.

The people inside the holding structure must have heard the commotion or felt the vibration in the ground as they began to come out of the main doors or out to their balconies.

All of us watched in awed silence as particles of metal came up from the ground, swirling in a circular motion beneath Christik's hands. Even though I'd recently witnessed her doing this, I was still seriously impressed.

Before long, Christik had a lot of silver metal collected in mini tornadoes under her palms. The wind and the earth tremors gradually died down. She raised her arms before her as if offering the silver, and all eyes were on her as her outstretched hands grew even brighter.

The silver began to melt together until there were two large discs of silvery metal spinning above each of her hands. With amazing speed, she threw one of the discs, and it spun like a Frisbee through the air, sliding underneath the floating Marilian. She threw the other, and we watched it fly just as fast, stopping and hovering above the monster's head.

Christik glided right up to the Marilian, raising her arms either side of his imprisoned form.

"You will not harm anyone on this planet," she declared to him in a voice full of fierce authority.

A flash of light released from her hands and instantly a barrier appeared between the two spinning silver discs, encasing the terrifying Marilian.

There were many sighs of relief among us humans and the angels, once the monster was trapped completely. As I looked around at my people, many were hugging each other, shocked that they were witnessing one of our enemies literally so close to home. I understood how they felt.

Seeing the Marilian before us confirmed that the threat was real, and that they were definitely here already or on their way.

Christik glided over to us and Nalik. James still had his arms around me protectively.

"Thank you, Mel, for your quick thinking; you really helped with a difficult, and possibly deadly situation, which we were not prepared for," she said. "I have no idea how or when the Marilian arrived here, so we need to find out immediately. Would you both please come with me now?" she asked.

"Yes, of course," I replied quickly for both of us.

I was desperate to get answers too; the lives of our kids and unborn baby could depend on the knowledge we needed.

"Nalik, could you please go back to our rooms and explain what's happened to Holly, Abigail, and the boys?" I asked the angel, who was still standing next to us. "Make sure you tell them we are safe, and we'll be back with them soon."

"Of course, Mel," he replied, and with that, he was gone.

One of the remaining angels began to glide towards us as two others began to raise their arms around the imprisoned Marilian. With a flash of light, the angels and Marilian were gone, I assumed back to the main craft. When the single angel reached us, he put his hand on James' arm, and Christik did the same to me.

In a flash, we were back on the main craft, and I was shivering again with James rubbing my arms trying to warm me up.

We found ourselves in a large room that we hadn't been in before. It was a white room, and it was bare of furniture of any kind.

Towards the back wall was the Marilian, still wrapped in the metal vines and imprisoned in the energy barrier between the two silver discs.

"He's actually scared now," I told Christik, James, and the other angel. "I can feel his fear strongly."

James looked at me with either curiosity or worry, but I wasn't sure which.

"Do you think you could feel if he was lying?" Christik asked, taking me at my word.

"Yes, I believe I could," I answered with conviction.

"How the hell is my wife going to know what that monster is feeling?" James demanded.

'*Worry*' I thought to myself, "*Yep definitely worry.*'

Christik smiled at James with empathy, obviously understanding his concern and protectiveness.

"I think your new baby is enhancing Mel's already existing, strong emotional senses," she explained. Since I first met your wife, I was aware that she was attuned to people's emotions. However, I believe Mel wasn't truly aware of it herself."

James' eyes widened with understanding and maybe acknowledgment of what he already knew about me.

"We need to get as much information as we can from the Marilian. It would be more than helpful if Mel could tell us whether he is lying or not," she added kindly.

"Of course, I totally get it," James admitted. "Do you want to do this, baby?" he asked as he turned back to me.

"Yes, I do! I will do whatever it takes to protect you all," I answered, determination in my words.

Christik took my hand in hers and began to glide towards the Marilian who was watching our every move with his fiery eyes.

Suddenly, Christik's voice was in my head. '*I will have to speak in his language, but I will share what he says with you and James.*'

She touched a glowing hand to her throat and then began to speak to him in Marilian.

All my ears could hear were various snarls, but in my mind, I heard her loud and clear, word for word.

'*How did you get to this planet so quickly Marilian?*' she demanded forcefully.

'*You brought me here weak one,*' he replied scornfully.

'*You think us weak, and yet you were hiding all this time, and you are our now our prisoner Marilian,*' she reproached him.

'*Why did you hide on our ship to come here?*' she asked.

'*I do not need to tell you anything; you are beneath me, weakling!*' he spat out venomously.

'*Is that right?*' she told him, raising glowing palms to face him.

As her hand shone brightly, James and I watched as the metal vines became tighter around his body.

'*If it were not for us saving your planet, you would not be alive Marilian. I would have thought you and your race would have more respect for us,*' she reproached.

'*You tell him Christik!*' I heard James say in my head.

Christik subtly smirked at James's encouragement. The Marilian began to writhe in his bondage, obviously feeling extremely uncomfortable now.

'*You do not know much about the human race, do you Marilian? They have been killing each other since they existed and can be just as barbaric as your race,*' she told him. '*This man, James, would not even hesitate to torture you to retrieve the information I want. So, I will ask you again, why did you hide on my craft to come here?*' she demanded.

I turned to look at James, and he was playing

the bad guy very well. He was giving the Marilian a death stare, looking deep into the Marilians blood red eyes.

If looks could kill, the Marilian would have been already dead. '*Damm, my husband is a good actor,*' I thought as the hairs on the back of my neck stood on end.

I looked back at the Marilian just in time to see him visibly deflate in defeat. He must have realized he was in a no-win situation, with zero back up.

'*I hid on your craft as I was ordered to do by my ruler*" the Marilian answered, his eyes now looking down to the floor.

'*For what purpose?*' she demanded.

The Marilian ignored her. Still holding his death stare, James walked forward threateningly just as Christik tightened the vines a little more.

'*I will do whatever it takes to protect my family, my planet, and your race too, Christik!*' I heard James say to us both.

Christik turned to look at him, her eyes wide with surprise, but when she saw the determination on his face and maybe felt the protectiveness he was feeling, she nodded her head at him in understanding.

'*For what purpose?*' she demanded again, more forcefully to the Marilian.

'I was supposed to find the angels we corrupted and help them prepare for the arrival of my race,' he unwillingly admitted, his voice straining with the tightness of the metal vines.

'I see, and what abilities does your race have that I do not know about?' Christik asked as James took a few more threatening steps towards the Marilian.

The Marilians eyes began to dart from Christik to James and back again.

'We can transfer our essence into objects,' he replied.

'Yes, we assumed as much when we discovered our fallen ones. Tell us the things we don't know!' she told him.

'Our race can control the fire on our planet,' he told her hesitantly, "I do not know if that is the same on this planet."

'Anything else Marilian?' Christik demanded.

The Marilian shook his head, but Christik obviously didn't trust him to tell the truth. She turned to look at me.

'Is he being truthful, Mel?'

'No, he's not completely being truthful; he already knows he can control fire here,' I said confidently.

'I did not think he would be completely honest with us, but it does not matter. We will be even more prepared now,' Christik told us. *'Come, we must tell the others.'*

CHAPTER 20

We left the holding room in silence; the true weight of the situation was really hitting home. There was no longer any doubt that the Marilians were on their way to invade. In a way, it was a blessing that our Marilian prisoner had stowed away on the angels' craft. At least now we knew a little more about them, and I was pretty sure that his presence was going to get us well and truly motivated in our defense.

James held my hand as we traveled down the main corridor; it was a comfort, but I had a heavy feeling in my gut.

"The Marilian was still hiding something, I don't know what, but he was hiding something for sure," I said to James, Christik and the other angel.

"Do not worry, Mel; we will prepare for as many instances as we can," Christik replied. "We are going to the main meeting room; the others are meeting us there, so we can inform them of what we have learned so far.

"Let's hope your dreams give us some more info since your dream about the Marilian coming was so spot on," James said as he gently squeezed my hand.

The meeting room was full of people when we arrived there, including our kids who were mingling with everyone. As well as our usual group, there were also some people from the holding structure such as Shawn and Luiza. I didn't know if James, Christik and I were giving off any serious vibes, but when we entered the room, everyone fell deathly silent.

As we took our places around the table, Hulaz raised her arm and created the sphere to enable us to communicate with the Viziers once again. Within minutes, the Viziers had filled the slowing turning sphere and were ready to hear the news.

Christik stood and looked around at the faces of angels and humans.

"As you all know by now, we have captured a Marilian, who apparently hid on one of our crafts by the order of Drakron. We have questioned the Marilian, and although he hasn't told us everything, we do know they are definitely coming here to invade. We also now know that they are able to control fire on their home world and here. The Marilian was sent here to help the fallen ones. Obviously, when we captured and healed the fallen angels, he was then alone," Christik explained.

"How was the fucker found?" Tracey asked, in her usual blunt way.

"He was discovered as he was scouting the holding structure by two of our angels," Christik answered. "He is now very well secured in a holding room. So, he will not be able to pass on any information to his race when they arrive."

"We are lucky that Earth has such an abundance of water if they can control fire," one of the Viziers stated.

"Yes," agreed Christik, "and that we can use our power to control all that water."

Luiza, who had been quiet up to then, stepped forward confidently.

"Please be honest with us all Christik. What are our chances against these bastards?" she also asked bluntly.

Christik looked into Luiza's eyes, sensing her anxiety just like I was. We both knew that our races needed the whole truth, no matter how scary the truth was.

"I believe we are going to have a brutal battle ahead of us," she said honestly. "Which is why I will not take any chances, nor will I take anything for granted. I have decided to contact the elders of our race. I believe we will need them to make sure we can defeat the Marilians," she added.

Luiza and everyone in the room nodded their heads to Christik in acceptance and respect. I could feel the worry in the room emanating from everyone.

"Viziers are you in agreement with my decision?" Christik asked the angels in the sphere.

"We agree with your decision Christik," one of the angels replied. "We will carry out our current plans and wait to hear from you when the elders arrive," he told her.

Hulaz closed her hand, making the sphere instantly disappear. I noticed that her hand was shaking slightly as she lowered it, her eyes connecting with Harrik's.

The worry I felt coming from her matched my own, and as I watched her go to Harrik, I realized that nearly everyone was holding or touching another for comfort and support.

Abigail was being hugged by Harrison, Holly was in Nalik's arms—not surprisingly, and a very pretty young lady was in Anthony's.

I assumed the young lady was his new lady

Friend, Christine, as both her and Anthony's hair were damp from their swim.

"I think we all need to take some time to rest for the remainder of the day. I have already arranged angels to guard and patrol all holding structures. So, you will all be safe," Christik said. "Please continue your defense plans tomorrow morning. I will organize the contacting of our elders."

In a bustle of movement, everyone started to leave quickly. It appeared that all of us couldn't wait to get back to our rooms.

Just as my family and I were about to leave, Anthony came up to us with Christine holding his hand.

"Mom, Dad, I'd like you to meet, Christine," He nervously told us.

She was a very pretty young lady with freckles complementing her tanned skin and long, dark-blonde hair flowing past her shoulders. When I smiled at her, she smiled back with a smile that lit up the room.

"Hi Christine, it's lovely to meet you," I told her shaking her hand.

"Great to meet you, young lady," James added, shaking her hand also.

"It's nice to meet you all too," she replied

warmly.

I had a great feeling about her, and Anthony looked like the cat who got the cream.

"Would you like to join us for dinner, Christine?" I asked, getting the impression that Anthony would like to spend more time with her.

"Yes, I'd love to," she said, giving Anthony her winning smile.

We were soon back at our rooms enjoying a meal with our kids, Christine and Nalik. After the day we'd had, it was soothing to my soul to watch our kids enjoying themselves.

The girls suggested that we should all play charades, which was hilarious, especially watching Nalik's utter confusion.

Both James and I were very impressed when he decided to have a try himself. It took us about half an hour of laughing and guessing before James guessed the answer, which was Braveheart.

"How on Earth do you know about the Braveheart movie?" James asked, seriously impressed because it was his all-time favorite film.

"I like to talk with your people, and Derek was telling me about films. It happened to be one of his favorites apparently," he answered.

"Maybe when our battle with the Marilians is

over, we can use your green energy to set up a TV, DVD player and watch the film together," Holly told him sweetly.

Poor Nalik looked completely confused.

"What is a TV and a DVD player?" he asked.

"You'll see," she told him, shaking her head and smiling.

After lots of talking and playing games such as 'What am I', Nalik kindly took Christine back to her cabin. Abigail, Harrison, and Anthony all went to bed leaving James, Holly and I left in the sitting area.

"So, how is it going with Nalik?" I asked.

The resounding smile she gave us seemed to say it all.

"It's going really well," she replied excitedly. "We actually have a lot in common."

She paused a moment as if she wasn't sure what to say next.

"I think I'm in love with him," she admitted with sudden seriousness.

James reached over and held her hand, smiling reassuringly.

"You don't need to be embarrassed or worried darling," I told her sincerely. "As you know, I met your dad when we were young, and we've been together twenty-eight years now. People can find their soulmates at a young age. We're pleased that he's making you happy."

"He is making me happy, and I think he is my other half," she said.

She came across so sure of her feelings. I felt pleased and relieved that she was so happy with the angel. We all went to bed feeling a little more light-hearted after the pleasant evening we'd all shared.

I know I'm dreaming, but I can't wake myself up from the nightmare I'm in; there are Marilians everywhere.

I'm hiding down the side of an abandoned building, and I can't find James or the kids anywhere. Panic is rising in my chest; my heart is pounding so loudly that I think I can hear it hammering.

There are fights happening everywhere I look, between angels, humans, and the Marilians. As my eyes scan the area for my family, I witness a man and Marilian fighting.

The man has lost his gun; I can see it on the floor a short distance away, and he has no chance of retrieving it.

In each hand, he has a knife, the blades glistening in the bursts of light from the nearby angels' power beams and the fire the other Marilians are throwing.

The Marilian is so much faster than the man; his sharp blade-like talons slash at the man's body. It feels like slow motion as the Marilian flashes forward just as the man raises an arm to strike.

The Marilian grabs the man, pulling him towards his body, so they are face to face. Watching the man in the Marilians grip is terrifying, but I am helpless.

I can't use my com because I don't know who is still alive, and I don't know the names of any of the angels I can see.

The man is struggling violently against his foe, but the Marilian is so much stronger. Suddenly, the Marilian puts his head against the man's, their noses literally touching. '*What the hell!*'

He almost looks as if he's about to kiss the man. Instead, the Marilians blood-red eyes become fiery, and the man's eyes start to glow red too.

I can't grasp what is happening between them, but when the Marilian releases the man, the fight between them is over. The man isn't changing into one of them, but he appears to be just as evil as the Marilian now.

When the man turns, facing my direction, his eyes are the same as the Marilians, exactly the same.

I woke abruptly safe in our bed covered in a

cold sweat. My body began to shiver as I thought about the man with the fiery red eyes. James was still fast asleep, his clothes folded neatly on the floor next to his side of the bed.

I slipped out of bed trying not to wake him and slipped on my dress. Still not feeling warm, I grabbed his smock and pulled it on over my dress. Not only did it feel warmer, but the scent of my husband made me feel safer.

'*I need to tell Christik,*' I thought to myself '*Right now.*' I knew I wouldn't be able to rest, let alone sleep until I told her about my dream.

Touching my pregnant stomach, I whispered to my baby, "thank you, my baby girl."

After quickly brushing my hair and teeth and getting a drink of water, I touched the com on my chest. '*Christik, I need to talk to you; are you awake?*'

I had no idea what time it was, and glancing at the window, I could see it was still dark. There was no sign of the sunrise yet. I didn't even know what month it was to be completely honest.

'I am awake, Mel. Are you alright?' she answered, concern in her tone.

'*I'm fine, a little shaken though. I had another dream, and I need to talk to you about it,*' I replied, knowing that she'd pick up on my emotions.

'*I am coming to get you, Mel; meet me outside your room,*' she said.

I headed for our room entrance knowing that she'd already be there waiting for me. I was not mistaken; as soon as I was out of our rooms, there she was.

'Would you like some fresh coffee, Mel?" she asked warmly.

It was as if she'd read my mind.

"Mmm, yes please," I replied without any hesitation.

"Harrik, Hulaz, and Zanika are waiting for us," she said as she touched my arm.

In a blink of an eye, we were at the meeting room next to the large control room. The angels were there sitting at the table, and the fresh coffee was waiting for us with, an added bonus. There was now fresh honey on the table too. My heart leaped for joy at the sight and aroma.

"Thank you so much for doing this," I told them as I took a cup of honey-laced coffee while trying to steady my shivering hand.

It was heavenly and began to warm me instantly; it was just what I needed.

"Please tell us about your dream, Mel," Christik said, her concern still evident.

I told the angels about my dream in as much detail as I could. Luckily, because I awoke so abruptly it was still very fresh in my mind.

"So, the Marilians are able to take over your people and turn them against us all, without changing them," Zanika said, her eyes wide with worry.

"Yes, I think so," I told her. "I believe that was what the Marilian was hiding from us. What concerns me is that we don't know if he was able to corrupt some of our people before he was caught."

"You said that the man's eyes turned fiery red like the Marilians, yes?" Harrik asked.

"Yes, they did. So, the only way a corrupted person could hide their corruption is if they were wearing dark sunglasses," I explained, giving them a mental image of what sunglasses were.

"If they were unable to get any from nearby houses, they would have to hide away from the others at the holding structure," Hulaz added.

"We will question the Marilian prisoner again now and see what else he reveals," Christik said. "In the meantime, Mel, would you like to have breakfast with your family and meet us here when you are ready?"

"Yes, that would be fine," I answered, feeling somewhat back to normal.

"I will flit you back to your room," Zanika

offered with a lovely smile.

I really didn't want to flit again, now that I was finally warm.

"Actually, I think I'd much rather walk," I told her, giving the angels a respectful nod.

As I was leaving the meeting room, all the angels disappeared apart from Zanika who seemed to be following me out.

"Would you mind if I walked with you?" she asked.

"No, not at all," I told her.

I was actually glad of the company to be truthful, and I liked Zanika a lot.

It was pleasant walking down the long corridor, running my fingers along the glistening wall. I could feel the energy through my fingertips, making me feel as if I were being recharged.

"I hear Holly and Nalik are bonding well," she said with a little smile.

"Yes, they are, and we're happy for them. I think it's serious between them. The only thing I worry about is, if they do pair, they won't be able to have a family together," I told her with disappointment.

"And why is that?" she asked, obviously confused with what I'd said.

I felt really embarrassed knowing that I'd

have to state the obvious out loud. I could feel my cheeks already starting to blush.

"You angels don't have any genitalia as we do," I stated, my cheeks now burning so badly I could have toasted marshmallows against them.

"Ahhh, I can understand why you would assume that, Mel," she said with another smile. "We do actually have genitalia; however, ours is only activated when we begin to be intimate with another," she explained. "We have the same genitalia as your race; the only real difference is that our bodies adapt to our other half's sexual needs."

'*Lucky fuckers,*' I thought, realizing Tracey was rubbing off on me.

"You mean to tell me that your males can sense how big they need to be to please their partners?" I asked, totally stunned.

"Yes, exactly, and our females can adapt for males too," she replied, clearly enjoying my utter surprise.

"Well, be fair warned Zanika, when my fellow humans discover this piece of information, there may be a whole lot more pairing going on between our two races," I told her as I began to laugh.

We both began to laugh as she started to understand what I was getting at. After the awful nightmare I'd had, it was another dose of what I needed.

When we got to my room, another angel was waiting for us with our breakfast. He nodded his head and passed the tray to me.

"Your family is still sleeping; I did not want to wake them," he said kindly.

I thanked the angel and thanked Zanika for walking me back. As I watched them glide away, I thought about the conversation I'd just had with Zanika. '*The girls are going to freak out when I tell them this gem of information.*' I couldn't help laughing again, knowing that they'd be just as stunned. '*I wonder what Holly is going to make of this new information too,*' I thought as I quietly crept into our room.

I placed the tray on the table and sat in one of the chairs, helping myself to the coffee and honey. I wasn't worried about talking with Holly about the angels' sexual differences. James and I were lucky in that we'd always been honest with the kids when they'd asked questions. Such as 'where do babies come from,' and 'why do you and Dad have hair in places?'

As awkward as some of their questions had been, we preferred the kids to know the truth, and my Holly deserved to know, so she didn't get embarrassed with Nalik.

She was always so much more mature than the other kids her age. Holly had what my own mother would have called an old soul, and with the situation we were now in, I wasn't going to try and stop or slow down her beautiful relationship with the angel.

Roughly an hour later, James and the kids began to stir. James gave me a kiss and looked at his smock I was still wearing.

"I was chilly," I told him. "Grab a shower to wake up and then we need to talk."

Not really being a morning person, he nodded his head and headed for the shower. It didn't take him long, and luckily, he was back before the kids opened the dividing barrier.

I explained to him about my dream and what happened to the man. He seemed just as horrified as I'd felt.

"This shit just keeps getting worse doesn't it," he said, flabbergasted.

"But at least we know what else we're dealing with, James," I assured him. "It would be a whole lot worse if we didn't find out until after they'd arrived."

"Well, yeah, there is that," he said quietly.

"And there's another thing," I told him with a smirk.

I explained how the angels could adapt their bodies when pairing, and he laughed just as hard as I had. He agreed that the information was going to stir a lot of interest as word of it spread around the holding structures.

Before too long, we were all dressed and eating our breakfast together, discussing our plans for the day. I explained to the kids the dream I'd had, and after a few moments of silence, they seemed to shake their momentary shock.

"I think we just need to make sure that everyone knows," Anthony said. "I'm sure if everyone knows, they'll keep a lookout for anyone who's acting odd, such as wearing sunglasses like you said, Mom."

"Agreed," I replied, to my always sensible son. "Now, before we do anything else today, Christik wants us to meet her and a few others at the main meeting room here on the craft. I don't know why, but I'm sure it will be interesting, knowing Christik."

Little did I know at the time just how mind-blowing things were going to get.

CHAPTER 21

We were all ready for the day ahead after the lovely breakfast with our kids. The dream I'd had that night still had me a little shaken. I couldn't bear the thought of anyone being turned into a Marilian or one of their minions.

The kids' banter with their dad was helping to chase away my fears, thank goodness. They were keen to find out what Christik wanted to show us, and I was too. We knew that she wanted to contact their elders as soon as possible, so I was assuming it was to do with them.

We didn't know very much about them, apart from the fact that they were even more ancient than Christik and the other angels. I wondered whether they looked like the angels who were now our friends.

"Right, are we all ready to go?" James asked us all.

"I think so," I replied, as I then turned to Holly. "Is Nalik not coming with us today, darling?"

Holly looked embarrassed, her cheeks turning pink as everyone's eyes were suddenly on her.

"He's actually waiting outside our rooms for me," she said while blushing even more.

Always the gentleman, Anthony approached his sister, wrapping an arm around her shoulders.

"Don't be embarrassed, sis, Christine is waiting for me outside too I think," he said with a huge cheesy grin. She looked at him with sisterly affection that seemed to say, 'Thanks, Bro.'

They were both obviously just as smitten with their new love interests. How could we not be thrilled that they'd both found love after everything that had happened?

"Come on then. Let's not keep your lovebirds waiting," James said, wiggling his eyebrows at Holly and Anthony at which point both of them started to blush as much as the other.

We left our rooms, and Christine and Nalik were both waiting patiently just outside the archway. The moment Nalik's eyes connected with Holly's, his body and eyes again began to glow rhythmically with his heartbeat.

I didn't know if it was just my observation, but his love glow seemed even brighter. I wondered if it was because Holly's feelings were becoming stronger towards him. Holly and Christine both gave their beau's beautiful smiles which showed how much they felt.

Walking to the meeting room was a pleasure with the kids. Listening to the light-hearted small talk between the couples and Harrison telling Abigail about the building work. Not only had our kids grown closer as a family but they also appeared to be best friends too.

Christik was waiting for us at the meeting room with Harrick, Zanika, and Hulaz as well as Toniz and Anglik. They were all clearly pleased to see us as there were hugs all round as well as the dipped heads of respect.

There was a nervous excitement in the air from the angels in the room, which I gathered was the anticipation of what we were going to do that morning.

"Good morning everyone," Christik greeted warmly, "Today is a big day for all of us. We do not go to our home world very often as we are usually drawn to the next failing planet while we finish healing the one we are on," she explained. "It has been centuries since we have physically seen our elders, two of which are my paired creators."

"Do you mean your Mom and Dad?" Abigail asked respectfully with wide eyes.

"Yes Abigail, they are my parents," she answered kindly. The elders are far more ancient than we are and are very wise. They have seen and experienced more than any other race we have encountered. I will be extremely honored for you all to meet them when they arrive."

"When will they get here?" I asked, feeling excited to meet them.

"We will summon the elders this morning from Stanhenge. I hope that they will be here within two days," Christik answered. "Come, let us go to the smaller craft; my other angels are waiting for us. Please take the hand of the nearest angel."

"I've heard of Stonehenge before—but not Stanhenge," Holly stated, her expression looking thoughtful.

"Stanhenge is what you know as Stonehenge Holly," Zanika told her.

At the mention of Stonehenge, James and I locked eyes and smiled excitedly at each other. It was one of the places we'd always wanted to take our children, as they'd all learned a little about it at school.

We all stood next to the nearest angel. Unsurprising, Nalik already had Holly's hand in his, and

Anthony reluctantly released Christine's hand to take Hulaz'. We all vanished from the room the moment everyone was connected to an angel.

Within seconds, we found ourselves standing next to a craft in the angels' version of a huge hanger. The craft was larger than the one we'd been in before when we traveled to Peru, and it was located on the outer edge of the room, allowing us to see the length of the room and the many rows of crafts of various sizes and shapes.

Hulaz glided forward using her power to open the craft, and we all boarded with Hulaz taking the pilot position. We watched again in awe, especially Christine, who'd never been on one of their crafts as Hulaz activated the craft, and the door closed.

Hulaz glowed as she raised her arms reaching for the craft's energy and instantly the craft's power reached for her. The silvery vines once again reached for her and wrapped around her hands and arms.

This time, when we sat in the craft's bucket seats, I was prepared for my body being gently sucked into the seat, securing me in place. Christine obviously wasn't as she gave a little shriek of surprise, making all of us chuckle. Anthony leaned over, giving her hand a loving squeeze, making my heart melt.

"Are we ready to go?" Christik asked with a smile.

"We were born ready," Anthony, Harrison, Abigail, and Holly all said in unison, making Christik's smile even bigger.

"Hulaz, if you wouldn't mind," she said.

Instantly, Hulaz had the craft lifting off their hanger floor and moving slowly towards the now open exit.

The moment the craft was free of the hanger, we began to travel at speed across the country.

"Why are we going to Stonehenge Christik?" I asked. "Is it a magical place like Peru?"

Christik looked thoughtful for a moment.

"Yes, it is a magical place; however, it does not have the same purpose as the Star passages, or the Gate of the Gods," she explained. "We use Stonehenge to summon our Elders; we have similar sacred sites on many planets."

"Have you ever needed to summon the elders before?" Harrison asked.

"Not to my knowledge, Harrison, and never in my lifetime. However, we have never before encountered a race as barbaric as the Marilians," Christik answered.

The rest of the journey was full of light

conversation and questions while we sped across land and oceans. It was amazing to travel across such a distance in such a short space of time.

We are all so engrossed in our conversations that we arrived at Stonehenge in England in no time at all.

Hulaz landed the craft softly near a long road that ran along the side of the monument. As we exited the craft, the sun was starting to set, creating warm yellows, oranges, and reds in the sky. The soft, green grass under our feet was damp with rain, and the distant trees were full of swaying branches thick with dark green leaves.

As we stood together taking in the Wiltshire scenery, I was instantly blown away by the English countryside. The angels had obviously been busy in the area as there were healthy, green fields as far as my eyes could see. All of us were turning slowly, admiring the rural views.

Christik began to glide towards the stone ruins of Stonehenge.

"Come," she said softly, "my angels await us."

I hadn't even noticed any other angels, but as we started to follow Christik, I could see angels already there and others appearing around the large sarsen and blue stones I'd read about.

As soon as an angel appeared, he or she would walk towards what seemed to be an outer circle, only evident from the shortness of the grass. Everywhere else, the grass was long and wild apart from inside and around the stone formations.

As we curiously watched, more and more angels appeared, and not only were they walking to the outer circle, but they were also forming their own circle.

I tried to keep count of the angels as they appeared, and I counted over fifty before some app-eared behind the stones making me lose count.

The angels were a mix of male and female, all of them stunning with long, golden hair and win-gs. Christik glided forward to what would have been the entrance to Stonehenge and then she stopped.

As she began lifting her arms in front of her, the ground began to tremble beneath our feet. We all soon realized that two huge stones were starting to rise from the ground.

Both of the stones were partially buried, one more buried than the other, but once they were both free, they started to glide towards us, and they see-med to be repairing themselves as they moved.

Bits of stone rose from the ground, being drawn to the stones as if they were magnetized until finally, they were whole once more and hovering either side of Christik.

Slowly, she used her power to place them either side of the entrance, letting them sink back into the soil where they began to glow, one glowing red and the other blue.

"You may begin!" Christik commanded.

Abruptly, one by one, the angels in their circle raised their arms up, putting their hands together. Their wings opened, revealing their beauty and sheer size.

Their wings sparkled against the warm sunset and started to move forward—encasing their tall, slender bodies until they all looked like golden chrysalises.

Just as we all started to feel power in the air around us, the angels began to turn slowly in their places, dispersing the soil beneath their feet.

The entrance stones glowed even brighter as the angels turned faster and faster, creating large holes in the ground with each rotation.

Before long, all we could see of the angels were their touching hands.

"Can I see one of the angels please?" I asked, desperately wanting to see down one of the holes with an angel in it.

"Of course, you may all take a look," Christik

replied warmly, obviously understanding our curiosity and eagerness for knowledge.

We all walked over to the nearest angels and peered down into the deep pits.

"Wow," I whispered under my breath as my eyes looked over the golden angel beneath me.

The angel was a male with broad muscular shoulders showing within his shimmering wings. His golden hair ran down the length of his back and down to the backs of his knees.

Right at the bottom of the pit was a large gold disc that the angel was hovering over. I wondered if the gold disc was there already, hidden from us humans all this time.

Had it been buried underneath all the earth the angel had moved or had he created it as he created the hole? With our curiosity now sated, we walked back to Christik and the others. Just as we approached them, Christik spoke again.

"Begin!" she ordered again.

Instantly, we turned back to the golden angels to see what they were going to do next. I don't think any of us wanted to miss anything as it all seemed so magical and surreal.

None of us spoke at all as we continued to watch in awe as they all opened their hands, leaving their thumbs connected while spreading out their fingers.

The sunset seemed to be at its peak of brightness as the angels' hands started to glow a blend of gold, orange, and red.

Again, the earth beneath our feet trembled. Only this time it was stronger as if a large earthquake was about to strike. The angels' power abruptly pulsed forwards towards the center, where the stones stood or laid.

"Look," Harrison and Abigail shouted above the noise.

Both of them were pointing to the Sarsen and blue stones. We watched stunned as all the stones immediately commenced moving around.

The smaller stone rose high into the air and began to circle while the biggest stones slid into place.

As the whole stones moved and continued the part circle that had survived through the centuries, the lost and destroyed stones were beginning to form before us.

Not only was the outer circle forming but five pairs of stones were forming in the center, creating a horseshoe shape.

I was so engrossed in the scene before me that I couldn't tell how long it took before all the larger stones were all whole and in place.

Just as swiftly and effortlessly, some of the smaller stones started to gently land on top of the outer ring stones and the horseshoe stones.

While the smallest blue stones created another circle around the center stones and lined the inside of the larger horseshoe.

When all the stones were in place, the angels reined in their power and immediately rose from the holes. Once they were out, their wings began to unfurl, spreading outwards and upwards.

In one swift movement, their wings came back down, lifting the angels high into the air over the stones, and as they started to descend, they landed on top of all the smaller blue-colored stones, all with their wings poised in midair.

They were all magnificent.

"Woah," Holly uttered.

It was as if she had read all our minds—because we were all just as enthralled.

"Please follow me," Christik said as she glided forward towards the central stones.

We all followed her—with Harrick, Zanika, and Hulaz taking up the rear. I noticed that Nalik was again holding Holly's hand, and Christine was holding Anthony's, making me smile.

James gave mine a little squeeze as we walked, grabbing my attention.

"Are you okay, baby?" he asked, seemingly worried. "You look really flushed."

"I'm good James. To be honest, I feel better than good. It's as if I'm being recharged," I told him genuinely.

The responding smile he gave me made my heart swell in my chest. '*Bloody hell, I love this ma-n,*' I thought to myself.

Christik led us through the stone monuments and angels until we reached the absolute center of Stonehenge. It was so surreal being in the middle of such an amazing sight.

As I scanned the scene, I noticed not only an unoccupied blue stone in the middle of the horseshoe but also a large flat stone that looked like an altar. Christik came to a halt and turned to Nalik and Holly.

"Nalik, I would like you to take the remaining power stone. You are in love which has increased your power greatly," she told him. "Everyone else please follow me while Zanika, Hulaz, and Harrick take their places."

While Nalik followed the golden angels' act-ions—taking off and landing gracefully on top of the remaining blue power stone, the rest of us followed Christik.

She led us to the furthest power stones, so we were all facing the large five stone arched structures.

Our angel friends glided around behind us linking their hands together.

The sight before us was breathtaking. When I imagined seeing Stonehenge for the first time, I had no idea it would be like that, renewed with all the stones in the right places.

Who would have believed that the ancient site was meant for what we were all witnessing? It was blowing my mind to see all the golden angels and Nalik surrounding us on top of the power stones in all their splendor. I couldn't wait to see what would happen next.

None of us spoke, but we all kept looking at each other in stunned disbelief, our wide eyes of amazement saying it all for us.

James held my hand tightly, and I didn't know if it was due to worry or excitement. I hoped it was excitement, because I was truly buzzing with the magic of it all.

Christik glided towards the altar stone, coming to a full stop about ten feet away. We all stood mesmerized as she lifted her arms out to her sides, suddenly releasing her power to the two golden angels at the ends of the power stones' horseshoe.

The moment her power reached the two angels, it seemed to start a magical chain reaction.

The angels began to spin in the air just above

the stones—which were now glowing a true-blue color. As they spun, their power traveled outwards to the angels next to them, and so it continued.

One by one, the angels began spinning, powering up the blue power stones—until every one of them was glowing brightly. Their gold wings reflected the light from their shared power, sending flashes of colors in all directions.

It was nothing like I'd ever seen before.

Within minutes, the power was flowing freely between all the angels in the outer circle, as if the energy was passing through them all, and the same thing was happening to the angels in the horseshoe.

I felt James gently squeeze my hand again getting my attention.

"Look at the large stone arches, baby," he said, as he pointed in their direction.

When I looked over to them, it appeared that a blue ball of light was forming in the middle of the arches, growing steadily larger with each second. Before long, the blue light filled the voids completely, and as we stared, the light turned into a fluid, rippling softly before turning to a solid mass. It was as if they were blue shimmering mirrors reflecting the scene before them.

"Elders, I respectfully request your presence," Christik said loudly and with confidence.

We waited with bated breath to see what would happen next. I was acutely aware of the excitement in the air from James and the kids; it was so strong.

I glanced at my family quickly, before I missed anything. I could see Anthony and Christine still holding hands with amazement on both of their young faces. Harrison was holding Abigail's hand, and Holly was staring directly at Nalik's spinning form with her mouth agape in awe. When I turned back to the arches, I had a huge smile on my face and love in my heart.

We all heard the elders before we could see them, their voices loud and clear above the humming energy.

"You have never summoned us before, Christik, why do you summon us now, my own?" one of the elders replied.

My eyes strained to see the images forming in the glistening blue mirrors, the images becoming clearer with every second.

Moments later, the elders were clearly visible within the arches, and they were just as beautiful as the angels. We could see the elders so clearly, it was as if they were stood there, and they were very much like the angels who were with us.

The elders had the same long, shimmering

hair, which was bright silver and appeared to be held at the napes of their necks, but then splayed out around their broad shoulders. Their larger wings sat higher above their shoulders and seemed wider than our friends' wings. They were a lot more muscular overall, giving us the impression that they were more warriors than healers of worlds or peacekeepers.

"I will be brief, Lindaz, my own," Christik told the elder, who I assumed was her mother. "The Marilians are on their way to Earth to conquer it and take the humans as their own. I respectfully request your assistance in defending this planet and the human race," she added with conviction.

The elder, Lindaz, appeared thoughtful for a moment, and I could feel my anxiety building as we waited for her to speak again.

'*Please don't say no,*' I thought to myself over and over like a mantra.

"Never before have you asked us for assistance Christik. We do not take the threat you feel lightly," the elder said with compassion. "We know of the Marilian race. If they are on their way to Earth, you will indeed need our help."

"We will arrive through the Star Passage, the day after tomorrow Christik, my own," a male elder added.

Again, I had to assume that the male elder

was her father.

"Do my elders concur with this decision?" he asked.

The other elders all voiced their agreements, and I sighed with relief. The elders came across so powerful; I was sure they would give us a big advantage in our upcoming battle.

"We will take our leave now, my own," Lindaz said more warmly. "I will hold you soon enough," she added, giving her daughter a loving smile, then dipping her head in respect.

The other elders followed suit, all dipping their heads to Christik who returned the gesture. Moments later, the elders began to disappear as the shimmering mirrors again turned to liquid, then back to the bright lights. I could feel the energy around us begin to lessen as the ball of light shrank to nothingness.

The spinning golden angels and Nalik began to slow above the blue power stones, which were also starting to darken as the power ebbed and dimmed. Christik slowly lowered her arms as the angels came to a full stop. Each of them opened their wings and lowered themselves to the soft earth.

"Thank you, my angels," Christik told them warmly, "it is done. Our elders are coming; please return to our craft and rest."

All the angels apart from Nalik dipped their heads at Christik and then disappeared one by one. Nalik immediately started to glide toward Holly, dipping his head to Christik on his way.

When he reached my daughter, she reached for him, wrapping her arms around his waist and holding him tightly. Nalik responded just as affectionately, holding her tightly as his body began to glow.

"You were amazing," I heard her say to him sweetly.

His resounding smile and his body glow showed just how much Holly's words meant to him. I think we could all feel the love and respect between them.

CHAPTER 22

Holly, Nalik, Christine, and Anthony were still holding hands as we walked back into our rooms. We were all still so stunned by what we'd all witnessed that the journey home had been one of silence. I did notice Christik smiling knowingly at each of us in turn; obviously, she knew that none of us had ever seen anything like that before.

That evening, as we all sat together around the coffee table chatting and enjoying some well-deserved family time, it was all we could talk about. What we'd all seen, how we felt, and how impressive Nalik was.

Nalik was steadily blushing. He was a very modest angel; they all were. None of the angels seemed to have negative traits that we humans had such as ego, greed, and a need for power or material things. Hell, they didn't even feel like they needed clothes.

It suddenly dawned on me that if humans were able to change the size of their genitalia like the angels, without the need to wear clothes, that there would be humans all over the place with massive cocks and huge boobs, flaunting them for all to see.

Although probably not as many people now as before. I didn't think any of us were feeling vain about our looks anymore. We were all just grateful to be alive.

"Mom, Nalik, and I are going to watch the sunset down by the Cruiser," Holly said, breaking me from my humorous thoughts. "Anthony would you and Christine like to join us?" she asked her big brother.

Christine looked delighted, and when Anthony looked at her to ask if she'd like to go, he instantly took her big smile as a 'Yes' and closed his mouth again.

"I think I can safely say yes, sis," he answered smiling widely.

James stood from his seat with a serious fatherly look in his face.

"Please stay near where the angel guards are. If there are any corrupted people in the Cruiser, I want you to be able to get away instantly, and Nalik can only flit you one at a time, okay!" He told them all.

They could all tell how serious James was, and I was glad he'd told them, so they'd be more aware of their surroundings.

"Do not worry, James; I will flit them to and from the Cruiser, next to where the guards are," Nalik told my husband.

James nodded his head in respect to Nalik, showing his appreciation. James worshipped our kids and had always been very protective. He was even more protective now and who wouldn't be after everything that had happened?

We watched the four of them leave together; the two couples holding hands and sharing smiles. My heart felt full, seeing them so happy. When I looked at Abigail and Harrison, they were rolling their eyes at each other, and then Harrison started to pretend to make himself sick. James and I started to laugh at their funny faces and reactions.

"You wait until you meet someone you like, you two!" I told them as I ruffled Harrison's hair. "You'll be just as smitten as your siblings, and then it will be your dad and I rolling our eyes," I told them, laughing even harder.

Just then, I felt a flutter in my stomach. It was the baby. I could actually feel the tiny movement of our baby daughter. I instantly stopped talking and placed my hand on my small baby bump. James looked worried for a moment, his eyes scanning my face and bump.

"Are you okay, baby?" he asked, worry showing in his handsome face.

I gave him a reassuring smile as I got up and walked over to him.

"I'm good, baby," I answered as I wrapped my arms around his waist. "I just felt the baby flutter."

I looked up to his face just in time to see his eyes widen and a huge grin appear.

"You felt the baby move?" he asked.

I nodded, smiling at the happiness on his face.

"What did it feel like, Mom?" Abigail asked curiously.

"Like little bubbles," I told her with a smile.

It made my heart happy to see our kids interested in the new baby. They seemed just as excited about our new family member as James and me.

We spent the rest of the evening playing eye spy with them, and Abigail entertaining us with the amazing dance move she'd learned.

We were all getting ready for bed when Holly and Anthony came back. Both looked like cats who'd both got the cream. Anthony had a blissful smug look on his face, and Holly literally looked like she was dreamily floating on air.

'Well, that mini sunset date obviously went well,' I thought to myself, smiling at their very happy expressions.

"I gather you had fun, you two?" James said, beating me to the punch.

Anthony instantly started to blush, his cheeks turning a deep red.

"Yeah, we did, it's beautiful down by the water, and we saw a stunning sunset. The colors were amazing," he told us. "Now I know what you mean, Dad, about having a real romance."

"It was very romantic," Holly gushed breathlessly, her cheeks turning pink also.

Both of our kids went to bed very happy. Abigail and Harrison were already asleep by then, not being able to keep their eyes open any longer. When the barrier closed between our rooms, James and I followed suit and climbed into our own welcoming bed too.

Within seconds, James pulled me into his arms and rolled me, so I was laying on top of his muscular body. I lifted myself up, straddling his hips with my legs, looking down on his sexy ass form beneath me.

As I looked down at my husband, the love of my life, I thought again how lucky I was that he was mine. He looked back at me with a look of awe. My love for him was so strong, and my need for him was even stronger.

I could feel his desire stirring beneath me, pulsing between my legs. His hands moved to my thighs, and as he softly moved them up my body, he lifted himself up, bringing his lips to meet mine. His kiss was deep and full of passion, my lips plumping with his passionate onslaught.

I could feel his chest hair graze against my hard nipples, making them even more sensitive as he lifted my body to lower onto his arousal. As I felt him enter me slowly, he started to kiss my neck and ear.

"I love it when you're pregnant; you are always so ready," he whispered.

He used his teeth on my earlobe, his breath hot on the side of my neck. I lifted myself and arched my back, inviting him to pay attention to my tingling nipples. As soon as his mouth took one, I slowly lowered myself down again. He moaned loudly as I took him all, clenching my muscles around his arousal.

I began to raise and lower myself, enjoying the feel of his fullness inside me. The friction against my hyper-sensitive nipples added to my quickly building climax. James lowered his mouth to them again, grazing them with his teeth in turn, making me lose control. His hands gripped my thighs as he released with me, his head buried in my neck and long, blonde hair, his moans adding to my pleasure.

As our climaxes ebbed away, leaving us both content and relaxed, James lowered himself back to the bed taking me with him. While laid on top of him with my ear resting against his broad chest, I listened to the rhythmic beat of his heart. Soon, I could feel him stirring again.

We took it slow and really made love, pleasuring each other until the early hours. As I laid in James's arms, content and relaxed, my mind wandered as I listened to him breathing deeply.

I couldn't dispute his words while we made love at all. Unlike my friends when they were pregnant, I was always hot to trot as James called it. In fact, when I was pregnant with the twins, James had complained that I was wearing him out.

I'd had to remind him of all his friends that had gone months with no sex, telling him that he was a lucky bastard. He'd laughed and agreed at the time. '*It was me who was the lucky one,*' I thought as I could feel myself falling asleep, safe in the arms of the man I adored.

'*Mel, are you awake?*' I heard, as if someone had said the words right in my ear.

I came around from my deep sleep state

feeling very confused, '*What the hell?*'

I lifted my head off my pillow and looked around the room. James was still sleeping soundly next to me, and the barrier between our room and the kids' room was still closed.

'*Mel, it is Christik, are you awake?*' Again, I heard her speak, realizing that I was hearing her in my head.

'*Yes, I'm awake Christik, is everything ok?*' I asked, feeling concerned.

It wasn't like Christik to contact me so early.

'*We've had word from the holding structure; a married couple there have been acting very strangely,*' she replied. '*Shawn and Luiza said the couple haven't been out of their cabin during the day for a while. They only come out at night when everyone else is asleep. I think they may have been turned and corrupted, by the Marilian we discovered,*' she added.

My mind was racing.

If Christik was right about this couple, everyone at the holding structure was in danger. My mind flashed back to my dream or vision—when the corrupted man had looked at me, his blood-red fiery eyes oozing evil.

I could feel my skin crawling, and I felt a shudder run through my body.

'*James and I will meet you at the meeting room as soon as we can,*' I told her.

I sat up in our bed and reached for James.

"James, wake up," I said gently as I brushed my hand against his forearm.

He looked so damn sexy, even when he was so sleepy.

"We need to meet Christik at the meeting room. Come on, we need to get going," I told him, trying to act calmer than I felt.

As we got ready to go, I explained to James what Christik had said. She'd arranged breakfast for us all, and as we quickly grabbed a bite to eat, we told the kids what was going on.

"You all do what you have already planned, and we will keep you posted, okay," James told them.

"But Harrison and I were supposed to meet Christine at the cruiser this morning with her dad," Anthony said, clearly disappointed with how the day was going so far and obviously worried about Christine.

"I'll ask Nalik to bring them here for you," Holly told him, sympathy showing in her voice.

"Thanks, sis," he told her, relief making him relax in his seat.

"Don't worry son, just tell them to stay in their cabin until Nalik comes for them," I suggested.

Fear suddenly gripped me, and I reached for the com on my chest.

'*Christik, you need to post guards outside the couples' cabin and quietly evacuate the cruiser without them knowing. We don't know what they are planning, and we can't afford any casualties,'* I told her desperately.

I could sense her sudden realization of the situation. I felt just as panicked, especially when I thought of all the adults and children there.

'*Yes, it will be done,*' Christik replied earnestly.

"Stay away from the cruiser today until you hear from us, okay," James told our girls.

Both Abigail and Holly nodded their heads at James, understanding how serious things were.

"Let's go," I said as I headed for our room's exit.

We walked at a quick pace down the long pearlescent corridor, occasionally passing angels. One had long, shimmering red hair, another with green. It was good to be able to tell straight away what roles the angels had just by their hair coloring. They were always friendly and respectful, dipping their heads as they glided past.

Christik was waiting for us in the meeting room when we arrived with Hulaz, Harrik, and

Zanika. They all rose from their seats the moment we entered. Christik's face was full of concern.

"The guards are outside the couple's cabin, Mel, and we believe the holding structure is now fully evacuated. Are you ready to go?" she asked, obviously eager to contain the couple.

"Yes, let's get them," I told her, as I reached forward to touch her arm.

James moved over to Harrik, placing his hand on the angel's forearm.

Within a second, we vanished from the meeting room, and my body felt on fire. I didn't think I was ever going to get used to flitting with the angels.

Just when my body felt like it was about to burst into flame, we arrived inside the beautiful courtyard area of the cruiser. The scents of the tropical flowers surrounding us instantly reaching me.

I took a moment to smell the floral scents as I tried to control my body's instant shivering. James took me into his arms to try and warm me, both of his hands stroking up and down my back.

As I looked over James' shoulder, I could see the angel guards dotted around the ground floor level and on the first-floor walkways, all on high alert. Their peacock eyes were darting here and there as they scanned the areas.

It felt weird being there with no hustle and

bustle of people. Or seeing and hearing the children as they ran around laughing and playing.

Four of the guards started to glide over to us as soon as they saw us. Their bodies were looking tense and no longer the fluid grace of their usual manner.

"Where's the cabin?" James asked Christik.

"It is five cabins down from yours, James," she answered, her stress level evident in her voice as she spoke.

The angel guards approached, dipping their heads in respect to all of us.

"Lead the way please," Christik asked them as we reciprocated the angels' gesture.

I slipped my hand into James', and we foll-owed the guards and Christik through the social areas of the cruiser, past the now-closed shops, and empty seating areas.

I was relieved that my body was warmed back to normal temperature. The last thing I needed was to be still shivering, on top of the growing anxiety I was now feeling.

We didn't know if the couple had been turned or not at that point, and if they were, we still had no clue as to how they would react.

I was very surprised that I'd been asked by Christik to come along, considering I wasn't asked to go when they were trying to find the fallen angels.

"Christik, how come you asked me to come with you all today?" I asked her. "Don't get me wrong, I am glad you did."

"You and James are able to think defensively very quickly, Mel," she said warmly, "If you had not suggested the Star of David entrapment technique when we were trying to catch the Marilian, I believe angels and humans may have been lost."

"She's right you know, baby," James agreed, smiling at me proudly, "I dread to think what would have happened if you hadn't suggested it to Nalik."

James affectionately squeezed my hand in his.

"I appreciate all your faith in me," I told them, suddenly feeling a little bashful, but it was a welcome distraction.

We reached the steps to the first-floor cabins, and Christik took the lead with James and me behind her; the guards followed in the rear.

As we reached the top, my nervousness grew. I knew I was holding James' hand too tightly as we began to walk towards the cabin, but I couldn't help it. James rubbed his thumb against the top of my hand reassuringly, but it wasn't helping.

I couldn't remember how far down James and

the kids' cabin was, but I could see some more angel guards towards the end of the row of cabins. They were standing guard quietly, just where the cruiser started to curve, and they looked tenser than the angel's downstairs.

Christik dipped her head to them, and then I heard her voice in my head.

"I will go in first. James and Mel, please stay here out of reach. Angels flank me and only move in if necessary," she ordered with conviction.

James and I stayed where we were. My heart was beginning to pound in my chest. I was surprised that James couldn't hear it; it was so loud in my own ears.

We watched Christik approach the door, and I held my breath.

She glided forward and politely knocked on the door. Nothing. No one came to the door, and no noises could be heard. Christik knocked again, louder this time, and we waited.

A few more tense minutes passed.

I had to assume Christik could hear something as she moved back from the door giving herself some space. The other angels changed their stance in preparation.

The door opened slowly, and male head appearing around it.

The man was wearing dark reflective goggles, the kind that skiers wore. If the situation hadn't been so serious, I might have laughed.

"Hello Peter," I heard Christik say in my head as she spoke to the man, "You haven't been out of your cabin, for more than a week. Are you both alright?" she asked calmly and politely.

The man didn't say a word—but even we could see from where we were standing; that he appeared to be baring his teeth.

A shiver ran through my body, making the hairs on my arms stand on end. I quickly touched my com.

'*He's been corrupted Christik, back away!*'

I shouted in my mind to my friend, who was now in serious danger.

No sooner had I said it than the man flung the door open and rushed at Christik.

He was so fast taking her by surprise. Within sheer seconds, he had her in his grip, and both of them were falling over the side of the banister.

"No!" I screamed aloud.

James and I rushed forward, leaning over the banister just as Peter hit the floor. We watched in amazement as Christik glided to the floor gracefully, her massive wings completely outstretched, breaking her fall.

Peter hit the floor hard, his body jarring as it hit the ground.

A normal person wouldn't have been able to get up; a normal person would have been a broken mess, but Peter was no longer a normal person.

I felt a huge rush of wind above me, and when we looked up, the angel guards had taken wing.

I could feel their power as their stunning wings came down, lifting them into the air. The angels leaned their bodies forward as their wings came down, propelling them forward.

As we looked back over the banister, Peter was getting himself back to his feet, just as the angel guards landed gracefully either side of Christik.

The angels who were already on the ground floor were flanking Peter, coming around behind him. He had nowhere to go.

Christik was calm and impressive as she looked at Peter, her eyes showing her understanding. I could feel his rage flowing from him in waves. His hand came up to his face, ripping off the reflective goggles he wore, and there beneath were the fiery blood-red eyes I'd seen in my dream.

My blood ran cold in my veins, making my body tremble. All I could feel from him was rage, hatred, and death.

"You do not have to do this Peter," Christik

told him calmly. “You are alone and unarmed; the Marilian who turned you is in our custody. Please stop this now. I do not want to hurt you.”

Her words appeared to enrage him further. It made me sick to my stomach when he started to snarl at her, spittle coming from his mouth with every angry sound.

“Hurt me?” he growled at her; “I’m going to tear you to pieces angel.”

Abruptly, he shot forward; the man was so much faster than a normal human. His hands reached for Christik, his fingers like claws aiming straight for her throat.

Within a split second, Christik raised her arm with her palm facing towards him, and a burst of power pulsed from her with such amazing force. Peter was thrown off his feet, back to where he started.

The rage coming off him escalated, hitting me like a ton of bricks, and I felt my knees buckle beneath me.

“Baby, are you alright?” James asked as he grabbed me quickly.

I looked up into his worried face.

“I’m okay, but the evil rage coming from the guy is horrific; he’s not going to let anyone subdue him,” I told my husband.

James touched his com on the wrist that was holding me up.

'*Christik, Mel says he won't let you take him. I think he's going to fight you to the death.*'

I heard James clearly, not only with my ears but also in my head. Something I was sure I'd eventually get used to.

'*I understand, James; we will try to make him sleep without hurting him,*' I heard her reply.

She never took her eyes away from watching the man in front of her. I could see the angels behind him moving slowly forward. Peter was so enraged that he didn't seem to notice.

Movement caught my eye to the left of me, and as I turned my head, I saw a woman.

She was coming from the end of the walkway. A tall, thick-set woman, and when I saw her face, my blood ran cold again.

She had the same fiery blood-red eyes, '*Peter's wife*', and she was heading straight for James and me.

There was no time to think and no time to run. I knew that my legs wouldn't hold my weight.

"Christik!" I screamed as the woman rushed towards us.

James instantly moved in front of me, shielding me with his body. He was ready to take anyone on to protect me, but this woman was no longer a normal human either.

James didn't stand a chance.

I couldn't see her coming after a moment or two because James was blocking my view, but I could feel her coming.

The evil rage rolling off her body was getting stronger with each second. I couldn't breathe, my lungs no longer wanting to take in air and I felt like I was about to pass out.

The next thing I knew, James was being thrown.

His body flew through the air as if he were feather-light. I could hear myself scream as though my heart was being ripped in two.

I watched in horror as my husband was tossed to the ground below like a rag doll. My heart broke as he hit the floor. He was motionless.

I felt rage rising in the pit of my stomach, a rage so strong I'd never felt anything like it before.

I turned my head to look at the monster who had just destroyed the love of my life, and I felt beyond murderous.

"You killed my, James!" I screamed at her.

I felt a power flowing through me that I didn't understand, but I knew it was coming from my stomach, *'Our baby.'*

Instinctively, I threw my arms in front of me, both palms facing the woman before me, and I let the power flow from my body.

The blue light bursting from my palms was blinding, so I closed my eyes, trusting my daughter to help me.

I could feel her power in every fiber of my being, and although I wanted to kill the murdering bitch in front of me, I knew my daughter did not.

As the power began to subside, I opened my eyes.

There before me was Peter's wife, but she was no longer standing or moving. The woman was floating in what appeared to be a bubble of shimmering blue fluid. It was flowing around her body as if it had currents.

I staggered to my feet, using the banister for balance and stumbled forward, still too sickened to look down at my broken, dead husband, knowing that when I did; it would become real.

When I reached the woman, I saw that her eyes were open, and as I watched, the fiery blood-red seemed to fade away. She didn't move or even breathe; it was as if she were frozen in the fluid.

I was relieved that she wasn't dead. That was something I knew I wouldn't be able to live with, no matter what she'd done.

'*James,*' I thought, *'My James is gone.'* I looked to my right, over the banister, and watched as Christik took James in her arms while the angels who were flanking her were facing off with Peter.

I touched my com at my neck, reaching out to Christik, '*Star of David,*' I told her, just as my mind shut down, and my body hit the floor.

Thank you for reading.
You can leave your book Review here.
https://www.amazon.com/dp/B07JDQ4Q8V
"The Marilians" book two of the
Earth's Angels Trilogy
Available now on Amazon.
https://www.amazon.com/dp/B07W76R667

ABOUT BETH WORSDELL

Beth Worsdell is an English born author, who now resides in California with her husband and three of her four children.

From a young age Beth always wrote poetry for herself, friends and family. Never knowing that she would eventually write a sci-fi fantasy fiction novel. Although, Beth has always been a big sci-fi fantasy fan, beginning with Star Trek when she was young.

When Beth and her husband had the opportunity to move to America in 2011, they jumped at the chance, knowing that it would be a great family adventure.

After five wonderful years of living in South Carolina, Beth had a strange dream which wouldn't leave her thoughts. So, after moving to California and two more years of the dream popping into her head, she decided to write it down.

One chapter led to another, and Beth suddenly realized that she was writing a Novel. Before long 'Earth's Angels' was created. A novel full of action, adventure, humor, love and magic.

Beth Worsdell's new debut book trilogy has a completely original concept. Earth's Angels is-NOT a religious book in any way, but rather it delves into the mystery of ancient aliens and our ancient ancestors.

She would tell you honestly that her story wrote itself, she only held the pen.

Beth has recently released 'DESTINATION UNKNOWN' which is book three in the 'Earth's Angels Trilogy'.

Don't forget to follow Beth and 'Earth's Angels' on Facebook, Twitter and Instagram. Please show your support for Beth and the 'Earth's Angels Trilogy' by inviting your friends to her social media pages, sharing her pages and posts. Tell your friends about the Earth's Angels Trilogy today.

LINKS

https://www.bethworsdellauthor.com/

https://www.facebook.com/BethWorsdellAuthorFantasyFiction/

https://www.facebook.com/EarthsAngelsTrilogy/

https://twitter.com/bethworsdell

https://twitter.com/EarthsAngelsNo1

https://www.instagram.com/bethworsdellauthor/

https://www.instagram.com/earthsangelstrilogy/

WAYS FOR YOU TO BE AN EARTH ANGEL.

Use energy efficient appliances and light bulbs.

Turn off computers, Tv's and other appliances when not in use.

Buy foods and items in eco-friendly packaging.

Always recycle as much as possible.

Use cloth diapers when possible.

Air dry clothes.

Use less paper napkins when dining out and use washable napkins at home.

Minimize stationary waste by using both sides of paper.

Use a whiteboard or chalkboard instead of paper notes at home.

Recycle newspapers and magazines.

Use reusable bottles instead of disposable.

By Beth Worsdell

Plant trees in your garden. Tree shade on your house helps reduce your AC usage too.

Save gas by using cruise control on your vehicle when possible.

Use reusable gift bags instead of wrapping paper.

Try to buy used items instead of new. Vintage items are generally made to last, that's why they are still around.

Buy local produce and products to minimize your gas usage and suppliers' gas too.

Adjust the thermostat in your home, it will save you money also. using a timer so, it isn't on while you are out, will also save you money.

Use a travel mug instead of using coffee chain paper cups. Some companies may give you a discount for doing so.

Run your errands in a batch to save your gas and time.

Turn lights off when you leave a room.

Use solar lights in your garden and home.

Don't use lots of water to pre-rinse dishes.

2,500 gallons of water is used to produce a single pound of beef. So, have a vegetarian day when possible.

Try to wash laundry in full loads on a warm or cool setting.

Use reusable water bottles to help prevent plastic waste in our oceans.

Take a shower instead of a bath.

Share a shower with your partner.

Shorten the length of your shower.

Don't leave taps running when brushing your teeth.

Water your garden at night to prevent quick evaporation.

Use a watering can to spot water plants and areas.

By Beth Worsdell

Use vinegar to kill weeds instead of pesticides, which kill wildlife and poison our earth.

Compost your kitchen waste to save you money and create organic fertilizer for your garden.

Recycle your old cell phone as cell phone batteries leak acid into the soil at waste dump sites.

Keep your cars performance up and check your emissions on a regular basis.

Always recycle your cans. Less energy is used to recycle than to make new cans.

Use paper matches instead of lighters. Paper matches are made from recycled paper.

Don't throw away anything that could be used by another. Advertise it as FREE locally and online.

Save water by using a car wash service. They use minimal water and emissions.

Use cloth shopping bags instead of plastic.

Take advantage of e-tickets instead of printing them out.

Instead of buying discs, download the program, music or movie.

In the winter try to buy a pet-safe, non-chemical de-icer for your needs. They don't contain the harmful chemicals.

Use biodegradable cotton buds/cue tips instead of plastic.

Cancel paper bank statements and paper bills, so you can do it online and save paper.

Buy and use rechargeable batteries.

Empty the lint filter on your dryer after every use. Your machine will work more efficiently saving you money. Plus reduce the fire hazard. You can also safely save the lint, to use as a fire starter in the winter, for your log fire if you have one.

If you have a cat, why not try a biodegradable, flushable kind of litter.

When buying fish, try to buy a fish that was wild caught.

Going somewhere local? Take a nice walk or blow the cobwebs off your bike.

If you're a student, why not share a load of washing at college.

Plant wild flowers in your garden to encourage bees and butterflies.

Recycle your vehicle oil, by taking it to your nearby recycling center or gas station.

Buy and use a low-phosphate or non-phosphate washing-up liquid and laundry detergent. Phosphates encourage algae growth which removes the oxygen from water, which in turn, kills the water wildlife.

Try and buy organic foods.

Ride share with people you work with.

Save left over food for meals and store in your freezer.

Use crushed eggshells and used coffee grounds to feed your planets.

Insulate your house to save you money.

Use solar power when possible.

Grow your own food produce.

Use public transport when you can.

Let your hair air dry instead of using a dryer.

Join local wildlife groups.

Support global animal organizations.

Join litter a clean-up group.

Collect rainwater off your roof for watering your garden on dry days.

Grow plants in your garden which don't need a lot of water.

Keep blinds and curtains closed during hot and

sunny days to keep your home cooler, so you don't use your AC as much.

Buy food items in cardboard packaging instead of plastic.

Use an organic bamboo toothbrush instead of plastic.

Use can now find toothpaste drops, instead of using tubes.

Kitchen towel made from bamboo is also available.

Buy toilet paper which is wrapped in paper and not plastic.

Grow fruit and vegetables from the tops after preparing food.

Thank you for being an Earth Angel.

#BeAnEarthAngel

THE MARILIANS.

We are bad-ass human survivors, working with very powerful ancient angels, who came to save us. They have been healing Earth and they have activated magical ancient ruins, we didn't even know existed on our planet. We had no idea that Stonehenge and the Gate of the Gods were so magical and that our planet had star passages to other worlds.

We have already been through hell. First, our planet began to die and we lost people we loved. Then, after the angles arrived, we discovered fallen angels, who had been corrupted by the Marilians.

Now we have to fight the second battle for our lives, against the evil and vicious Marilians monsters.

The Marilians are coming to take it all, and change us into their own kind…..

A fate worse than death.

We will do whatever it takes, to protect Earth and each other. We have been through too much, to lose it all now. Mel, her family and all the human survivors have been busy helping Earth's angels to heal our planet, and prepare for the Marilian invasion.

The ancient angels have called upon the

Elders to help, and the Elders have something up their sleeve, which may give them and us the upper hand.

The magic, action, love, humor and intrigue will have you hooked.

Our planet dying, was just the beginning……